Advance Praise for 1

MW00412748

St. Joan manages from the first page to
about sisterhood, coming of age and the ways women can cross generations, borders
and cultures to weave from the tatters of oppression enduring fabrics of deliverance and
justice..

> – **Susan Greene**, the *Colorado News Collaborative*

From the scarf to the shawl and finally the shroud, *Shawl of Midnight* is a provocative
story of women entrapped by patriarchal norms [which] leave little room for self-identity
or discovery. St. Joan accurately describes this phenomenon through an interwoven story
of women ... challenging the norms. Spellbinding events engage the reader throughout.... An excellent text for Women's Studies courses and Cultural Sociology. Highly
recommended.

> –**Zahra Deborah Buttar**, Ph.D.: College of Southern Nevada

The Shawl of Midnight is a mesmerizing second novel from Jackie St. Joan that takes
you into the frightful challenges and drama of gender crisis in Pakistan and India through
the experiences of a family we know well from St. Joan's breakthrough book, *My Sisters
Made of Light.*

> –**Fawn Germer**, Author, *Hard Won Wisdom, Coming Back,* and other books.

Women's stories to fall into, women to challenge our notions of "what life is like" in
different areas of South Asia, women to cheer on and cry for—all of this in *The Shawl of
Midnight*. A dangerous trek, surprising allies, and a touch of magical realism make this
an absorbing read that also illuminates some of the geography and history of Kashmir.
An absorbing sequel to *My Sisters Made of Light.*

> –**Ronnie Storey**, Diseuse/Storyteller

The Shawl of Midnight takes readers onto the streets, through the forests, and into the
minds of women fighting for justice and freedom in Pakistan. A captivating novel and an
inspiring read.

> –**Cora Galpern**, University of Michigan student activist studying sociology
> and social work

Its depiction of time and place, its evolution of character, are told with convincing
detail; it has the ring of truth. *The Shawl of Midnight* is a compelling story that belongs in
the annals of literature.

> –**Harry Maclean**, Edgar Award-winning author, *In Broad Daylight*

The Shawl of Midnight

Jacqueline St. Joan

Golden Antelope Press
715 E. McPherson
Kirksville, Missouri 63501
2022

ISBN: 978-1-952232-71-8

Library of Congress Control Number: 2022938586

Published by:

Golden Antelope Press

715 E. McPherson

Kirksville, Missouri 63501

Available at:

Golden Antelope Press

715 E. McPherson

Kirksville, Missouri, 63501

Phone: (660)349-9832; (660)-229-2997

http://www.goldenantelope.com

Email: ndelmoni@gmail.com

for Zea Lucia

Contents

Nafeesa's (Maternal) Family Tree

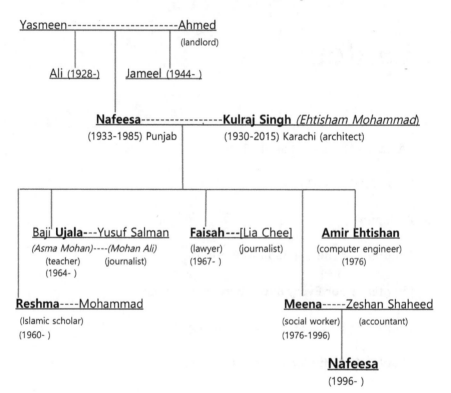

Yasmeen----------------------Ahmed
(landlord)

Ali (1928-)   Jameel (1944-)

Nafeesa----------------Kulraj Singh *(Ehtisham Mohammad)*
(1933-1985) Punjab   (1930-2015) Karachi (architect)

Baji **Ujala**---Yusuf Salman   **Faisah**---[Lia Chee]   **Amir Ehtishan**
(Asma Mohan)----(Mohan Ali)   (lawyer)   (journalist)   (computer engineer)
(teacher)   (journalist)   (1967-)   (1976)
(1964-)

Reshma----Mohammad   **Meena**-----Zeshan Shaheed
(Islamic scholar)   (social worker)   (accountant)
(1960-)   (1976-1996)

Nafeesa
(1996-)

Relationship Names Most Used by Nafeesa's Family

Ammi --Mother
Abbu --Father
Nanaa --Grandmother, Father's Mother
Babba --Grandfather, Mother's Father
Baji --Elder Sister, Auntie, Older Woman
Mamou --Uncle, Mother's Brother

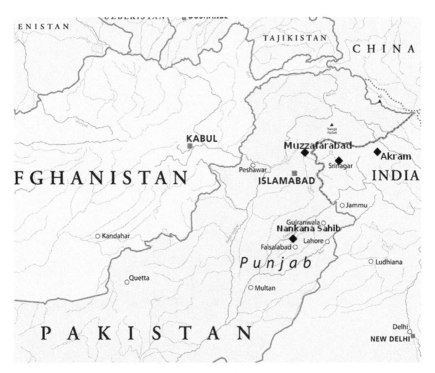

Map of Novel's Main Setting in Pakistan and India.

To hell with all your vows and prayers;
Just help others through life, there's no truer worship.

-Lalla (Lal Ded)

Prologue

Islamabad, Pakistan, 1996

The hundreds who rallied on the mosque's lawn that day were only a peep of dissent in the body politic. Dominating the skyline was the Faisal Mosque where the people of Islamabad surrendered five times a day. Its four minarets pointed with certainty to the promise of heaven. Set against loden pines, cedars, and palm bushes of the rolling Margalla Hills, the modernistic mosque bewildered—as if it were an eight-faceted diamond laid in an emerald, or a heavenly tent for one hundred thousand worshippers. Perhaps it was a spaceship preparing for liftoff, or a giant bug trapped on its own back. Its front yard entombed the despised General Zia, who died almost eleven years earlier in an exploding airplane, and people still joked that the relics in the grave were not Zia's at all, but the tailbone of an ass. Human rights lawyer Faisah Ehtisham, hid along the side of the crowd, away from the stage, with her dupatta pulled across one side of her face. Beside her a family friend, journalist Yusuf Salman, was fingering a pistol out in the open. Faisah quickly scanned for police. "Put that away!" she ordered and, for the first and only time, Faisah saw the rage that her authority and insistence caused in him. For just a moment, his eyes glared, then, without a word he returned the gun to his pocket and turned away.

Up on the platform, Meena, her younger sister, introduced the speakers, and one by one each ascended the few steps, spoke for five minutes and descended. After one local politician finished his comments, he handed the microphone to a Catholic nun from the Peace and Justice Commission. She wore the white veil made famous by Mother Teresa.

"Whether legal or not, Baji Ujala's actions to save those girls were just," she said softly. "They were destined to live tortured lives or to be killed by their families. Baji is a model for all who seek justice. She should be released from prison at once! May God have mercy on Pakistan." The nun returned to her chair as the crowd politely pumped their homemade signs that they had tacked onto sticks.

At the microphone again with her fist in the air and her pregnant belly high and round, Meena roused the chanting crowd: "Free Baji! Free Baji! No honor in honor crimes! No honor in honor crimes! Free Baji! Free Baji!" The crowd responded, loud and intense, as if the volume of their voices alone might spring open the prison doors to release their Baji or change the social conditions they protested.

Mynah birds with white-tipped feathers were feeding on seeds in the expansive lawn. At a distance a line of police formed a wall and pointed the gun barrels of their Kalashnikovs into the sky. Beneath a cascading orange jacaranda, a group of thirty women in black burqas watched the protest from afar. Bearded men from Islamic University milled around two idling motorcycles. Several wore the green turbans of Jamaat, the Islamist political party. They looked hostile and seemed to be shouting at the protesters in front of the mosque.

Yusuf watched the Islamist students but could not hear what they were saying. He saw Meena lift her chin in his direction, signaling that Yusuf would speak next. He climbed the stairs and stood at the podium in a white caftan and skullcap. He riffled his notes and brought Ujala's face to his mind. Adjusting his wire-rimmed glasses, he looked out over the crowd.

"My statement today reflects jihad," he began, "meaning struggle, the struggle I have engaged in, as a Pakistani, as a Muslim, as a man. I come from an old family, from the hills above Karachi, where my father's father built the first mosque of this century in his town. Many years ago, I left this country to work in America as a journalist. But today in Pakistan I have found a story I cannot stop telling—one that was invisible to me when I lived here. It is the story of the suffering of women under the harsh rules of our society, an injustice that contrasts with the compassion of the Q'ran I learned at the tables of my grandfathers.

"It is because I am a human being and because I am a Muslim that I will tell these stories. To be a Muslim is to surrender to the will of God by living in such a way that one can always know what the will of God is. Then one can act on that will, even at the risk of losing one's own freedom, or reputation, or even one's life. It is not hard to be a good Muslim when we have models of goodness such as Ujala Ehtisham—a teacher who has followed the path God directed her to. May the light of Allah bring peace to those who are persecuted."

Then there was a mysterious event that many would try to describe later, but no one would ever succeed in doing. First, there was a commotion in the back of the crowd, then a migration of crows began—tens, hundreds, thousands, tens of thousands of black wings silhouetted against the hazy sky. Magnificent, they raced from the void with great intention, and fast, as if the kernels of their hearts might pop open. The crows swept by the crowd for many minutes, blackening the day, and the experience itself carried the people away to something they knew, something they needed to remember, something older and even larger than the courage it took for them to demonstrate their beliefs in public. The ground to one side of the mosque became a carpet of crazed, calling crows. One tree was so full of birds that it blackened and tilted forward from their accumulated weight. Only the sound of overhead jet planes drowned the birds' complaints. Then, as quickly as the spectacle had appeared and cast midnight into the midday sky, the last bird sped by, and the mystery dissolved like an image on film.

Faisah, Baji Ujala's younger sister, waited for the effect of the birds' drama to subside before she mounted the platform. Over one eye a hospital-green patch was fastened by an elastic cord tied around her head. She wore round, plastic sunglasses for protection. When she reached the top step, she tugged her dupatta down onto her shoulder and faced the crowd, leading with her chin. The air emptied of words, as her friends saw—many for the first time—the extent of Faisah's injuries from a recent acid attack. The scars on her cheek and neck were red ribbons of flesh welded to her bones. Someone in the back of the crowd began a cautious tribute to her—a slow, rhythmic clapping. Others joined in one by one, but Faisah could not bear the tentativeness of the crowd's response, and she interrupted their nervous, ambivalent effort. She did not want them to linger on her face. She stepped closer to the microphone.

"Today in Islamabad," she began, gesturing toward the mosque, "here in the shadow of God's house, we are outraged by the crimes of violence committed against women everywhere, including in our own country. Last year, here in Punjab alone, nine hundred women were murdered in so-called honor killings. In Sindh, in the first three months of this year, over a hundred were reported—that is one per day. For many women the pain of being female is so great that they find their own relief only in suicide." She lowered her voice. "People of conscience must continue the work my sister, Baji Ujala, has begun—and we must do it even if we are afraid. We must listen to our consciences, not to our fears. This is what we face."

At the mention of the word *face,* Faisah hesitated. With her good eye, she could see that another crowd was growing near the wild jacaranda across the park. She inhaled deeply and continued. "And do not be frightened by what you face. This woman you are looking at is yourself. Yes, these scars are not mine alone; they were intended not only for me, but also for you. I was merely selected to receive them. We earn these scars together because we value our consciences more than our faces, our daughters more than ourselves, freedom more than security." For the first time, Faisah smiled as she spoke. "You know, they say that a lion knows danger like an old friend. And a lion with one eye is to be respected—she's tattered and a little crazy." As Faisah grinned and Meena reached to hug her, the protesters broke into applause.

All at once a frightening popping sound split the crowd into pieces, as people ducked and hurried apart. If God had been watching from the minaret, He would have seen one body of people exploding into pieces, winging apart, a churning mix of movement and emotion. He would have seen people yelling and running to avoid a spray of bullets. But there was no spray of bullets. There was only one shot. If it was intended for Faisah, it missed its mark. A single, hot bullet drove into Meena's chest, and, standing next to her, Faisah felt the impact, too. A numbing burn tunneled into Meena's body. Faisah pulled her down to the platform. Meena gasped for air as her neck seemed to collapse and turn, and her quiet eyes calmly surveyed the blood pooling beneath her hair. The heat of Meena's blood was saturating Faisah's clothes, and she knew what it meant.

Meena! Not Meena! She curled herself around and over Meena, covering her with her body. The rustling sound of mass movement and the calling of people to each other continued in a lower range. The high-pitched war cry of police sirens came faster and closer and faster and closer and slower and closer and stopped. The pile of people protecting Meena moved aside so that Yusuf could lift Meena carefully and carry her from the platform.

Armored vehicles circled the patch of grass. Uniformed police streamed out of their vans and lined the street between the protesters and the Islamic University students. Police pointed their weapons in the opposite directions, alternating one by one—half at the protesters, half at the students. Several officers began a foot-chase around the mosque, searching for the shooter; others followed on motorcycles, and their sirens split the air.

Meena lay on a pile of shawls both women and men had spread on the lawn. With her head in Faisah's lap, Yusuf scanned the crowd for an ambulance. Meena groaned as she bled. "I'm here, Meena," Faisah whispered through her tears. She could see the entrance wound where Meena's shalwar kameez was ripped apart. Her flesh was seared, a gash, open like a pocket. Meena swooned with pain. "The ambulance is coming. The hospital is nearby. Hold on, Meena. Breathe with me. Look at my face." Meena's eyes gripped Faisah's, as the sisters inhaled each other's desperation. "Here," Faisah said. "Watch me again. Just a little breath, like this." Meena may have tried to follow Faisah's lead, but she could only cough and cough. Faisah pinched Meena's cheek. Meena's lips stuck together, but a teaspoon of air slipped through one corner of her mouth. "Stay with me, Meena. Oh, stay with me."

"Here they come!" shouted Yusuf above the crowd, waving his arms to the hospital truck.

"Call Zeshan," Faisah whispered to Yusuf, as she climbed into the truck with Meena, "and Abbu and Amir."

Two porters lifted Meena onto a gurney. "Ammi," she whimpered, calling for her mother, staring at a distance.

Faisah looked where Meena was staring. In a flash under the blazing jacaranda, Faisah imagined she saw the ghost of their mother there—a silver-haired woman in black with a scar at her hairline. Faisah froze in that moment, utter sadness filling every pore for the motherless children that they had been for so long. "How has the world come to this, Ammi?" she asked.

And her mother whispered, "It has always been so."

Faisah snapped out of it. "And tell Baji what has happened," she instructed Yusuf. "You have to tell Baji."

The ambulance sped along the brick wall lining Airport Road, past rows of simple signs attached to the wall and extended like open hands. Each sign bore one of the ninety-nine names of Allah. Faisah read them to Meena as they flew by: Allah, the Merciful. The Wise One. The Only One. The One Who Brings Good News. The One You Can Expect Something From. God of Our Ancestors. The Giver. The Omnipotent. The Greatest One. The Innocent One. The Righteous One. The Alpha and the Omega. The Inner and the Outer. God of the Orphan. One Who Talks About God. The Friend. The Just. The All-Seeing. The Protector . . .

Meena died at midnight. Minutes later, surgeons separated her baby from her womb. Meena's final act in this world was to give birth to a daughter.

"You are Nafeesa," Zeshan said to the infant when he first held her, "named for your mother's mother, as Meena wanted. Welcome to the world and bid goodbye to your mother." He curled the squalling baby into Meena's neck, between her cheek and her shoulder. "She has given her life for you. She is a martyr for all the daughters of Pakistan." Then Zeshan placed his face next to his wailing child and they wept together. The room filled with the pain of birth, the pain of death, and all the suffering of life between the two.

Chapter 1

"The She-Lion of Punjab"

Akram, Jammu & Kashmir, India, 2014

Eighteen years later, two men are meeting inside a dark teahouse, a place like any other, a place for men to share their memories, their plans, their gloom. The journalist and the publisher of *The Convoy,* an Indian magazine, are meeting to discuss a story Yusuf has submitted for publication. Before this story can be told, he must let the editor know how the story ends. Yusuf sits in a single ray of sunlight across a small table, explaining to the man with the note pad: "My beloved is gone," he says. "My wife died last winter."

"Baji Ujala? My condolences," the editor counters coldly as steam rises from their cups. He pauses and then pursues what he wants. "But, Yusuf, now you must tell the world about the infamous prison break in 1996 and how you two escaped." Then Yusuf hands him this manuscript:

The She-Lion of Punjab

It was in a visiting room at Adiala Prison where I first saw Uji after our ten years of separation. I had left Pakistan in the late 1980s when she rejected my marriage proposal, telling me "maybe someday," but insisting she had a teacher's vocation to fulfill first. I took my heartache to

New York and spent those years building my reputation in journalism, publishing a poetry book or two, working on my novel, devouring every book by Ernest Hemingway, trying to imitate his style in my own work. They were years Uji spent on the roads of Pakistan, teaching children, training other teachers, and rescuing women who seemed destined to die in honor killings. When I learned of her imprisonment, I returned to Pakistan as soon as I could. In that prison hellhole, all concrete and steel, she was even more beautiful than I recalled from our university days. Her thick hair was covered by a filmy white cotton dupatta and her head's shadow was dark beneath it. I shivered recalling how it had felt to touch that hair. Uji's skin had the glow of an ancient Sufi, feverish and saintly. She nurtured a fervor for those she loved and I could see that I was still one of those.

"Puuh! I'm no saint," she said across a table, and tried to change the subject. "Tell me about your life in America."

"You are a saint," I insisted, but she would have none of it.

"I've only done what others before me have done quietly. The difference is that the eyes of the media have turned my way."

"They have," I agreed. "So, we will use that, too, in service to our cause."

She shrugged. "I don't want all the attention. But what can I do?"

Really, there was nothing more she could have done to save herself. Faisah, her younger sister, had mounted a legal defense the press touted as "fresh and brilliant." Reshma, her older sister, had testified as an expert in some weird version of feminist Islam. Their father and their brother occupied the front pew at every hearing, lent their moral support, and fed the entire defense team at their country home each night after the trial ended. What cooks they were! And sharing those meals kept our spirits up. In the end, the verdict from the Shariah Court was past due and we feared the spectacle of Uji suffering a public hanging or a life sentence, invisible to the world. Time was short. The many who loved her agreed that something had to be done.

The details of the escape are unimportant and, besides, they could incriminate the innocent. All that can be written here about what happened next is this: a scheme was devised, diversions were created, and trickery was carried out on visiting day at Adiala. Certain resources were gathered. A rusty Nissan waited outside the prison gate with its engine running. When they realized Uji had escaped, Pakistani police searched for her, and Indian police pushed for bribes at the border. Bullets flew across Kashmir's Line of Control, but Uji and I arrived in the Himalayas along with winter and its ageless power, its white, killing presence.

Let's go back many months before the 1996 escape, to Lahore High Court, a nineteenth century structure as dingy as Dickens, where worked a slow-moving bailiff, a notoriously lazy judge, and curious spectators on all sides of the case against Ujala Ehtisham. Right outside the building was an ocean of lawyers and clients, tables and typewriters. Protesters abandoned their "Free Baji" signs there and took their seats, squeezed into pews right next to the opposition-- Islamists in their bright green turbans proclaiming their virtue, Sindhis wearing caps hand-embroidered by their women, and Pathans, sitting stock-still with their plain, flat wool hats in their laps. Maybe a hundred observers and reporters filled that bleak forum while security officers encircled them, firearms fixed onto their hips and batons slanted in their fists.

There were two charges of kidnapping filed against her. One was signed by the father of Chanda Khan, a teenage girl who was present in the courtroom that day, and the other was filed by the husband of Khanum Wazir, a woman who was still missing. The judge saw the case for the celebrated and messy thing that it was, so he maneuvered a pass to Islamabad's Shariah Court, intoning the language of the law:

"We request that august body to accept jurisdiction of this matter in

order to interpret for the High Court, the language in the Q'ran to ap-
ply to the claim of the defense—that these two young women were not
kidnapped, but rather sought out the assistance of the defendant, Ujala
Ehtisham, left their families willingly with her, and were, in fact, agents of
their own destinies." The gavel was pounded, the case was transferred,
and microbits sped the Lahore High Court files north to Shariah Court in
Islamabad.

It was weeks later on an early fall day that Uji stood in that court
next to her sister Faisah, a one-eyed lawyer with a pale green hospital
patch over her blind eye. She wore the formal attire of the legal profes-
sion, black shalwar kameez with black suit jacket. She faced the insensi-
tive and dim-witted prosecutor who recoiled when he saw the nasty scar
across Faisah's face. Faisah lifted her white dupatta from her shoulder
to cover her head before the judges entered. She cleared her throat and
scratched her nose, so eager was she to address the court.

At precisely nine o'clock there was a splash of morning on the opposite wall, and the three associate judges of the Shariah Court, nondescript as most judges are, took their seats the way judges do. Surely they
had already reviewed the court file—the charges made, the defenses as-
serted, the law to be applied, and the list of witnesses to be presented.

Chanda Khan was a Pathan girl in purdah, who had disobeyed her father by leaving her home unaccompanied. She dressed in her brother's
clothes and tucked her hair inside her brother's cap to walk to a forbidden part of Lahore where a friend taught her to dance. Her brother and
father, suspecting her transgression, followed her. The brother pinned
her arms against a wall, while their father raised a knife and sliced off
half her nose. Really, there was nothing the courts could do for the child.
She belonged to her father and had no legal recourse, so Faisah and Uji
made a plan to get Chanda Khan out of Punjab. She asked the girl to join
her in Chitral and they spent the winter in the Northwest, where Uji led

a teacher-training program and Chanda Khan danced.

I never saw Chanda Khan myself, but once Uji described to me how Chanda looked the day they departed the bus station together. She said Chanda was light-skinned and slender and was wearing a full burkha to hide from the nosy neighbors when she sneaked out of the family home. Only her frightened hazel eyes showed. She followed Uji onto the bus, dragging their food bundles. Many hours later, Uji said, it was a great relief to arrive in Chitral, a place where Chanda would have a chance of survival.

The trial proceeded. Words exited Faisah's mouth strategically, like soldiers. "For helping this child find safety in another province, away from the father who defiled and disfigured her, the defendant has been wrongfully charged with kidnapping, for interfering with a father's control of his daughter, for violating the Quran. It's her father and her brother who should be on trial here."

Witnesses were called. Promises to tell the truth were made to Allah. The jurisconsult testified that a fair interpretation of Shariah required Ujala Ethisham's release. Issues were argued and the law was analyzed. In the end the President Judge surveyed the audience, and cut a horizontal slice of air with his hand, signaling it was enough. The questioning was over. The game was called. The court took the matter under advisement. And now, eighteen years later, the verdict is still pending.

***

What did it mean to be on the run, wild animals in a forest fire, fleeing with the one I loved, from whom I'd been separated by ten years, by seven thousand miles, by prison bars? I was almost giddy at first, disbelieving she was sitting next to me in the front seat of that Nissan. My heart raced, young and ripe, excited by the danger we were facing together. I remember I was so nervous that I ground the gears twice before they fell into place and at last we pulled away from the gate at Adiala Prison. I glanced in the rearview mirror to see, standing outside the jail, Rahima Mai, the Women's Prison Supervisor. She had folded her arms over her ample chest and her face was flat and emotionless. Once I interviewed Rahima Mai for a freelance assignment. She had befriended Uji in prison, but she despised me. "Whatever does she see in you?" Rahima Mai had yelled down the outside staircase when I left the interview. And on the day of the prison break, she had wrapped a deep pink and orange Kashmiri shawl around herself, which looked truly odd over her prison uniform. Her shawl was dark with a paisley pattern, identical to the one in Uji's lap.

We entered a traffic circle and I searched for a southern road to take us out of the area. I had planned to head for interior Sindh to Fort Abbas where friends would help us cross into India. But the N-5 was under construction and both police and military vehicles surrounded the area, so I pointed the car north. I drove as fast as I dared while my heart pounded. I had a million questions, and worried about driving the popular Expressway north. We needed to focus on what to do next.

"All this air, all this sky," Uji said, gazing out the car window. "It's a shock to be outdoors, to see partridges in a drainage ditch." A flock of the brown and white-flecked birds rose together and floated over a wheat field.

"Uji, I think we should abandon this car, find another way to travel. By now the police may have its description." She wasn't listening and her shining public face was exposed to the world outside her window. "Uji, pull your dupatta closer. Cover your face."

I checked each corner, each truck, all the while on the lookout. I could not understand how Uji could be so calm. She opened up the shawl that was folded in her lap and removed two items wrapped inside. One was a leather pouch she spread open and shook into her hands. Out spilled white, red, blue and yellow stones—precious stones we could use. I recognized them—they were the same gems that the missing woman, Khanum, had sent from Karachi for Uji, the same ones I had offered Rahima Mai as a bribe. She had thrown them back at me, calling me a stupid boy, but I had left them there on her desk. I begged her to use them somehow to help Uji. The other item inside the shawl was a paper drawing. She opened it.

"It's a map of the Neelam Valley, where Rahima Mai grew up in Kashmir. Look. She's marked a trail she told me about. As a child she used to climb it with her pet donkey." Her voice rose. "Yusuf, this trail crosses the mountains into India." She breathed audibly. "It's an escape route. Rahima Mai is showing us a safe way out." The old gal came through for us after all—both jewels and a map. I laughed.

"But first we must get out of Punjab," I said. Taking the Expressway into Azad Kashmir would be fastest, but too risky—the police might expect us to choose the quickest route to a border. I was eager to leave Rawalpindi behind. There was a green road sign: "MURREE."

"Murree," she said, bowing her head, turning it away from the window. She drew the shawl closer to her face, fingering its weave. "Let's drive to Murree. There are people there who will help us."

"Who do you know in Murree?"

"Some teachers I met at a training. They live together in the nearby hills. It's a boarding school. I'm sure they'll help."

I questioned if it was a good choice, but went along with her suggestion anyway. Away from the military headquarters in Pindi. Murree was a mountain resort, a place with gem shops and restaurants, outdoor sporting equipment and ice cream stores. Not a likely place for fugitives. Next we passed a park so nondescript that even the birds are not worth mentioning. "That's where they hanged Bhutto in '79," she said, pointing at the grassy area. "Afterward they tore the jail down and built Adiala."

We passed a petrol station and crossed a bridge. "And that's where they tried to assassinate Musharraf in 2003." An assassination tour, I laughed to myself. Loudspeakers from the mosques of Rawalpindi emitted competing calls to evening prayer. We followed Benazir Bhutto Road to the roundabout that carried us out of the unknown into another unknown. We rolled up the windows as the heater pumped and rattled, ridding the Nissan of the mountain chill.

The countryside was pale magenta with fiery sunset clouds and the hills were red clay and white salt deposits with tunnels and tracks. Motorbikes, trucks, camels, donkey carts and cars crowded the back roads. Oncoming headlamps flashed on the sides of trucks, reflecting their ornate decorations, rich and complete, a corona of highway convoys, beautiful and shining in the twilight. The two of us were beginning to relax with darkness coming on and the thrumming of tires on the road. Although I wanted to speed to safety, it was safer to crawl. Nightfall and the constancy of the sounds accompanied our own vehicle of intimacy.

"Tell me about the matching shawls, yours and Rahima Mai's," I said. Uji smiled at me and for a moment my mind was lost there, re-absorbing the reality that she was sitting next to me, her face soft and lips parted to reveal that endearing gap between her front teeth.

"I once told Rahima Mai a story about such a shawl," she said. "One I gave to Khanum as I put her on the train to Karachi." Khanum was the first woman Baji rescued from a husband's abuse, so the shawl became a souvenir of that victory. Now I understood what it meant to her.

The closer we came to Murree, the more intense was our scanning for police.

"There's one on a motorbike up ahead on the right," she'd say.

"And another around the corner of that shop," I'd say.

Police were everywhere, but they seemed more interested in traffic violations than prison breaks. We drove past shops strung with white lights and posters of dark-eyed women in video store windows. There were larger, glassed supermarkets with signs in English: "1st class!" "Super!" There was a jewelry shop, clean and empty, except for the merchant, who had a soiled turban twisted around his head. Next to the shop was a petrol station with an adjoining room where men bowed repeatedly and prayed into their hands.

It is never summer in the Murree hills. Always cool weather. People come from the far regions of over-heated Pakistan just to experience snow—the snow at the baby toe of the Himalayas—a puny hint of the monstrous northern mountains we would soon face.

Uji broke the silence. "What do we have for resources? And what do we need?" I had brought a gallon of water, chapati and butter. Some fruit. Enough for a day or two. I had rope and tools for the car, of course, and notebooks.

"About 50,000 rupees," I said, "plus the jewels from Rahima Mai. But nothing for cold weather. I was expecting we'd be in the Sindhi desert."

She grinned. "How many sleeping bags?"

"Two."

"Good. We're not married, you know."

I was unsure for a moment if she were teasing. "But, Uji, you promised . . ."

"And where can we find someone to marry us, Yusuf? No imam. No license. No I.D. with which to obtain a license." That was when I became excited.

"We do have I.D.s. Zeshan Bhai arranged for that." I reached into my shirt pocket and handed over two cards. "Your driver's licenses, Madam."

"Asma Mohan," she read. It was an Indian I.D. with her photo on it. Fuzzy, but it was her face. She looked at the second one. It was a Pakistani I.D. with a different first name, a male name "Ali Mohan."

"One identity is male—you are my younger cousin, Ali—as long as we are in Pakistan. Then, in India, you are my wife, Asma." I paused. "And now—meet your cousin and your husband," I said with a flourish, handing to her my new I.D.s "Both are Mohan Ali. One is Pakistani. The other is Indian." She laughed. A warmth spread inside me as I felt what it would be like to have Uji as my wife.

***

All that can be written here is that we departed Murree late the next afternoon without the identifiable Nissan that later was thoroughly doused with kerosene and pushed into an abandoned quarry. A match was lit and tossed by some unnamed persons. We also left behind on the floor of our friends' home almost all of Ujala's long black hair. Then we traveled as Pakistani boy cousins in the back of a commercial mini-van up and down hills growing cold with the coming winter. The foothills were steep but the van climbed fluidly. The fields were brown and gold rectangles of late crops and there were old fig trees and orchards, and a wind from the north. Town after town that we passed had been con-structed many generations earlier, and along the hillside, there was a crumbling British fort, old but still used. Everything was used. Every acre planted, every tree pruned, every ox harnessed or milked, worked or slaughtered.

We sat side by side in the kind of van anyone would prize, quiet and new. Buses unloaded their passengers along the side of the road, buses so full that many riders just jumped on and hung onto the back bumper or were offered a hand up so they could sit on the top. From the roof one could trace how in the valley below tiny streams merge, forming a mighty river, one that mixes with its sister rivers, becoming the mighty Indus that feeds Pakistan and splits its map in two, rolling and rolling until finally it meets its destiny in the Arabian Sea, the sea that never fills and never empties

For a moment, cramped in the back seat of that van, I longed to be atop, to witness for myself the rough rimrock where the lips of those cliffs narrowed and almost kissed across the canyon divide. I wondered where she was walking to, the woman in the field wrapped in cloth with a basket of mustard greens on her head, rambling toward something, toward what I did not know, any more than I could know the future we in the van were rambling toward.

***

By the time we arrived in Muzaffarabad, an old city of alleyways, it was in the half-shadows of nightfall. Doors clicked closed and shutters covered windows, and wooden stalls slammed shut and the steel of storefronts were being rolled down and locked. There were two soldiers every few blocks in a pattern so regular that one could only conclude an officer with a plan must have assigned the posts. Shellfire had hit a few houses at some point in time, but from the color and texture of the repair work, it appeared the hits occurred years before. Or perhaps they were not caused by shellfire, but from earthquakes that rattled the area from time to time. There was a mix of wood smoke and roasted mutton, spicy and peppered on a spit, a delicious smell in the air.

The driver dropped us off at an ordinary hotel. We wore wool gloves and coats we had found in Murree, and underneath our woolen caps, we had fresh-cropped haircuts. For the first time in months, I was clean-shaven, like my younger "cousin." We carried two backpacks and laid them on the floor in front of the registration desk. A last ray of sun blinded the desk clerk for a moment. He squinted, stepping backward, lifting his hand to block out the light. Outside a muzzein, full-throated and reverent, sang the call to evening prayer. Uji stood in a shadow while I waited at the desk to rent our first room together.

The room had two small beds, although I had not requested that, but

I thought it was right since we were not married yet. In the pitch black outside the window, there was nothing but emptiness and my own reflection, the unshaven face and buzzed cap of dark hair, my eyes and brows were almost invisible in the glass. I looked more frightening than frightened. I turned away from the window. It was just as well that it was night, because to actually see the militarized city could have been terrifying, as we were close to the Indian border, and the war zone that is Kashmir and the challenge of the Himalayas loomed to the north and to the east.

I decided to light a fire in the stove but first I turned to light a candle. And there was Uji, who lay across one bed fully dressed, the coat, the gloves, the wool cap, even the boots. I called to her. No response. She was sound asleep. I put the candle in its holder and set it down on the small table between the beds and sat on the edge of mine, filling with the pleasure of looking completely at Uji for as long as I liked. I could admire her eyelashes, their curling, wiry, wily way of framing her eyes where the light of her lived, and now had rolled down and shuttered for the night. Firelight flickered across her cheeks and I wondered which was softer—her face or that spot below her ear that was warmed by the blood in her elegant neck. The circles dark beneath her eyes were a dramatic inheritance from her mother and all her grandmothers, from the sleepless nights of generations of women awake with sick children or sick themselves. I had noticed earlier, when she had difficulty lifting her pack, that her body had weakened from so many months behind bars. Still, I could imagine others would view her as a boy in the shapeless clothes we wore. Her breasts were small, I knew, though I had never touched them. I wanted to touch them. I laid the palm of my hand on her head imperceptibly, weightlessly, almost nothing at all, just to sip for a second what it was like to touch her. Then I covered her with a blanket, removed my boots and, remaining completely dressed, lay down on my bed and I listened to distant gunfire and Uji's breathing.

I awoke in the morning to the roar of a motorbike in the street. The room was cold and dark and we drank tea, tepid and drab as it was. Still, the hotel had provided a hotpot, teabags, sugar and powdered milk. We began to unwrap our packs. Inside were the things I had packed for the two of us and several items that our Murree friends had kindly folded inside, including sweaters and several suits—shalwar kameezes, ironed and fitted for each of us. We remained wrapped in our clothes, sitting on the floor together, sharing one blanket across our laps, pouring tea for one another, placing cups on a short table beneath the one window. I heard a motorbike backfire and speed away. We huddled together in a slim slant of daylight that fell on the floor. She spread out the wrinkled map from Rahima Mai. Its folds crinkled as she flattened with her palm a sketch of the trails around Kotha, the town we must find.

We discussed the details of our plan. Uji would remain in disguise. For fear her voice would betray her, she would not speak. She would pretend to be both deaf and dumb, a lip-reader who could pretend to use sign language, and she would never smile so that no one would want to engage with her. We would need to avoid both police and military, who might have our photographs by this time. If we were captured, I would likely be tortured and killed. She would be tortured and returned to court. Capture was foremost on our fear list, and it was both real and pervasive. We would leave Muzzafarabad in a few hours and board a bus north into the Neelam Valley toward Kotha, a remote tourist retreat, fifty miles away, a four-hour bus ride if snow or landslides did not block the road. Kotha lay on the bank of Jagran stream, close to the LoC, the Line of Control that marked the boundary between what Pakistanis called "Free Jammu and Kashmir" and what Indians called "Pakistan Occupied Kashmir." There we would buy additional mountain gear in the Neelam Valley, where the wildest, most fanatical mountaineers could be found. We would always carry our own supply of water and matches. From Kotha we would find and follow Rahima Mai's donkey trail over the border into India.

"One more thing, Mr. Map Man," she said, reaching for my hand. I looked up. "Promise we will never be separated again." Then her face was nuzzling my neck. I kissed her cheek and she kissed mine and I started to nibble, to inhale the scent of her. I was motionless, restrained, not leaning my face into her face, but allowing her space and assent. She stopped herself, exhaled loudly and our eyes locked in our promise.

I patted the pocket of my down jacket and said, "I still have the pistol." It was the nine-millimeter handgun she had carried on her rescue missions, and later had given to me for safekeeping. She reached in and took the gun.

"Good," she said. "We may need it."

At the Muzzafarabad depot, we pushed our backpacks deep in the hold of the bus, alongside cardboard boxes and plastic bags, suitcases and bubble wrapped hunting rifles, aluminum frames and climbing gear of the others on the bus—all men except for two grandmothers traveling with their grandsons, returning to the north from shopping expeditions in Muzzafarabad. The driver and his helper jammed the cargo to the limit before they would allow the passengers to board. Then, one by one, the helper checked each ticket, offered a receipt, and stepped back to allow entry. Uji and I huddled in our seat at the back of the bus, where fewer eyes would fall on our faces or observe us fumbling with our fake lip-reading and hand signing. I eyed passengers as we boarded. Good, I thought. No police. No military.

The sky was blue and seemed to be higher than usual, and the sun shone helplessly against the freeze arriving from the north. The temperature was close to freezing and would drop as we climbed from 2000 to 7000 feet above sea level. There was a great relief shared by all the passengers as the heating effect of our collective, bundled bodies caused the temperature inside the bus to rise a few degrees. Uji stared out the window where cattle huddled under a small shelter constructed of wooden planks. I did not speak but motioned from time to time and she responded, mouthing words or signing gibberish in the air with her woolen gloves. I watched her lips, those wide, rosy pads that fascinated me.

The driver turned on a speaker that played a recorded prayer and the bus backed out onto Neelam Road. Fifteen minutes later, Uji was asleep or pretended to be, her wool cap against the bus window, while I made a shopping list for Kotha, anticipating what we might need. I wondered what kind of terrain we would cover and for how long. Surely some of the time we might be above timberline but we would have to cross valleys as well. Wherever we were, we would need protection from the weather, plus food and water, a place to rest, and it occurred to me for the first time, we might very well need a guide.

The bus re-entered the same agricultural landscape we had passed through from Pindi to Murree the day before—a land of farm workers and donkeys, irrigation ditches and green fields. The palette changed from the new green of crops to a darker, shadowy evergreen. The bus was a mere pinpoint creeping into the Neelam Valley, majestic and forested, its river parallel to the side of the road, traveling in the opposite direction. It rushed downhill beneath an unending sky. I imagined what it would be like to drink from that river, to cup water so cold that my hands would ache, to let it freeze my insides, my teeth, the back of my throat, to feel the chill before it disappeared into the furnace of my bloodstream.

I was not an experienced climber, but I would be able to traverse a mountainside like the one across the road, to weave back and forth between pines, junipers, shrub oak. I imagined it. Yes, we could do that if we were careful and slow. I worried about altitude, about the effect of climbing five thousand feet in only one day. I realized how little I knew about altitude sickness. I would seek information at a clinic along the way, I decided, so we would know what to do if we lost our breath or our brains and our bearings. I thought I could feel the weight of high altitude on my lungs already.

***

An hour later, with tires on muddy Neelam Road, a haze of cloud cover began to form, and I felt the effects of high wind, dropping temperature, increased humidity from all the lungs exhaling in the closed bus. At Bara, the bus stopped to allow passengers to unfold their prayer mats onto the ground or use the toilets or purchase drinks. When we stepped off the bus, I did not help Uji down. She shivered, startled by the frosty cold. There was only one toilet for everyone and the grandmothers were first in the ladies' line. We stood in line with the men—the driver's helper in front of me, Uji behind.

"After this, the road worsens," the helper said. "But we will make it, inshallah. We always have."

It began to snow. Nearby, rows of wooden houses on stilts were watermarked by the depth to which snow had accumulated in previous years. The moment I left the toilet and Uji started to enter, two soldiers came around the building and entered the line. They wore thick green sweaters, brown camouflage helmets and flak jackets loaded with grenades—border patrol. Uji's eyes flashed and she stepped into the room, closing the door firmly while I tarried outside. The soldiers did not queue up. They examined the faces of those standing in line, looking for someone. For us? Then they walked into a field where one pissed while the other dropped his pants and squatted.

Uji and I circled the building to return to the bus. She stopped along the way and reached down into a mound of dirt next to a fencepost and rubbed some of it across her face. I hoped the bus would be empty so we could talk. But when I pulled the door handle, I discovered we were locked out. The driver and the helper were still shopping. Alone, and without exchanging a word or a glance, Uji and I were of one mind about what to do. We crossed to the far side of the bus, out of the soldiers' view where we could not be seen or heard.

"Are we drawing attention? We look like we're hiding here," she whispered. "All the others are over at the tea stall."

"Yes," I agreed. "The soldiers may move on to the tourist shop."

"Then it will be safer if we return to the toilet line," she said and we walked back in that direction. The line continued to shorten. One of the grandmothers' boys returned to the line as well.

He spoke to Uji. "How much longer to Kotha?" Uji shrugged and pointed to me to respond.

"About three hours away," I said. The boy was staring at Uji. I spoke sharply. "Don't stare, boy. It's impolite to stare at someone who is deaf and dumb."

"Sorry," he said, turning away.

I patted him on the head. "It's okay. It happens to my cousin all the time."

"He can't hear or talk?"

I was relieved to hear that Uji was seen, by this boy at least, as male. "He can talk with his hands and he can read your lips to understand what you are saying."

"So he knows we are talking about him?"

Uji laughed soundlessly, nodding, pretending to sign, "Of course," and I translated her signs to the boy.

"Can you read their lips over there?" he asked her. "What are those soldiers saying?" By that time the soldiers were at their jeep, conferring with others. "They have two photos. I saw them myself. They are looking for a man and a woman. They would not say why. Maybe if you read their lips, you can make out what they are saying."

My stomach clenched, but Uji only laughed again, shaking her head, pointing to her squinting eyes. "It's too far away," she mouthed and I told him, "It's too far, boy."

The helper sounded the horn of the bus to signal we would be leaving. The boy went to find his grandmother. Uji and I inched toward the bus, step by step, not wanting to appear too anxious, but anxious we were, not wanting to be the first to board, but wanting to be inside, dry and safe. We returned to our seats and Uji sipped water from the thermos and passed it to me. Just as well we didn't drink too much in order to delay the need for another toilet stop. I imagined she must be dreading the idea of coming to a stop somewhere ahead where the toilets might be separate and she had to use a men's toilet or worse, would have to share one with strangers.

Then two older, higher-ranking soldiers boarded and looked around. The shorter, balder one stalked down the aisle toward where we sat in the back. He stopped, checking faces again, from one to the other, passing his eyes over the boy and his grandmother and pausing on Uji's smudged face. Suddenly the soldier reached across my body and pulled off her wool cap, and she turned, startled. Her head was bare, her hair cropped, almost shaven. She looked directly at him, her eyes dark and wide, the corners of her mouth turned down. She sniffed loudly, sounding rheumy and sick and she coughed something into her hand from deep inside. She let a plug of snot drip from her nose. The soldier threw the cap back into her lap and looked away, disgusted. He gave me the once over, then turned his back and moved to the front of the bus, re-checking faces before he signaled to the driver that he could leave. The driver turned on the loudspeaker, causing the recorded prayer to squawk again as the bus pulled out, now several passengers lighter, as some had remained in Bara to return to their homes, or to hunt or fish, or perhaps just to rest and warm themselves.

The snow continued its flaking, floating, slow accumulation on the road. The sky and landscape were empty of birds. The dirt road was narrow and curvy, but it was smooth with bad patches here and there. Then the helper would open the side door and guide the driver over the ruts to avoid breaking an axle or blowing a tire. To me it was nerve-wracking and claustrophobic inside the bus with its small windows, the valley walls closing in, snow banks accumulating on each side, ice forming on cedars, nothing but the narrow unknown ahead.

I tried to think of Allah's blessings. No other vehicles on the road, thank God, as there would be no lane for another vehicle to pass. We had avoided detection by the soldiers, and within a few hours, before nightfall, we would be safely in Kotha, inside a guesthouse. Tomorrow we will find a clinic, purchase supplies, and ask about a mountain guide. We were just a couple of cousins on a mountaineering getaway.

I had to wonder what thoughts were moving around in Uji's mind as she pretended she could not hear or speak. She slept a lot until she couldn't sleep at all. The altitude was affecting both of us. I felt light-headed and my heartbeat seemed to quicken without reason. I couldn't ask her about herself openly, but when I mouthed the question—how are you?—she gave me back a relaxed smile and leaned away from me and into the side of the window. Outside the wondrous snow-covered holly bushes and short cedars, and rows of honeysuckle vines clustered next to the road that narrowed as the bus crawled along and climbed.

Uji pulled out of her daypack the shawl Rahima Mai had given her. She stretched the loosely woven wool over herself like a blanket, and stuffed it between her arm and the inside wall of the bus. She fingered it, first patting it like one might pat a small child, then weaving her fingers in and out of the web of fabric, folding it first one way, then another and another. She ran her fingertips along the threads as if she were blind and reading Braille. I noticed that the colors were more refined than the shawl itself, the dye having tones from purple, deep and rich, to a pink that deepened to magenta along the edges. And the orange threads, too, seemed to have more life than before when they had been like a jacaranda, bright and wild, and like a persimmon, pale and evenly colored. Now the color wasn't orange at all but ranged from amber to rust to clay. The threads wormed like the pulp inside the rind of a tangerine. I became thirsty, outrageously thirsty, turning the water bottle upside down and emptying it into my mouth. Uji had to pound my upper arm to stop me, and stare into my eyes to calm me down. I was panicky, but I read in her eyes, even without a word, that she understood me—that I was terrified.

She wrote me a note: Just imagine the sheep. Keep your mind on their warmth, how they can climb, can stay with their flock and make the mountains their home. Just remember the generosity of the sheep who have given us their wool.

I nodded in her direction, wondering if she was losing her mind too. I was eager to rent our room in Kotha where we could at least talk in whispers. When I looked in her eyes I could not imagine how the soldiers could have believed for a moment that she was anything but a radiant, beautiful woman. That was all I could see.

Soon the snow stopped and the landscape changed from narrow canyons to vistas, miles high and miles wide. The bald and snowy crags above timberline were bright in the afternoon light, and the valley was white with green patches where sunshine had melted the snow. A wall of ice formed on the surface of small waterfalls along the road and rainbows and hawks played above them. The bus turned into a driveway of trucks and SUVs. We were parked next to a guesthouse, a few shops, and a petrol station. There was a small mosque and a sign that read

Jagran Creek Clinic. At long last, we had arrived. Our donkey trail out of Pakistan would be nearby.

We removed our packs from the cargo bin and hiked a short distance to a guesthouse. When Uji stumbled, I caught her.

"Dizzy," she mouthed. I felt a little dizzy myself. "And weak," she added. I pointed to the clinic sign and we were first in line to talk with the medic. We looked over the brochures about altitude sickness—of course it would be common here—and it seemed to me that I had two of the six symptoms mentioned. I rated myself as "mild." The sickness could be fatal, it warned, and recommended departing immediately for a lower altitude if symptoms are moderate or severe. But there was no way we could return now—the bus would be continuing higher up to Kel and wouldn't return until the following day.

"The nurse will help you next," the clerk said to Uji, who backed away. Naturally, she would not allow herself to be examined by a nurse. I interrupted.

"My cousin, he is shy and has no money to pay. Perhaps we can just follow the recommendations in this brochure?" I asked, waving it toward the nurse.

"As you wish. She turned to the next person in line. "But be warned. People die from altitude sickness," she shouted after us. We walked to the guesthouse that provided some privacy at last. We could hardly wait for the door to our room to close. Uji took my hand at once.

"I am familiar with this, Yusuf. I lived in Chitral. I recognize the signs and for me they are mild—my head throbs and I'm exhausted, but that's all. Resting a few days here and drinking lots of water before I exert myself is all I need. But what about you?" She reached up to stroke my face and we kissed.

"Feeling much better already—a little lightheaded and having some trouble breathing, but that could be because of your kiss. Maybe we should lie down."

"We should eat something," she said.

"Not hungry."

"We should eat anyway."

But first we lay down together on one of the beds.

For a week Uji and I were in Kotha, a kind of heaven with cool days of blinding sunshine and clear nights of stars without end. Each day we prepared for the next step in our journey, a journey that would last a lifetime if we could only find our way over the mountains into India. We rested in our room at the guesthouse, learning about each other without chaperones, without prison walls, with no ocean between us, nothing but a cotton sheet, a woolen blanket, the surface of our skin.

The guesthouse was a plain, recently built shelter, and the town was little more than a hillside of gravel and mud. There were clusters of wooden buildings faded gray with worn, slanted roofs, and row houses with well-insulated vinyl siding for tourists who could afford them. Once in Kotha, there were no signs of the police, but because we were so close to the LoC, we assumed that soldiers must be patrolling nearby.

Each day we practiced climbing into the hills, and our hikes became longer and longer. At the town's only restaurant, I purchased take out and brought the dinner to our room at the guesthouse. Uji set up the small table for the two of us with a lit candle in the center. I sat across from her, spooning yogurt over the potatoes and wild onions on her plate, cutting half of my goat meat and offering it to her on the tines of a fork. "Here," I said. "Meat." I wanted to strengthen her to prepare for the climb ahead. She opened her lips and I slipped it inside.

***

On the second afternoon in Kotha, she stood at the window of our room studying a distant line of soldiers moving along the top of a steep wall. She pointed.

"Pakistani or Indian?" she asked and I came over and stood behind her squinting.

"Who knows?

"How do they ever tell each other apart?"

"Is that a Sikh turban on that soldier standing at the end?"

"It is."

"Then it must be the Indian Army," I said, closing the shutter.

It was our first sighting of a military patrol along the fenced line between the two Kashmirs. We had heard that Indian security forces sometimes tortured and killed civilians, especially women. Accusations ran in both directions, of course, but I had read the human rights reports of the detaining, burnings, beatings, abuse and rape of men, women and children and the retaliations that caused one brother to rush into the field to avenge the death of another and so on and so on. It was a case of both official and unofficial terror, and any incident could cause outrage to arise, a mob to gather, a deployment to occur, an international incident to be reported, with the potential of nuclear disaster on both sides.

Gradually we became used to our dual roles—cousins outside the room, a married couple inside. In public I did the talking, keeping up the pretense of signing and lip-reading when others were around. In the tourist shop I spent most of my cash on equipment for the trip—flashlights and walking sticks and special gloves and goggles, fur-lined hoods for protection from high winds. I returned to the room and spilled the items out of a bag and onto the bed. Uji looked bewildered and then she laughed.

"I doubt Rahima Mai would have given me a map to cross the border if it required all that," she said. She picked up the new woolen mittens that promised protection. She fingered them.

"But it's impossible to know what to expect," I said.

"Impossible without help. Yusuf, we will need a guide."

"But you will have to be able to talk. We can't have this pretense on the mountain."

"We have to find the right guide. I will pray for help."

Her words, "pray for help," surprised me. After so many years away from Pakistan, I was often surprised by the constant religious tones to everyday conversation. Somehow I had not expected Uji to be religious and, I admit, it made me uncomfortable.

"Does it bother you that I don't attend Friday services?" I asked.

"I am not on my knees throughout the day, am I? Like the women who always remember the five times."

"But something has changed from your being in jail."

"It's not due to my imprisonment," she said softly, "and I am not sure how much I should say about something I myself don't completely understand." She looked up at me. "You are like my husband—no, not *like* my husband. You *are* my husband, so I must share my soul with you. I will tell you that there is something about these mountains that affects my soul—the silence, the stillness, the dark nights, the stars. Perhaps it is Allah. I don't really understand, but those distant things touch me here."

"I know what you mean," I said, but I was not sure I really did.

When I woke on the third day, I heard feral noises I did not recognize. Uji was murmuring, pulling me closer in her deep sleep. She squirmed like an animal with a pitiful desperation. My mouth wanted to nestle in her neck. I shook her and she woke, warm and dreamy.

"Stop," she said, keeping her eyes closed, reaching for my hand. "Shh!" I relaxed back, watching her, silent, biding time. Then she laughed out loud. "I was trying to capture my dream before it slipped away. You'll never guess. I was dreaming of Rahima Mai!" She paused. "That's it—

that's what the dream means!" She was suddenly awake and in charge. "Her people will help us. We can start by asking around about people who knew Rahima Mai when she lived here. Perhaps they can point us to a guide. It's risky, but we must find a guide we can trust, someone with whom we can be who we really are. At least until we cross over."

It was not my way, to follow a message from a dream, to put confidence in something like that. I began to question if we were exaggerating the risk of discovery that seemed so unlikely in such a remote area. This far into the Neelam Valley there was no television, no internet, and few radio signals to spread the news of Uji's escape. We were only two days away from the prison in Rawalpindi, but it was an entirely different world.

In Kotha the teashop owner poured Darjeeling at the counter, where Uji and I were the only customers. The cups are ceramic and small. I asked about Rahima Mai.

"Ah. I knew her. She's my cousin. As children we played in the hills." Her bloodshot eyes grew wider as she spoke. "My cousin and her husband left here many years ago, but I sometimes think of her still." She poured us each another cup of milk tea. The journalist in me tried to think of something friendly to say.

"She told us about her donkey," I said.

"You must mean that husband of hers?" the cousin joked. "He was a donkey." She laughed, carrying the pot of tea to a table on the shadowed side of room that was draped in rugs and blankets so that the starkness of sun and snow could not penetrate them. "Rahima Mai had lots of donkeys. The family raised them as pack animals, rented and sold them to riders, climbers, traders and so on." The woman spread her hands over the belly of her apron as she recalled the past. "Lots and lots of donkeys, but always Rahima Mai would always have a favorite." Uji raised her hands and moved her fingers, as if signing to me that she had been Rahima Mai's favorite donkey at Adiala. I interrupted reminiscing.

"We are looking for someone to guide us through the backcountry," I said. It was a serious admission to make to a stranger—an illegal border crossing. It got her immediate attention. "Someone good." Uji watched the shopkeeper's lips, pretending to read them.

"Oh, there are lots of guides around here." She mouthed her words in Uji's direction. Uji gestured toward me.

"We want someone who is like family," I said. "Maybe someone from Rahima Mai's family?"

"Oh, they are in the cities now. The young ones move away, you know. The old ones die before they ever leave." She turned to walk away and then turned back, pointing her finger to the north. "Auntie Beezah is still here. She lives up the stream. All alone. She's Rahima Mai's auntie, her mother's elder sister. She would have an idea who in the family could help you--if any of them are still around."

***

By the fourth day we had recovered our strength and our clarity. In the morning there was cloud cover to the east, a gray flat-bottomed thing that hung in the sky, a full presence, potentially ominous. We explored the floor of the Jagran Valley, toward the stream the shopkeeper told us was the course to Auntie Beezah's house. There was little snow on the ground. The sun dried the sap from the pine needles that crunched under our feet, a playful percussion as we trekked along. A gold toad startled us on the path. There were squealing chirps and calls of peregrine falcons, and one sudden, surprising roar of a jet plane not far above. We lugged small packs with lunch, water, compass, and some of the smaller equipment I had purchased, and, of course, Rahima Mai's map. We stuck to the stream until we found an unmistakable trail to the west, a defined hillside path that wound around cedar and sage, traversing the mountain, creating a long, slow and steady route, the kind of trail that anyone might manage, even in the snow.

Near the top of the hill was a structure—not a house exactly, more like a stone hut built into the mountainside with a door and one small window, a chimney smoking from a fire inside, a pen with goats and donkeys, two outbuildings, crude and wooden. Dogs barked and a person appeared in the doorway with a rifle cradled in her arms. I was alarmed.

"Assalam aleikum," I said, eyeing the gun.

"Waleikum salaam," she replied, not moving the rifle. She was wearing men's clothes—not the shalwar kameez of the towns, but heavy trousers and a homemade wool cardigan, Pathan style flat hat over her headscarf, and gloves, thick, leathered, and dry. Her face was a wiry bundle of muscles and nerves with fierce eyes. Not a soft spot on her.

"Beezah Bibi?" Uji asked. I was surprised to hear Uji speak. Now there was no point in pretending to be unable to hear or speak. The woman gestured us inside.

"Quickly," she said. Uji and I responded immediately to her authority.

The room was dark and deep, larger than one would expect. We sat on pillows over rugs that covered the dirt floor. The table was a round slice of a pine trunk, old and thick. A fire smoldered in a corner pit. There was a large open cage with three big dogs inside. They stood and watched us, but did not growl. The old woman lit her kerosene stove under a kettle and turned up the wick on a lamp. She grunted softly as she moved around the room completing her tasks. At last, she sat at the pine table alongside us. Two of the dogs lay down on their sides, back-to-back pressing into each other, the other one remained on its haunches, calm and alert.

Beezah directed her piercing eyes at Uji. "How may I help you?"

"I am Asma Mohan," Uji began. "I am friends with your niece in Pindi—Rahima Mai. We are like sisters." Beezah perked up at the mention of Rahima Mai. "Since Rahima is like a sister to me and you are her auntie, you are my auntie, too." The old woman held the handle of the teakettle with a dirty rag. She turned to me.

"Yes, but who are you?" she asked.

"Ali. Asma's husband, so you are my auntie as well."

"Good. Then we are all related," she said, wiping the insides of two mugs with the same cloth. "Related," she repeated and hesitated a second, holding the gaze, "but then, after all, who isn't, huh?" She cackled. I wondered just how old this woman might be. There was a raw, worn beauty about her. Her lips had disappeared into the pit of her mouth, but her teeth looked big and strong. Her eyes were extraordinary—one blue, one brown—and they seemed lit from deep inside, especially the blue one.

"And where is your husband?" I asked her. Uji cringed. Beezah's eyes flashed.

"No husband. Puuh! What a worthless thing that would be." She laughed. "I know husbands. I've had husbands." She began pouring water from the steaming kettle into a pot she had stuffed with stringy plants she fished out of a paper bag. "How is Rahima, that old Russian? Ha! She always did look like a Cossack, don't you agree?" Beezah was enjoying herself, unconcerned about whether or not Uji agreed. "Tell me whatever you can tell me. And how is that worthless husband of hers, eh?"

"Her husband passed away several years ago," Uji said. "Rahima has a government job and she's in good health."

"Good. Good. But she'll be lonely, bless her. Rahima always needed a man." We were silent while she poured more tea into our thick ceramic cups. Then Uji unfolded the map Rahima Mai had drawn and flattened it on the table.

"Auntie, we are looking for someone to guide us over the old donkey trail, past the LoC into Jammu and Kashmir."

"Why the old trail? Why not cross at a checkpoint?" Beezah was look-ing away, drinking her tea as though her question were only a casual one. I hoped Uji would not reveal too much.

"Because it's the way that Rahima Mai recommended," Uji said matter-of-factly. "Are there any guides in the family that we could hire?" She paused. "We have money."

"It will require money and more," said the old woman. "That trail is a good one—" she began, but seeing the relief on Uji's face, she spoke slowly as if she wanted to be sure we were listening. "That is, when there are no snowslides, or landslides, or snow leopards, or wolves, or India militia or thieves or night raiders, or—." She stopped, reading the alarm all over our faces. "Or yetis," she shouted, spitting out the words, smack-ing the table, laughing out loud. "Oh yes, yetis, too! Abominable snow-men! And sea monsters! Lots of sea monsters!" Beezah paused to read her success. She had made us feel foolish. It was her pleasure. "But, all right, I'll do it."

"You will do it?" I said. "We were thinking perhaps a nephew or a brother?"

"You insult me," Beezah snapped. "Who knows these mountains bet-ter than I? A pup? A kit? I was just ten years old when infidels shot my mother down in the 1948 war. These mountains and I are like sisters—sisters who sometimes love each other and sometimes hate, but they understand one another completely." She faced me. "You think I am not strong enough? Try me," she challenged, placing her elbow on the table, raising her forearm. I backed off. "All right then," she continued, "We will have to leave soon, before the next freeze. We need a few days to pre-pare, and we will wait for good weather. If we start out early, the three of us can cross over in a day." Beezah's eyes grew smaller, receding into the block of her face. We looked at each other and nodded in unison. "A thousand rupees," she said. "Plus expenses."

Each day we traipsed back and forth from Kotha to Beezah's property. One day the sky was cloudy and the winds blew. The next, the sky was high and the air was still. In the mornings there was frost that coated the fences, but no real freeze to prevent our journey. Little by little we carried to her hut all of our possessions.

"Bring everything," she insisted. "All of it—so I can decide what to take and what to leave behind. And, what it is that you two are made of."

On the third day, and for the last time, Uji and I scaled a path away from Beezah's hut to a distant crest above timberline. We held hands in an awkward way, pulling and pushing against each other for support, as we slid repeatedly on the slippery scree deposited there by millennia of landslides. The morning's pervading cold dissipated on the burners of the sun-soaked boulders and the view below us became a curvy furrow of river and heath, dark and rich. I knew from my study of the maps that what we were looking at was the area where the old donkey path would take us.

Since we first boarded the bus in Muzzafarabad, a kind of silence had grown between Uji and me, fed first by the ruse of deaf and dumb we fostered at the hotel, on the bus, in the shops. Then a different kind of silence arose, not between us but all around, enveloping us in something we had never shared before. Uji tried to talk about it on the way back to the hut. I took her hand to lead her to a rock where we both could sit but she insisted on walking alone.

"I remember in Chitral I had this same feeling," she began, pushing my hand away, "—that the earth and the sky were two forks scrambling my brains, and sometimes my mind would float in silence for hours." Suddenly Uji's foot slipped on a patch of mud and pine needles and she fell to her knees. I reached for her and as she tried to stand, we glimpsed there, beneath the rock, a kind of cave just big enough for one person. "That certainly looks familiar," said Uji, gesturing for me to look deeper.

Inside was a flat surface with bowls of water, mountain flowers, incense, candles and a hand drum. There were photographs and drawings, images of Sufi saints with colorful auras. "It's a shrine," she said, surprised, "something like my father's, but these saints are different. They are all women."

"Well, this one's completely naked," I pointed out, peering inside the cave. I picked the photo up for a closer look and Uji flashed a naughty grin. I reached for a statue. "It's Sanskrit. But this third one—ugh! Look at these ugly claws and the huge tongue hanging out, the necklace of skulls, and fire eyes."

"I recognize her. It's Kali, the Vedic goddess," she said. "And this shrine is well-tended. The flowers are fresh. I think this must be Beezah's shrine. Perhaps this is her form of religion."

After our glimpse of Beezah's curious interior life, we let go of any misgivings that she might cheat or abandon us, and we began to trust her completely. By day five, we had moved into her hut and were sleeping on the floor together, with the dogs, not wrapped up into each other, but close enough that we could smell each other's breath, and the dogs. In the morning when we woke, a fire had been lit but Beezah had vanished. Uji and I bundled up in blankets outside in a sunbeam with mugs of milk tea. The early frost melted wherever the rays hit. Her donkeys brayed in their pen.

"I see you found my shrine," Beezah said when she returned. Uji and I glanced at each other. Neither of us had mentioned our discovery of her shrine. "Footprints," Beezah said. "One of you must have fallen. Probably the clumsy one," she added, eyeing Uji with a grin. She turned to me. "And it was probably you who moved my photo of Lalla."

"The naked one?" I asked, embarrassed.

"Exactly. Six hundred years ago she roamed these mountains dressed just like that—in her bare skin—winter and summer—she was a yogi and a mystic unburdened by the cares of this world. The Sufis recognize her as a poet-saint, and she belongs to all of Kashmir. Her poems live in our memories."

"May we hear one?" Uji asked, and Beezah began whispering words, as if conspiring with her own collar. We moved closer to listen:

> Impart not esoteric truth to fools,
> Nor on molasses feed an ass.
> Do not sow seed in sandy beds,
> Nor waste your oil on cakes of bran.

I thought her choice of poem was a part insult, part joke, but I felt only amusement.

"The other saint is the ferocious Machig Labdron," Beezah continued, "the Tibetan *dakini*, dressed only in bones from the charnel grounds of cremation where she dances with a drum in her raised right hand. A mighty mother goddess. Don't get on her bad side!" Beezah laughed out loud, accepting the mug of tea Uji offered.

"And the third?" Uji asked.

"She interests you?" Beezah responded. "She's the Sikh warrior-saint, Mai Bhago, the Guru's bodyguard. Back then she wore men's clothes to lead troops into battle. Like you, Mai Bhago was a cross dresser." Uji's eyes widened. "Oh, I heard about your charade in the village. Pretending to be male cousins. Ha! It was quite amusing to everyone."

My heart raced in fear at this revelation. Still, something in me trusted that Beezah would not endanger us by telling the villagers what she knew. I really wanted to know how she could be a Muslim and also revere these strange creatures. "Are you a Muslim?" I asked.

"Of course," she said. "I wash. I pray. I am on my knees throughout the day, am I not? You are needy and I am giving to you. Look at this skinny body—does it not fast during Ramadan? There is no God but Allah and Mohammad is his prophet—but—is he the only prophet? Are there not others Allah has sent to us? Are some of them perhaps females?" she asked. "Women?"

"That's only four of the five pillars," I said. "What about the hajj? Will you journey to Mecca at least once?" Beezah stood up slowly and assumed her stance, fists on her hips. She opened her arms.

"This is my sacred city," she said. "Every day is my intended journey, my hajj." Then she sang out, slowly, full throated:

> *We will all go to Mecca on the Hajj*
> *We'll wear only warm, clean garments on the Hajj*
> *We will circle the pine tree on the Hajj*
> *We will drink the Mother's milk on the Hajj*

Beezah sang the words over and over. Then her eyes wandered as she hummed and when she was done, when the last note dissolved, she collapsed in a heap. Uji rushed to her and felt her pulse. Beezah's eyes fluttered.

"Cover me with a blanket," Beezah whispered. "I need to sleep now. I need to die a little."

***

When five days of blue skies had passed and Beezah could sniff no tempests in the near future, we rose in the dark morning and wrapped up in layers of warm clothes for the day's journey. Beezah insisted that we carry only what would fit in our daypacks.

"Remove anything that's heavy—like that flashlight," she commanded. "The pack is ready when it is full but at the same time, feels almost weightless." I was annoyed to be leaving new equipment behind.

"They will only become heavier as we climb," Uji whispered.

"But we might need rope and extra sweaters, rain gear."

"I understand. But we have to trust she knows what she's doing. That's our situation."

Before we left, Beezah fed her dogs, her donkeys, her goats, her one cow. Then she led the way up the hill. A crow cried out as we passed the cave with the shrine inside.

"I hear the call to prayer," Beezah said, giggling at the crow. She dropped her pack from her back and she leaned inside the cave. She struck a wooden match. When she bowed down, Uji imitated her, and dropped to her knees, her face in her hands. I remained erect. Beezah lit a candle then extinguished it with a pinch of spit on her fingers. She took the postcard of Lalla, pulled open her jacket, then her sweater, then her shirt, until Lalla was warm against Beezah's skin.

Soon the rays of the sun reached us. We hiked up the first hill and down the other side. By noon we were hammering the surface of the Neelam River to cool our feet and drinking its icy snowmelt. I tossed a few pebbles in the water while Uji handed out cooked potatoes, carrots and butter. We drank cold tea and rested in a circle of young cedars.

Beezah showed us on the map that we were close to the donkey path. "The veil between worlds is thin on this trail," she mumbled and I ignored her. She was an odd creature and some of her comments were hard to take seriously. I was eager to be on that path, confident that then I could find our way over the LoC. But I also was aware that Beezah needed to rest. Again, she fell into a sleep that she entered deeply and, twenty minutes later, awoke from quickly.

We hiked up the mountain on the other side of the river just a kilometer from the Line of Control. It was steeper, requiring a broad traverse. The blue sky was clear without even a white cloud to break its monotony. Beezah said it would take us four hours to cross more hills and valleys until we would find a road inside India, in Jammu-Kashmir, and then we would separate—Uji and I to the Muslim town of Akram and Beezah back on the donkey trail to her home.

The landscape became a Kashmiri weave. Coral and magenta shrubs covered the hillside. Some small birds hunted for insects and others snipped blue berries off the plentiful junipers. The roots of Himalayan green cedars twisted just beneath the ground, and we would trip on them and stumble, feeling the snap of branches on our faces. The landscape became a tangle of colorful brambles and eventually the donkey trail itself disappeared. We entered the world of the wolf, the red deer, the marmot and the pheasant.

Beezah hacked at the undergrowth and I chopped pine branches as we went. We spent the afternoon that way. Uji did not complain, but she showed the strain of physical exertion. She would stop to rest against a tree every ten minutes or so and she soon lagged behind. Six months of sitting in prison had weakened her legs. I wondered if we would cross the LoC and meet our destination before dark. Uji was so far behind she was almost out of sight. When Beezah caught up to me, we agreed to keep an eye on her as we went ahead. We climbed through the foliage together step by step.

"When do we cross the LoC?" I asked and the old crone turned with a friendly, unreserved face.

"When?" She pointed to the south and snorted. "We passed it ten minutes ago." At a distance was a gleam of light where Beezah pointed, a high fence layered with wire, a structure too thick to penetrate the barbed forest where we climbed. I called in a loud whisper to Uji, "We're in India!" We watched her panting to catch up with us. She and I hugged. We had made it this far. We had escaped Pakistan.

"India!" Uji said, grinning ear to ear. But Beezah's face crinkled into a mean-looking mask.

"India! Pakistan! Puuh! Politics!" She spat out the word. "It's all Kashmir!"

"But there are no soldiers, no military, around here," Uji said.

"Oh, they are here," Beezah murmured, gesturing with her chin. "Here. There. Everywhere. They don't maintain a post or a checkpoint here because there is no road. But they patrol the area, so keep quiet and watch out. You don't want the Indian army to catch you." She looked us in the eye—back and forth—as if she wondered which of us would give her the whole truth. "And I assume you do not want the Pakistan army to catch you either. Hmm?" Had she guessed we were on the run from the law? We were momentarily speechless as Beezah re-asserted her authority. "We need to pick up the pace now, my friends," she said, sniffing the air and pointing to the northern sky. "It looks like clouds are building and may be moving into the valley. I can feel the temperature dropping."

"That?" I asked, looking up at the thin cloud that did not appear to me to be threatening.

"Let's go!" ordered Beezah, ignoring me. And we climbed.

By midafternoon, snow began to fall. Beezah had recognized the scent of it. Her body knew, from spending a lifetime in one locale with its spiral of seasons, the vagaries of its natural events. Having lived her life both sweating in Sindhi sun and soaking in the rains of Punjab, Uji became like a child who had been denied the delight of swirling snow. Unlike the killing curtains of blizzards she knew in Chitral, this snow was friendly, like a display in a tourist shop, or a light show in a theater. The sun warmed the falling particles around us and transformed them into sips of refreshing rain on our lips. Uji raised her face to heaven and twirled around.

Beezah hustled us down the next slope like little children. The slick ground began to slip away beneath us and we used our knives to strip low branches off trees for walking sticks. We dug each one in place surely and firmly before the first step, then the stick, then the next step, then the stick. Uji's face had reddened from the physical strain but she seemed to have grown stronger. She was grinning now that we were almost at our destination. I turned to her.

"Slow down," I whispered as loudly as I dared. "More important that you not fall than that we arrive on time. There's no train to catch."

"Maybe no train to catch," Beezah agreed, slowing, "but you two had better prepare your story. You will have a ten-kilometer hike to town from where we separate. Soldiers will stop you on the road. It is inevitable. Who are you? Where are you going? Are you ready for that?" Beezah stared at me and I fumbled to reply. Beezah just shook her head, exasperated, as if she were the only one working on a solid plan for us. "Then I'll just tell you." she said, "You say you are on a day hike, vacationing from Delhi. . . now where do you live in Delhi?" She looked at Uji who had no answer, but I did.

"Zakir Naga," I said. "Never been there but it's a place where my friend lives. In South Delhi." Beezah looked pleased and continued her interrogation.

"And you are returning to Akram from your day hike." We nodded. "And where are you staying in Akram?" I exhaled and looked at Uji for an idea. We had no idea. "Just as I thought," said Beezah. "You tell them you left your things at the bus station and plan to find a rental tonight. You have your IDs in order, correct? And no weapons?"

"Yes. Yes," Uji said, patting her inside zipper pocket. "We have them. And a gun," she added. I removed the pistol from inside Uji's jacket.

"Give that to me," demanded Beezah. "They will certainly search you for weapons. If they catch you with a gun, they will give you a one-way ticket to prison!" She stuffed the gun inside her coat next to the picture of Lalla. "We must move faster now. We've lost time enough. That cloud is playing God with us," she said pointing to the sky. "It holds our lives in its hands."

"A cloud doesn't have hands," the editor in me said aloud and I swallowed hard, regretting my words. I heard Uji suck in her breath.

"That cloud holds our lives in its hands," Beezah repeated.

"Allah is just playing hide and seek with us," I said, trying to make up for arguing with her. Such a stupid thing to do.

"Don't you know anything?" Beezah shook her head. "It's like Lalla says:

> *I traveled a long way seeking God*
> *but when I finally gave up and turned back*
> *there He was, within me!*

"Ha!" Beezah laughed. "God is not playing hide and seek. God *is* hide and seek!"

Beezah and Uji held on to each other for support as they plodded downhill with hiking sticks. I picked up the pack Beezah left on the ground, threw it over one shoulder with my own pack over the other. By the time we reached the bottom, the sun was setting in a spectrum of wild reds behind the closest ridge and the air was freezing inside our nostrils. We stopped again to drink tea and eat more goat cheese.

"We will be able to see the road from the next peak," Beezah promised.

I felt annoyed that Beezah had made us leave all of our extra clothes in the hut. We could have used them now. But all we could do in the face of the changing weather was zip our down coats, fasten our fur-lined hoods, adjust our wool socks and boots, and protect our skin with thick mittens and face masks. The swirling snow was beginning to accumulate, making the hike treacherous. The pine needles underfoot were no longer visible, and the untrampled ground ahead was completely white. The footprints of small animals disappeared in a world smoothed by degrees of whiteness. We entered another dimension, one defined by fate, circumstance, and coincidence. In the snowfall, with the view framed by only a slit of fur around the hem of our hoods, we were like blind survivors endlessly seeking exit.

"Up this mother mountain and down the other side," Beezah announced. Her spirit had lightened. The wind rose from the north and the pines began to clack against one another as their tops swayed. Uji was using all her energy to support Beezah who leaned onto Uji's right arm. She wrapped her other arm around Beezah's shoulder as we hiked.

Even in the snow, green patches of tall grass appeared amid shorter brown blades burned by the wind. Their roots were alive through the grace of the sun and the damp earth that held them. Lines of cedars were scattered here and there across the great expanse of the mountain's foot. The trees drank from the underground rivers-to-be, the landscape fertile and lush. The snow never let up, yet never worsened. We avoided the fearful paths in our own minds--frozen toes or racing hearts, hunger or thirst, a grip of terror at the sound of gunshots, the rumble of thunder. And that was how we found the Akram road—step by step, as constant as the snowfall—moving in our own dream worlds, cold, exhausted, in danger, on a common donkey path over an ordinary mountain.

But what would happen to Beezah if Uji and I followed Akram Road? How would she return home in the dark in the snow? With a forest filled with wildcats and bears? We tried but there was no point in trying to talk her into joining us—she had no false ID and to be caught by the Indian Army was worse than hiking the donkey path in reverse alone. Uji worried about Beezah.

"We could camp nearby for the night and you could leave tomorrow when it warms up," she suggested. Beezah looked straight ahead, not turning toward Uji.

"And who says it will warm up? Tonight is probably warmer than tomorrow will be at noon. Do not worry about me. I have Lalla." She patted the lump under her coat where Lalla's picture was tucked next to the pistol. "In a way I am Lalla now that I am old and care less and less about this world. Allah calls to me and I search in the forest. Then he calls me from the sky and I run into the field. I will head back to Allah and hide in the mountains. In our game, now it's His turn to seek me."

Beezah chose two hiking sticks and accepted my help in strapping her pack over her shoulders. I felt a strange warmth around her head, then I surprised myself. I went down on my knees in gratitude, bowed my head, and I kissed Beezah's shoes. Now she looked surprised.

"I did not expect humility from you," she said sincerely, holding out her open palm. I looked at it quizzically. "A thousand rupees, please!" Beezah laughed and we laughed, too, at the three of us and the crazy world we found ourselves in. I filled her hand with bills and then Beezah hugged Uji one last time and turned away.

Uji and I traipsed toward the road. From time to time we glanced back to catch one more glimpse of the old woman, and there she was, moving step by step, slowly and studiously, hiking stick over hiking stick. Beezah stopped then and removed her hat and coat, stepped out of her trousers and shook her matted headful of gray braids from under her headscarf. She began to circumambulate a pine tree, circling and circling, and except for her high-top boots, she was completely naked.

"Look!" Uji pulled on my arm. "We must go back for her. She will freeze to death."

"She seems like a crazy old woman," I agreed, "but she knows exactly what she is doing."

"You're right, Yusuf. She is not of this world. And she does not want our help. Still, I can't leave her there." Uji started to drift away from me, and I pulled her back by her wrist. She was stronger than I expected and pushed me away, always moving toward Beezah across the field. I watched her tramp back through the wet ground. As shadows spread and the space between us expanded, both Uji and Beezah looked like tiny creatures creeping along a vast plain. I felt exposed and foolish there on the mountainside with long even folds of snow cover folding into themselves, like a blanket of wool from the whitest sheep. There was a mere fringe of starlight peeking through the mysterious weaving, a thing as profound as a spiderweb. At a distance the lights of Akram were a mere outline of a low-lying town twinkling. Between here and there was a vast, open expanse of land.

I felt a wave of nausea and exhaled sharply, shaking my upper body. A part of me wished to run back and hide in the trees. I looked around and saw ahead, about a quarter-kilometer away, along the thread of a dirt road, two beaming headlights of a vehicle with four soldiers—two seated in front and two standing in back. I called out to Uji then, pointed to the military vehicle, and she stopped and came running back to me. We returned to the road together.

"Allah hafiz, Auntie Beezah," Uji prayed, and I joined her in the wish, "God protect you." When we searched the slope for Beezah, she was gone.

"Allah hafiz, Auntie Beezah, God protect you," repeated Uji. The four young soldiers in the Jeep accepted the backpacking tale I spun for them and checked the IDs Uji presented. They searched our packs and patted my clothes, and they drove away, parallel to the Line of Control. Then we trudged toward Akram.

***

The sky was immense, dark and clear. Stars clustered, overlapping their edges of fire light-years away where galaxies and moments co-exist. We scanned the sky, encompassing the entire cosmos in one view.

"Impossible," I stated. "More stars than ever could be visible in one lifetime, but all in one night." But Uji had stopped looking at the sky. She was looking at me. It was as if she could not take her eyes off me.

"I cannot believe my good fortune." She removed her black wool cap to reveal the profile of her shapely head. "I have not felt so completely at peace in my entire life." Ahead of us a single eagle swooped, and we could hear the call to evening prayer from loudspeakers afar. We were so tired as we continued down the road.

At the bus station near the edge of town Uji and I stopped and warmed ourselves. We bought a copy of *The Akram Times,* and sat near the wood stove to eat the last of our potatoes and butter. I searched the headlines for any news of the prison escape. We purchased milk tea from a vendor and rested on a wooden bench. Uji had covered her head with a dupatta and removed her coat and mittens. She placed them near the fire.

I was able to confirm that several buses arrived from Srinagar that day. If asked, we would say we were passengers on one of those.

"There's nothing in the newspaper about you or Adiala," I told her. "Mostly political news from Delhi, and lots of local military stories." I showed her an advertisement for a hotel located around the corner from the bus station. "Shall we stay there? Expensive, but we can find something else tomorrow." When she did not reply, I whispered her new name. "Asma." I shook her shoulder. She was sitting up perfectly straight, sound asleep.

That night we slept in the depot and the next day found an affordable guesthouse with a shared kitchen and we did some shopping. We slept some more and began to outline what our ordinary and uneventful life together would be. The next day we walked by a nearby elementary school and Uji pointed to the windows. The sight of children's paper cutouts taped on the glass thrilled the teacher in her. On the third day, dark clouds floated in from the north. The first storm of winter blew into the valley and remained for two weeks. As avalanches closed the roads, a winter hush enclosed the town.

We would not be able to leave until spring when the roads cleared and the ice on the Kishenganga River cracked open. But deep below, the river continued its year-round journey, where floating, smooth-coated otters and leaping salmon rolled in the life between its riverbanks, joining with the Jhelum River farther on, after it merged with the Neelam that drained the valleys. As the river grew and ran freely below winter's ice, in a day's journey it entered Rawalpindi, less than one hundred fifty kilometers away, not far from Adiala Prison from which only two weeks earlier, some say, a prisoner and her accomplice successfully fled.

It soon became clear that the Akram District was a pocket of hell deep inside a natural paradise. Majestic and ancient, it was criss-crossed by barbed and razored fences of the LoC. Life was dominated by extremes of weather and war. Thousands of Hindus had fled the area when Muslim extremists conducted systematic and ongoing ethnic "cleansing" of the area. Most of the Pandits, the local Hindu scholars, had become refugees elsewhere, although the Sikh warrior class considered it a matter of pride and remained to fight. Now the district was more than ninety percent Muslim. At first the local Muslims welcomed the protection of India in the conflict with the Pakistani fundamentalists. But when Indian police and security forces engaged in widespread use of torture, in retaliation, Pakistani militants slipped over borders to plant bombs. The Indian army killed both suspected insurgents and innocent civilians, burning entire Muslim neighborhoods, engaging in gang rape, torturing, maiming of women of all ages, as well as beatings, electrocutions and detainment without charges. Thousands of Kashmiri men disappeared. Many believed that in the bed of the Kishenganga River that had been born of the glaciers and snowfall to the north, the bodies of their brothers lay in mass graves, bullet-ridden and covered not by clean, brown earth, but by shallow sand and ice. The loyalties of the Kashmiris were split, not because they were half-Muslim, half-Hindu, but because they were all-Kashmiri.

This was where we, Akram's newest couple—Asma Mohan, the teacher, and her husband Mohan Ali, the journalist—settled down to life in a new country.

"Never will I lose sight of who we are and why we are here," Uji said. She never lost hope of returning to Pakistan, of kissing the face of her dear father. "May Allah watch over him always," she prayed each day.

For me it was a more difficult adjustment. I'd come to love the cities I'd lived in—Karachi and New York were my forms of heaven. In Akram there was not even dial-up access to the internet, so I turned to what I understood: putting words on paper, making stories. When Uji left for work in the mornings, I would sort my notes from our journey and boot up the used computer we bought. I began two projects—my personal journal and a story I intended for publication someday, the story of the escape from Pakistan of the one I called "The She-lion of Punjab."

Chapter 2

For Every Soul There Is a Watcher

Lahore, Pakistan, 1996 and 2014

The sky filled with crows. Ambulance sirens wailed down Airport Road. At Jinnah Hospital, a long incision ripped open Meena's body. A baby was pulled into the light, and the cord was cut. Birth and death collided that day as Meena died twice—once to herself, and once to her daughter, Nafeesa.

Eighteen years later, Nafeesa eases into a molded plastic chair outside her grandmother's room at that same Jinnah Hospital, where now her father's mother, her Nanaa, is losing her life. Nafeesa fingers the fringe of her paisley shawl. She was at school when the firebomb hit her home, killed her great-grandfather, then smoke surrounded everything and filled her grandmother's lung and her body succumbed, the body where Nafeesa has taken comfort for her entire life.

Whenever the nurses scurry in or out of Nanaa's room, Nafeesa pops up to peek in before the door eases shut on its hydraulic hinge. She can see her father on his knees in there beside the bed that bears his mother. There are white bandages wrapped around her head, tubes that transport life's liquids and gases in and out, and there are black holes where her nose and mouth should be. His face in his hands, a shawl of sadness wraps around him and Nafeesa can feel its pressure pull her own shoulders forward, one weight for her grandmother and one for her father. She and her father, Zeshan Shaheed, have never been close; she pities him and sometimes resents him, but she knows she loves him. Nanaa always said that something in his soul broke years ago when her mother, Meena, died. Nafeesa has learned how to live without her mother, but she wonders now, however will her father be able to live without his?

Zeshan exits the hospital room, looking like an old man with tears soaking his beard. As usual, and as expected, he is in one of his depressive moods. Nafeesa lingers near the door as a nurse slips out of the room and passes by, whispering, "Risk of infection," she warns. "Best not to enter. Your grandmother is unconscious anyway. She would not know if you were there or not."

"What do we do now, Abbu?" she asks, searching Zeshan's damp blue eyes. Always dressed properly, today Zeshan wears the type of triangular fleece cap made famous by Pakistan's first Governor General, Muhammad Jinnah. The front of the cap barely conceals a large mole centered on his forehead. Zeshan bends his index finger in Nafeesa's direction, and reaches out to tug the edge of her headscarf. He does this with thumb and index finger, careful not to touch either her hair or her skin. It is a corrective move that adults in a family feel they are entitled to. She pulls away and tucks the tendrils inside her dupatta herself, then tightens the fringe around her neck.

"Come, let's go home," he says, leading Nafeesa away by her elbow so quickly she is unable to catch a last glimpse of her Nanaa. He says "home," as if they have one. Outside is a waiting Toyota with its nameless driver, then interminable traffic on the familiar road to whatever may remain of the house in Faisal Town. Alone in the backseat, Nafeesa imagines the house is still ablaze from the terrifying bomb; she pictures long flames licking the clouds, steaming into winter's sooty sky. And her heart hears all the burning questions: Who has done this thing? Why? Will we ever be safe again? Maybe it is my fault. If I had been home, maybe I could have gotten Nanaa out. Maybe this never would have happened.

"Pack your things as soon as we get home," her father orders. He uses his military voice from the front seat without turning around. "Then the driver will take you to Nankana Sahib. You will stay there with your grandfather and uncle for now."

Her eyes open wide at his insult. With just a few words, he is sending her away, to wherever he wants whenever he wants, away from her Nanaa, the one person in the world who loves her. She cries out as tears pour down her face. Her tears always defeat him, and for a moment, both father and daughter stop breathing.

"Until Ammi recovers," he gasps, gesturing behind him, toward the hospital. Nafeesa hears the split in his voice between his paternal authority and his filial grief. "Until I compute the cost to rebuild our house," he adds, his eyes flitting as panic flashes across his face. "Until I figure out what to do next."

Ah, yes, my father, the figurer, the reckoner, the accountant, she thinks. This is how he talks when he has no answers. He is numbing himself with numbers. Everything has a cost to be calculated. Sometimes when she watches him staring into a bowl of dal, she imagines he is counting the lentils. If ever he has something to say, he uses the fewest, most efficient words. When planning a walk, he will compare the number of steps on the shorter route with the scenic value of the longer one. Nafeesa pities him—his house is in cinders, his grandfather is at the morgue, and his mother is probably dying. She knows that her father, in his dark blue suit and meticulous white shirt, is retreating again into life's arithmetic, computing what has been given minus what will be taken away.

Nafeesa's eyes take hold of the packed residential streets—plain, flat-roofed living quarters; colorful food stalls with tidy stacks of tangerines, turnips, and carrots; squeaky bicycles, sputtering mopeds, and careening buses. A road full of people entering and leaving Faisal Town, an up-and-coming middle-class area, now with a bomb crater blasted through it. Above the area she sees the smoke that still lingers in the afternoon light. It seems that every few weeks venomous clouds appear somewhere in Pakistan–a suicide bombing at a market, a church on fire. They say no one is safe anywhere anymore, now that the Taliban is stretching from the North West into Karachi, and other zealots are storming, even in Lahore.

The car stops where once a house stood. Nafeesa stares at the snake of smoke that smolders on the ground and floats now like a ghost from a deathbed. The entire city must be inhaling the molecules of their life in that house. Its frame and a partial wall are the only traces of its structure. Pink stucco is blackened and fuming, hissing, sounding as if something small and alive is suffering inside a scalded wall. Shattered glass refracts the disaster in the late afternoon sunlight. A storm of debris is strewn across the street. Nearby men with stick brooms sweep sidewalks in front of their shops. A bright green parrot lands on a branch of the old neem tree. Neighbors watch from their windows and passersby stare at what remains.

Nafeesa gets out of the car without a word and faces the emptiness of it all. Her home is both there and not there. And, she wonders, might something explode still? Then, unpredictably, unbelievably, a once-in-a-lifetime event in Lahore occurs—it starts to snow. It is the kind of snowfall that makes children run around with their tongues out to catch and swallow every snowflake, letting them melt and vanish. Large white flakes are falling loosely while large black ashes are rising in the spaces between them. They play and toss and mix together in a light wind. The snow is as pure as white flower petals showered on a holy procession. It falls reverently as it blankets the charred skeleton of their house. One flake covers her eyelid and she blinks it away, as she searches for what her father described as "her things." What things can there possibly be? Together they tiptoe solemnly through the charnel ground of what was a modest house, a respectable house, not extravagant, but enough. Now, as chemicals oxidize and squeeze through wood, air, and plaster, the house's interior continues to squeal strangely like mice.

Although the structure is succumbing, Nafeesa knows where they are standing. "My room," she says and they both stop. The strange snow has also stopped. "It's my room," she repeats. "Once it *was* my room." She steps over the stump of a slat bed where snowy patches are already puddling. She circles bright green-painted shelving that now lies on its side, and she pokes the tip of her finger at the back of a surviving metal desk chair. This is where she completed her algebra assignment that very morning. Her shoe slides across a charred book with scorched pages and extinguished words. She slips and Zeshan catches her; she rights herself and scans the wreckage, the spaces where there once was a hallway leading to other rooms. All that is left of the kitchen is a propane stove that exploded—a burner and sheet of metal folded in on itself.

Nafeesa recalls Nanaa in the kitchen flipping parathas in the pan, pointing the long fork at her, crowing, "Don't take things so seriously, Nafeesa—really, life is just a dance." Then Nanaa turned back to the sizzling pan and corrected herself, admitting with a smirk, "Well, not a dance exactly...." Nafeesa sighs at the memory, starts to tap her foot to the rhythm of a folk song Nanaa once taught her, one they would sing together—first in Punjabi, then she would sing in English while Nanaa pranced around the kitchen. She still could conjure the cooing music that signals the elevation of the mind and the expansion of a moment. And there, in the snow-wet waste of the old kitchen, Nafeesa raises her arms high in the classical style, as Nanaa taught her. She twists her wrists and shapes her hands—first, palms up, offering an imaginary cup of water to an imaginary guest, then an imaginary plate of food, next an imaginary flame and the strum of strings, granting them all in her mind, first to Nanaa, as if an honored guest in her own kitchen, then to the world which is everyone, everything, and finally to those in need, which also everyone is. She steps first to the right, then to the left, another step and she bends her knee, as if she were spanning a stream, hopping from rock to rock. She can still recall the music so clearly in her mind—-the even tapping of fingertips on the tabla, the reverberating drone of the tamboura strings. She sees her father watching, frowning. She stops her dance.

From inside the house—and it would be the last time she would think of herself as being inside—she sees a small crowd gathering outside. The suffocating plume of smoke rises above Faisal Town, above Lahore, above Pakistan, and mixes in the sky with other poisons and inevitably will dissolve, but where the particulates may fall, only Allah knows.

Now it is clear to Nafeesa that there is no longer a place for her on earth— either in the walls of that house or in her grandmother's arms. Gone, she thinks–just like my mother, Nanaa won't survive. And the old ache pulses in the pit of her belly and the bone that protects her heart cracks open a bit more. Where is home now? She thinks about her father. Has she inherited his lifetime of loneliness? The accumulation of his dead is incalculable— first, his wife plus his father, and added to that today, his grandfather, and soon, she believes, his beloved, adoring mother. Now there is no number big enough to account for her father's losses. For him, it seems there is always one more loss ahead. Nafeesa has to wonder if she might be the next one he will lose.

Zeshan returns to Nafeesa and begins rummaging aggressively, kicking other things aside. He finds a bright yellow woolen cap. "This belonged to my grandfather," he murmurs.

"You think he was the reason for the bomb?" asks Nafeesa, but she needn't ask. She knows Shaheed was the target because he was an Ahmadi, a heretic in the eyes of fundamentalists. She remembers him as a prayerful man who was a religious leader in his youth. He often wore this cap while praying with his beads.

Zeshan makes a fist and wraps the cap around his bulging knuckles, opens his fingers, and stretches the woolen rim. He removes his Jinnah hat and places the cap on his head lightly, not pulling the edges down over his ears, but letting the thing sit there on top of his head like a circus hat. Then he reaches beneath a pile of singed clothes and pulls out a faded old shawl that somehow survived the flames untouched. He smiles at the shawl and doesn't look up.

"Do you remember this?" he asks Nafeesa, looking at it lovingly as if he rescued an old friend. He flattens the folds of wool against his thigh, pulling at the loose weave, opening up the shawl, letting it breathe. To Nafeesa, what Zeshan is holding so tenderly is cheap and old-fashioned, hideous really. She says nothing. "This is a kind of legacy your Auntie, Baji Ujala, left you," he says, not taking his eyes off the shawl. He is referring to one of her mother's sisters, one of several aunties that she has never known. He kneads the wool with his cindered fingers—the old, practically colorless shawl, his ashen hands, and the yellow cap. In an intimate tone of voice he says, "Yusuf knew she would want you to have it, so he gave it to me to put it with your things when you were a baby."

Then Zeshan wraps the old shawl over the yellow cap and pulls it around his shoulders. He slouches like an old woman and sighs. The thin line of a beard that edges his jawline drops and his mouth falls open. He whips the shawl up in the air and around their heads until it floats over and enfolds Nafeesa who sits cross-legged where her dance ended. Then he kneels to rest his head on top of hers and breaks down, wailing, moaning out loud. And she bellows, too. They are like two lost orphans in a crumbling world, as the two of them drift into that place life reserves for those who grieve, where rules bend, relationships are fluid, and age dissolves.

***

Before sunset Zeshan's friends bury what parts of his grandfather's body they can find, and Zeshan returns to his sacred station beside his mother at Jinnah Hospital. That evening, after prayers at her grandfather's burial, Nafeesa is driven to Nankana Sahib, a country town an hour's drive west of Lahore. She feels nervous about staying with strangers, as she has very rarely visited with her mother's family before–what remains of a family of seven – her grandfather, Kulraj Singh, and her mother's twin brother, Amir. She knows that Kulraj Singh has been a widower for many years; his wife Nafeesa (for whom she was named) died when Meena and Amir were children. Baji Ujala, the second oldest daughter became their mother then. Later, after Meena's death, the remaining three sisters (Reshma, Ujala, and Faisah) had all disappeared. Nafeesa is curious about them, of course, but knows little. Nanaa told her that her grandfather converted from Sikhism to Islam in order to marry his Nafeesa, and to prove to her that it must not always be the woman who converts. Then, after his wife died, he converted back, even taking back his former name.. Very unusual.

Kulraj Singh and Amir are very formal as they welcome her into their home, a mud-brick house shaped like a bracket, like an open box fallen to one side. Nafeesa's Babba is old, tall, and thin, wearing the white clothes and turban of a Sikh. Amir is young, tall and plump, sporting the so-popular intentionally unshaven look. He places Nafeesa's things in the women's quarter on the south side of the interior courtyard. The men have their bedrooms in the north wing.

Amir is her real uncle and he lets her call him Mamou, the Urdu term for a mother's brother. He has an IT job in Lahore, where he stays during the week and returns to Nankana Sahib on weekends. Nafeesa sees Amir as modern, educated, open-minded, and handsome—curly dark hair, wearing blue jeans and a starched shirt. Such a waste that he's not married. But he has no mother, no aunties to arrange it for him. And having a Sikh for a father, she knows, makes a Muslim marriage transaction very difficult, if not impossible.

Kulraj Singh is the only non-Muslim in the family; Nankana Sahib is

Pakistan's only remaining Sikh town. Like many old men, he spends most of his time sleeping, or pumping his harmonium and chanting, staring at images of his saints and all the family photos on his shrine. Behind the paisley cotton cloth that serves as its door, the little shrine room is aglow from morning to night with lit flames of thick, flickering white candles, and thin ones that burn down to blisters of wax.

A few days later, Nafeesa is on the phone with Rufina, her best friend in Lahore. "It's a firetrap, Rufina. A real firetrap," Nafeesa complains, lying across her bed. "And I have to put up with my grandfather's old-fashioned ways, his endless chanting."

"Oh, Nafeesa, don't say that," Rufina urges, "Grandparents are gifts—like shady trees in the desert."

"That's what we're always told," says Nafeesa, "but this old tree is crazy. Sometimes at night he shouts out and tramps around the kitchen, rolling out flour onto the table. One night when he was rattling pans, it woke me. Babba had flour all over his hands. His nose was dripping and it kept falling into the dough. He was squeezing the dough through his fingers. Disgusting! 'I'm making chapati,' he says, 'in case the girls are hungry when they come home.'"

"What girls?" Rufina asks.

"He means his lost daughters, my aunties, who aren't girls anymore and they aren't coming home either. They disappeared right after I was born." Her voice drops. "When my mother died." Rufina is the only person Nafeesa ever says anything to about her mother. That's how she knows Rufina is her best friend—when she hears herself telling Rufina about her mother. Rufina lets Nafeesa mention her mother casually the way other girls do—"I think Ammi would like this," she might say when they go shopping. Or "Ammi used to be a dancer, too." She actually has very little information about Meena, and only one snapshot of her with her sisters—laughing together, wearing sparkling clothes. She always wonders where they were when that photo was taken and why they were laughing. She wants to laugh with them.

"Oh, Nafeesa. Don't talk about it. It's too terrible to talk about."

"No, Rufina, it's all right." But Nafeesa knows it is not. Something is wretchedly wrong. She thinks for the one-thousandth time that there is a hole in her soul where her mother should be.

"How brave you are," Rufina says. But Nafeesa does not feel brave. She feels lonely.

"I miss our dancing together," she confides, thinking, yes, ten years of training in the best classical schools in Punjab, but now what?

"Don't think you are living there, Nafeesa. Pretend you are living here still."

Nafeesa looks around her room. "This house is so sad, Rufina. After my other grandmother died of a stroke, Babba raised the children all by himself. Ujala was the oldest sister at home at the time, the *baji*—so she became like a mother for Amir and my mother, Meena. The oldest daughter was already married, and there was one other one, too. Now everybody is gone, except Amir."

"Where is this *baji* now? Can't she help?" Rufina asks, sighing. Nafeesa can sense that Rufina is becoming tired of the obligation to continue asking her questions.

"No one knows. Ujala, the one they call Baji, left Pakistan around the time I was born. I've never met her."

"Oh," Rufina says, hesitating. "That's Ammi calling me to dinner now, Nafeesa. I must go. We'll talk tomorrow. *Allah hafiz.*"

Whenever Nafeesa asked her father about her mother's family, he always said the same thing. "I really don't know. Ask your Mamou, Amir. Your mother was his twin, after all."

But now when she asks Amir, he brushes her off. "Why bring all that up? It is history," he says. "Part of the pain of Pakistan."

Nafeesa misses her grandmother all the time, but not the way most girls might. With her strong opinions, her constant snooping, her fleshy bosom and sour smells, Nanaa was someone Nafeesa usually wanted to get away from. But there were times when they were close, like when Nanaa had one of her migraines–Nafeesa would slip into her room to leave tea by her bed, lukewarm in her best pale violet porcelain cup, just the way Naana liked it.

She feels guilty recalling it, but she remembers how annoying Nanaa could be—she yells at the servants and pushes her way through the markets, kicking aside a stray cat with her shoe, always having to be the first in line, the one to have the latest news, the most informed opinions. Nanaa strives to be the center of attention, the hub of activity, the centripetal force that draws to her the world that she believes was created for her. Nafeesa cannot imagine life without her. Even though the two of them never speak words of love to each other, for Nafeesa's entire life they keep moving alongside each other day after day. Nafeesa now wonders what is the point of visiting her. Still, she returns to Nanaa's bedside at the hospital whenever she can— if Amir will take her, or if Zeshan comes to bring her from Nankana Sahib, which is almost never. *Allah help me! Whatever will I do without Nanaa?*

***

After the fire, the house in Faisal Town cannot not be rebuilt, so Zeshan moves into an apartment near his accounting office. Nafeesa rarely sees him anymore, except occasionally when he visits Babba in Nankana Sahib. To her, Nanaa's impending death seals the fact that her family is all silence and ghosts. Will I suffer the same fate, she asks herself, some dark disappearance or death? She recalls how Nanaa, who was always willing to gossip about anybody, was never willing to tell her much about her mother's family. Nafeesa knows her own mother died when she was born, and she always

assumed childbirth itself killed her. Nafeesa's life has carried the weight of
that belief, and she has learned not to think about it, not to ask her father
or Nanaa about it. But she is curious about her mother's sisters and wants
some answers.

Later, on one of Zeshan's Friday afternoon visits to Nankana Sahib, Kulraj
Singh is in his shrine room, pumping on the harmonium, repeating and
holding the notes, pumping again. Amir is out shopping for fresh vegetables.
Soon she will help him prepare dinner—chickpeas and spinach in masala
sauce or potato curry. For now, she and her father are alone in the kitchen—
he, sitting on a high stool, and she, wiping the table and shaking the cloth
out the back door for the birds, the endless red ants, and all life forms her
Babba insists they feed.

"Please tell me," Nafeesa implores Zeshan later. "I need to know—who
are my mother's people?"

"Someday you will know all of it," he says. His brown eyes are calm.

"So there *are* secrets!"

"Every family has secrets. Ours is no different."

"I guess that's true. But when will I be told the truth?" This is becoming
a game, she thinks, turning her back to him.

He laughs. "That is not mine to decide, but perhaps when you marry."
He is mincing words, she knows, avoiding giving her a clear answer.

She hangs the cloth on the line above the sink. "Perhaps I should do my
own research then? I do have internet access and library privileges, do I
not?"

It is a small threat, but it catches his attention. His face twitches. She
thinks she has won a round. "You believe you are smarter than your elders,"
he shouts, pointing a finger in her face. "Don't be in such a hurry to grow
up and know everything." He shakes his head, waves her off.

His anger frightens her, but she refuses to let it show. She softens her
voice. "Please, Abbu, just tell me a little something about someone—about

my mother?"

"Never mind that. She is in the light of Allah."

Ah, now she wonders if the family is conspiring to keep her history from her. And why? The conversation is making her nervous. She decides to start with small requests. "If not my mother, tell me about my aunties, then? Faisah?" Her father looks away at the mention of Faisah's name. She recalls how he broke down on that day he found Baji's faded shawl in the debris in Faisal Town. "Ujala then," she persists. "Tell me about the one they call Baji."

His chest rises and falls in silence.

Nafeesa realizes that he is as nervous as she is. Why?

"All right," he sighs with defeat. "You are pushing me, but I will tell you only one thing." He wags his finger again. "Ujala was in prison. She was unfairly accused of a crime."

"What crime?" she asks and he looks away.

"Kidnapping," he mumbles. "Something like that."

"But who did she kidnap?"

He faces her. "No one. I told you. She was falsely charged under *Shariah*. Later she escaped and disappeared."

"With Yusuf?" she asks, recalling the name mentioned that day when Zeshan found the shawl.

He grimaces, "Yes, Yusuf Salman. Ujala left with Yusuf. Your Baji was a good woman who helped many people. You must always hold her in high regard. We cannot be sure if today she is dead or alive."

Nafeesa thinks it is too incredible—kidnapping, *Shariah*, prison escape, disappearance. He is weaving such a tale. "Have all the women in this family run away or died?" She raises her voice. "I should run away or die, too." Her face is red hot.

"Never say that!" shouts her father. Nafeesa sees his angry, panicked eyes flashing. In one circular movement, he raises his hand. She hears the slap before she feels the sting. She touches the heat of her cheek with the cool of her hand, and when she looks up, Kulraj Singh is standing at the door, holding a green mango. He looks frozen, stunned, as if he were the one Zeshan slapped.

Nafeesa runs to her room. She wants to slam the door, but she closes it without a sound. She thinks to throw herself on the bed and cry her eyes out, but she does not. No more, she thinks. No more.

Leaning close to a mirror on the wall she sees an adult woman with depth reflected in her hazel eyes, her square jaw, her determined mouth. Her hair has come undone and falls across her shoulders. Her lips are pink where she bit the bottom one. She pushes the tip of her tongue into the slight gap between her front teeth. Yes, the olive tone of her cheek has turned a little bit red. Reddish. Really, there is no sign of the slap, except for her memory of the hand striking, the snap of her neck, the humiliation that she deliberately left behind in the kitchen. The rapping on her door continues, but a part of her is still a child—she relishes the power of refusing to answer.

Who am I looking at in that mirror? Eyes steady. Mouth set. What is happening to me? She knows she was needling her father and that his slapping her is out of character for him. He can be controlling, but he is not abusive. Still, that slap changed everything. Nafeesa decides then she will no longer burden her life and waste her time with self-pity. She hates to think about it this way, but just maybe, she thinks, I should thank him.

The slap was the sword that flashed, and it cleaved the child from the adult, the girl from the woman. His slap gave her that. She vows that if her father, grandfather, and uncles are conspiring to keep her in the dark, well, that only means that it is her job to find out for herself what she wants to know. She will become the investigator of her own life. She will find her aunties or she will learn what happened to them. Now she will take care of herself. Now she will grow up.

***

The next morning Nafeesa wakes to a pool of blood between her legs. She forgot to plan for her menstrual period and she has no sanitary napkins—something Nanaa always provided. She rushes to the bathroom to clean up, but Amir is in there. She searches her room for something to stuff into her underpants, until she can leave the house to buy pads. With what? She has no money.

She hears Amir passing her door, so she slips into the bathroom. At least there is running water—even if it is cold. She soaks her nightshirt in the sink and wipes down and between her legs to clean off the blood. The wastewater runs pink when she twists the cloth. She pulls off a piece of the soft, old shawl that had once belonged to Baji, folds it and stuffs it in the crotch of her pants, fastens her shalwar at the waist and covers up with a kameez. Then she grabs a dupatta and a coat and heads for the kitchen.

In the hall she stops. Suddenly she wants to return to her room. She wants to hide. She closes the curtains, turns off the light and lies down on her bed in the dark. Where is my bravery from last night, she wonders? Both the memory of the slap and the menstrual blood remind her of her status as female. In her entire life, she has never purchased her own napkins. How will she be able to ask for them now in the store or hand the box to the cashier without dying of embarrassment? That is something women do for each other, but she has nobody to do it for her; she will have to ask the men for help. She refuses to talk to her father and she cannot bring herself to ask Babba for money to buy sanitary napkins. She will ask Amir. But first she will have to find him alone. She rolls her body into a ball. She is feeling crampy. Then there is a knock at the door.

"Nafeesa, may I come in?" It is Amir.

"Mamou," she says. "Yes."

He is wearing blue jeans, a stylish tee shirt, a casual suit jacket. "I'm planning to upgrade the operating system. Do you want to watch?" he asks.

She breathes deeply. "Yes, of course, but first I need some money for shopping."

"What do you need? I'll buy it for you when I shop this afternoon."

"No. I need it now." She squeezes the words out of her mouth. Inside, she is dying.

"What is it?" he asks again.

"It's personal," she says, being vague, hinting at the female.

"Personal?" He wrinkles his brow quizzically, "Oh! Oh! Okay, how much money?" He grabs his wallet and spreads the bills. "Take as much as you need," he speaks quickly, so Nafeesa grabs some bills and hurries to the door.

"Let me walk with you," he says, smiling his wide smile, his teeth gleaming. He follows her outside and down the walk toward the hollyhocks. Along the road a donkey in a straw hat is pulling an entire family in its wooden cart. "I can buy a few things and then I will take whatever you choose to the counter for you."

He is willing to do this for her! She looks at her shoes, relieved.

"*Shukriah*, Mamou" she says, overwhelmed by his kindness. "*Shukriah*."

Together they pass the field of sunflowers in the morning light. Amir on the outside along the edge of the road and Nafeesa on the inside, close to the bright fields. There are a few clouds in the cool day.

"Mamou, tell me your story," she pleads. "You know all about mine."

He smiles, "I thought you'd never ask," he says and begins as if he'd wanted to tell the story for a long time. "There are the stories of the ones who leave," he says," and then there are the stories of the ones left behind. My story is one of those—a boy, a man-child, a grown man—and mine is a

story that keeps repeating. The females in my family keep disappearing."
Nafeesa slowed down to walk at the pace of his telling. "Nafeesa, I was born
ten minutes after your mother, Meena, so I was the family's baby, the one
who didn't have to do anything to be loved by everyone. My life was easy
and happy until, when I was seven, my mother had a stroke. I was the only
one they could count on to always make her laugh."

Nafeesa had not known how Amir's mother, her own grandmother, died,
and somehow there is a strange pleasure to hear stories of her own people.
At the same time, her heart saddens, imagining that seven-year-old boy,
skinny and sweet and mop-headed, facing the death of a mother he knew
so well. Unlike herself, whose sense of a mother is distant and vague. She
wonders if her own mother had lived, if she would look like her twin brother
now. Maybe she would be like him?

"I learned Ammi's physical therapy routine and walked her through it
every day. They said she improved because of it. That was what they told
me, anyway, but who knows? I have forgotten so much about my mother,
but I remember every detail about my sisters. I had my GameBoy to get me
through the grief. And I had Baji, my oldest sister still living at home, who
was there when school let out, when it was time to practice the times tables,
and, later, when we all surrounded Ammi's bed.

"I remember Meena asking 'Is she sleeping? Why doesn't she say something?' 'Shh! She can hear everything we say,' Baji warned us. I remember
that part. But Ammi's eyes were closed so I was never sure what she saw
or heard. We moved the walnut rocking chair from my room to Ammi's.
Meena and I were the last ones to be cuddled in that chair, the lap babies,
and we took turns in the rocker, watching our mother, awake or asleep.
And when we were not taking our turns, then the grown ones swayed in the
rocker beside her bed—the teenager Faisah, the married sister, Reshma, the
college student, our Baji Ujala."

Along the road, Amir stops walking and faces Nafeesa. "When the time came, Baji found me in my room, playing a video game in the dark. 'Amir, my Amir,' she said. I remember I refused to look up—maybe if I did not look, I would not hear what I knew she was going to tell me. I felt her arm around my shoulder. 'Ammi is in heaven now,' she said."

Now both Amir and Nafeesa look away with tears in their eyes. Amir shakes it off. "I can still recall the weight of the big rugs and the heavy chairs that Abbu and I dragged outside and arranged for the funeral guests. I remember he turned to me and said: 'Remember when you were a little child and broke your arm? Remember how much it hurt? That pain passed, didn't it? You must let this pain pass, too.'

"By the time I was your age, Nafeesa, we had moved from Karachi to Nankana Sahib. One day the police arrived with an arrest warrant for Baji. When they handcuffed her and were taking her away, she turned her head and looked back at me. I will never forget those eyes that had kept the child in me alive. Later, in the kitchen, a radio program was interrupted to announce Baji's arrest, but I switched it off. Broke the knob." He pauses. "I have not seen Baji since her escape from jail."

Now that he is beginning to tell the story, it is as if he can't stop telling it all. He speaks into the air and Nafeesa knows not to interrupt him. She absorbs every word, every feeling as they walk.

"Thirteen years after Ammi died, my father and I stood at the door to that same room where, this time, your mother, Meena, lay on a bed. My sisters were washing her hair, rinsing, combing and braiding it. I remember I wondered whether, if she were in heaven, was she still my twin? My sisters prayed as they worked to prepare her body: 'Allah, this is Meena, the Twin Soul of her Brother, Amir. Send your angels. She is coming to you now.' As women, they were not allowed to help carry her to the grave, so I went in their place. Abbu couldn't go because he was no longer Muslim. All those foolish rules! Zeshan and I went for everyone."

Amir stops talking and looks at Nafeesa. They watch the cloud shadows in the silence of the sky. "It was before sunset," he continues trying to speak, to tell the full story, but all he can say are a few words: "Meena's shroud. Rose petals. A tractor path. Sunflower fields. A glint of light." And really those words are enough. He takes a deep breath.

"I think I cried harder when Meena died than when Ammi died," he spoke softly, then louder: "How many mothers and sisters must I lose? First, Ammi dies, then Reshma moves away, Baji is jailed, Meena is murdered, and Faisah goes to India. I still think of what Abbu told me at my mother's funeral—pleasure and pain are a set of robes that a human must keep on wearing."

Her mother was murdered? Nafeesa is in shock, but her heart is filled with all the words and images she both hated to hear and loved to hear. It is something she and Amir share—the deaths of their mothers and grand-mothers, the losses of his sisters and her aunties. She is now even more determined to find them. She wants to pump Amir for more information, but she knows this is not her moment. It is Amir's.

***

By April Nanaa's condition is no better. Each time Nafeesa visits the burn unit, it seems her grandmother's body has thickened from all the bandages wrapped around her, and her mind is soaking in morphine. Nanaa suffers skin graft after skin graft as the doctors try to piece her back together. First, they take a slice of Nanaa's thigh and sew it around her neck. Then they remove a sliver of her backside and weave it onto her ear. Eventually the doctors say the risk is too high for her to have any visitors, as they might escort that final infection into her room.

Weeks later, during a family midday meal in the courtyard at Nankana Sahib, Nafeesa asks her father about the police investigation. Zeshan ex-plains that it was an attack by fundamentalists. "Although there are a mil-lion Pakistani Ahmadis who believe their founder was the promised Muslim messiah, my grandfather—especially in his youth when he was a leader—dared to profess that belief publicly—which, as you know, is considered to be heresy, but also can have legal consequences– imprisonment, denial of a passport, and worse."

"Your grandfather was a good man—" begins Kulraj Singh reverently.

Zeshan interrupts angrily, scoffing, gesturing across the table. "They say my grandfather died on his knees. The Talibs bragged about it. He was praying by candlelight, when the screaming mob burst through the front, attacked him and then ignited the entire house." Amir glances at Nafeesa, who does not want to listen but cannot not listen either. "But to say he died on his knees praying to Allah—well, that is just sentimentality," Zeshan concludes. "A man beaten to death dies prone." He pauses and clears his throat.

Amir twists the corner of his mouth in disgust. Nafeesa has never seen her father like this.

Kulraj Singh shakes his head in distress and reaches for Zeshan's arm. "The Taliban is proud of their murders and mayhem."

Zeshan nodded his agreement. "I am worried, too, that visiting the hospital might be dangerous for Nafeesa. Who knows which fanatics committed this crime and burned down our house? What others could be watching us? I am so worried about her that it makes me angry. I don't even understand myself, but I must protect her. When her mother needed my protection most, I wasn't there to protect Meena ...." His voice begins to crack, and Kulraj Singh leans in his direction, but Zeshan recovers with a few words. "Yes, Nafeesa is much safer here," he says and exhales.

Nafeesa stops listening and looks out at the field, still bright with rows of young wheat poking up into the invisible light. A dozen sparrows are circling. All this talk of death and disaster and no Nanaa to be with me now. How, oh how will I learn to do what a woman must do? Who will find a husband for me when the time comes? Oh, shame on me! All I can think about is myself. She runs from the table and they let her go.

Later, from the kitchen, she can hear Amir calling out his farewells to her father and suddenly she feels alarmed. She hurries out to join them on the path, just as her father puts his lambswool hat on and offers Kulraj Singh his arm. They walk to the road where the driver had parked the sedan next to a flowering cherry tree now smothered with bees. Her heart is pounding with questions she does not know how to ask.

"Babba!" she shouts to her grandfather. "Stop! I have to know more! Where are the females in this family? And exactly who are my aunties? Are all the women of this family cursed?"

Zeshan snaps a harsh look in his daughter's direction, but he says nothing, as it is not his place to speak of another's family, even Meena's sisters.

Kulraj Singh straightens his spine to full height, and for a moment Nafeesa thinks he might shout. But his voice becomes a tender whisper. "You will know the women of this family, Nafeesa. And you will have your life. I promise you that." He sounds very confident, as if he is guaranteeing it—as if he could.

Zeshan folds himself into the back seat of the Toyota. The car lurches once and drives away, leaving Nafeesa alone with her Babba.

"God is too kind to curse you or any of the women of this family," he adds. For a moment he loses balance. He pushes one hand into the rough stucco of the garden wall for support. Her heart softens as she reaches out to let him lean into her, and they return to the house together, step by slow step. She helps him to the shrine room where he plops down cross-legged on the floor. She lights a stick of incense the way she has seen him do, and holds the match to a candle that burns in front of a black and white photograph of his beloved wife, his Nafeesa, her grandmother. She returns to her room and to her diary.

Maybe my mother is not dead, maybe Amir's calling it a murder is just a wild story they made up to explain her absence to me. Maybe she ran off with a lover and dishonored the family. Maybe she was kidnapped and my father refused to pay the ransom. Maybe she moved to Mumbai and became a famous dancer, one of those dressed in fuchsia and gold, tall and slim with one thick braid down her spine. Maybe she will come back for me. Sometimes when the drums are beating and my body matches their fury, I see someone over there by the door of the dance studio. A witness without judgment; a loving observer with no opinion. She offers no direction. She is someone for me alone, a woman I do not know and others cannot see, but who attends every lesson, every rehearsal, every performance, standing in the back over there where she has the entire view. She listens as the music seduces us. I dance to bring her back to me. Moving my body gives my grief a place to go.

If, as they say, for every soul there is a watcher, then whenever my soul dances, there must be a watcher, too; otherwise, dance would be soulless, without rhythm or sound, no form, no feeling. She is my deceased mother standing at the studio door, arrived from heaven, my Ammi with her flashing, hazel eyes and happy hands that clap in time with the music and applaud when my dance is done. But still, her hands do not make a sound.

***

Nafeesa passes the day in her room making plans and talking with Rufina on her mobile, now re-filled with plenty of minutes. Amir recharged her phone card at the shop. Later she finds him in the kitchen, which smells of freshly sliced ginger. He is glued to the screen on his phone.

"Mamou," she says, "there you are." Amir smiles his easy smile. "Our school break starts next week. Will you let me ride with you to Lahore so I can visit Rufina?"

"If it's okay with Babba," he says, crouched on the wooden stool, stuffing into his mouth a piece of chapatti loaded with spiced lentils. "Want some?"

he asks, handing her a plate of soft red lentils and spinach. He dives back into his game of Angry Birds.

"It's okay with him," Nafeesa says, wondering what Babba would say if she asked him, but she is not asking anymore. "Oh, and I'll need a little money to get me through the week." Amir reaches back for the billfold in his back pocket and hands it to her.

"Whatever you need," he says and she relaxes, feeling lighter, brighter.

"*Shukriah*," she replies, pulling some bills from the wallet. She gives him a little grin. "Mamou, I hate to ask, but I also need the password to your laptop."

"Okay," he says, "Okay. It's 92096–the date Baji escaped from Adiala Prison. September 20, 1996."

She hides her excitement. Amir has just handed over a clue: a date with which to begin her auntie search. She logs on to the archives of *Dawn*, the most popular of Pakistan's English newspapers, and the one with the best archive. She types Baji's name in the search box: "Ujala Ehtisham 1996," using the Arabic surname Kulraj Singh chose when he converted to Islam in the 1950s so he could marry his Nafeesa. *Could not find that page*, the website responds. She types "Faisah Ehtisham," and an address pops up: Faisah Ehtisham and Lia Chee, 11 Bhumi Marg, Parel West, Mumbai.

Auntie Faisah is in Mumbai! Nafeesa's spirits rise. Why did I not do this a long time ago? Why have I been waiting for somebody's permission, for somebody to do it for me? Quickly she types in the name of the oldest sister, "Reshma Ehtisham," but nothing comes up. She sucks her teeth in frustration, pounding the ebony keyboard with her fingertips. Of course, Reshma is married—she's the fundamentalist they say disappeared into that world many years ago. And I don't know Reshma's married name. But there is one other I do know. Nafeesa presses each computer key deliberately, gently, as if laying her mother's body down on the screen with letters: "Meena Shaheed." She adds the date from Mamou's password: "September 20, 1996."

No search results, the website taunts. Humph! Nafeesa lays out in her mind the next steps in her plan: Spend the week in Lahore, stay with Rufina, join her at the dance studio in the evening, and by day, conduct family research at Punjab Public Library and return with Mamou on Friday.

***

The wind is so fierce that the door to Amir's car flies open when he stops at Rufina's family compound in the upscale area of Gulberg. Nafeesa rings the buzzer at the gate. She hadn't called Rufina to let her know she was coming, because she didn't want to risk the possibility of Rufina's mother saying that Nafeesa could not stay with them. And she knew Rufina would be home. Amir sits in the car until Rufina peers through the creaky metal door. She looks surprised to find Nafeesa in the shadow of her doorstep on a Monday morning. Nafeesa steps out of the car, waves Amir off, and when Rufina hugs her, Nafeesa clings just a little too long.

"I'd have called but I ran out of minutes," Nafeesa lies.

"I was afraid you forgot about me," Rufina says. "I've missed you so much."

"Can I stay here this week? On Friday I can ride back to Nankana Sahib with Mamou."

"Of course. Ammi will be so happy you are here."

"Let's get the girls and dance tonight!" Nafeesa suggests, in a way that almost sounds naughty. The two of them have been attending after school classical folk dance classes along with other girls. They are allowed to walk together after school to the dance studio and afterwards they wait for their brothers to walk them home. They have never gone alone, at night, without the dance teacher.

"Yes, let's," agrees Rufina with a conniving grin and her endearing dimple. "Didn't the dance instructor tell us to 'Pwactice'!"

Nafeesa laughed, mimicking the teacher's funny lisp, her strange accent. "'You guls must pwactice!' Yes, I'll call the others. Tonight, we dance again!"

That night each girl tells her own family that the other's brother will accompany them to the dance studio, as they want the freedom to move about in the street on their own for once, and they lie to their families about the special evening class, saying it is a rehearsal for an upcoming festival performance.

The teacher's studio is deserted, but they have keys she gave freely to each student. Four other dancers join them, too, thrilled for an evening away from home, away from the hovering brothers, uncles, nephews, fathers. Once inside, with the doors locked, they turn the boom box up loud, but not loud enough to attract attention from the street. Mira plays the tabla, something forbidden at home. But here, in the studio, she taps, taps, taps the drums' edges, warming up to the rhythms with her fingertips, her rolling wrists, the slap of her palm. Noor, Shazhadi, Asma, Rufina and Nafeesa circle the room with their scarves afloat–the magenta, the chartreuse, the aquamarine, the goldenrod, all the colors of springtime stitched with the sparkles of female youth, trimmed and hemmed inside the forms of dance. One by one, each expresses with the shake of her hip, glance of her eye, the roll of her shoulder, something about the personal world inside her body, something that otherwise she never communicates to the world, even to each other. The roll of the shoulder, the sway of the hips as the bones loosen from their ligaments and the dance of life becomes more fluid. Asma bows low and tosses her long hair over her head, over and over to the rhythm of the music. Together, all in a line, they circle the room, promenading in their slippers, sensing the subtle aspects of their bodies, the heat rising, the heel stamping, the foot ready to spring. Rufina moves alone, undulating her spine, agile and confident. Shahzadi stops, finds a balance point and listens deeply for the precise sound in the music that matches her movement forward and back, side to side, until she leaves the point of stillness and flows into the room. For hours they sweat together, soaked in the perspiration of the work, the labor of private intensity exploding in a simple room where the mirrors reveal undeniably that they are growing into women. Each recognizes it in the others first, and then sees it is true for herself as well. When the dancers are exhausted, they call their brothers, button up in their long coats, and wrap their dupattas over their heads and around their necks. When the brothers arrive, they hurry home in the dark with all the secrets of the studio locked inside.

***

In the morning Nafeesa hails a rickshaw for the twenty-minute ride to Punjab Public Library, housed in a crumbling neighborhood of museums and university buildings. The air is chilly and the road is wet from the rainy night, coating the buildings with the beauty of aging. Originally constructed by the British over a hundred years ago, for Nafeesa the structure became a kind of private palace during her secondary school years when library membership was required by her academy. Its oversized arches and wide corridors, its marble towers and chipped surfaces were a place above and away from her grandmother's surveillance.

This library is a point of frequent return. Never before has she used it for personal research, but now that she is the journalist of her own story, she is fascinated by the question driving this research project: *Who are my mother's people?* She scribbles these words across the top of the second page of an old notebook with its friendly mottled cover. She jots down some of the facts she has garnered from the family and the internet:

My namesake, my grandmother, Nafeesa—died of a stroke
Kulraj Singh, my grandfather, Babba, was with her when she died
My mother, Meena, was only seven when her mother Nafeesa died

Oldest daughter, Reshma, married, living where? in Pakistan when Nafeesa died

Baji Ujala helped Babba raise Auntie Faisah, Mamou, and Meena.

Meena died the year I was born, in 1996.

Ujala falsely accused of kidnapping? in Shariah Court, escaped from prison. No contact with family, may have died.

My other aunties, Faisah and Reshma, have not been home in eighteen years?

Faisah may live in Mumbai with someone named Lia Chee.

Nafeesa drops her backpack on a long library table and crosses directly to the research desks for periodicals and genealogy. She recognizes a librarian wearing a designer headscarf.

"I'm researching my mother's lineage," Nafeesa says and the librarian is eager to help.

"*Achaa.* There are a number of ways to begin. Her family name would be one."

"I don't know that," says Nafeesa, cultivating her most inquisitive, innocent face so the librarian won't give up on her. It is very unusual not to know one's mother's family name.

The librarian hesitates. "Well, we can look at marriage records, perhaps. Another way would be to look at landholdings. If you come from landowners."

"I don't know about any landowners, but I do have dates of some public events about eighteen years ago that involved family members."

"Good. Then we can check periodicals. Unfortunately, they are not catalogued back that far, but we do have microfilm." She pulls open drawers full of small reels of microfilm. "Here are the records for *Dawn*. Do you want to research in English or Urdu?"

"*Dawn* is good," Nafeesa says. "I'll start with English periodicals."

"What year?"

"1996."

The librarian hands Nafeesa the correct reel, and Nafeesa gives her some basic facts—names of parents, grandparents, aunts, her uncle. "I'll look in the public records collection for marriage and birth records," the librarian says, walking away.

Nafeesa fumbles with the microfiche machine and begins scrolling. The rusty knob stops and starts but the film slides by in a dim blur of time. She speeds past January through June 1996 and focuses directly to her birthday, July 11, 1996. Nothing is reported about her birth or her mother's death. Nafeesa twists the knob to the September 20 date. Nothing about Baji Ujala. She scrolls to September 21, where a banner headline on the front page of *Dawn* read: "Woman Rights Worker Escapes Adiala Prison." There it is, complete with photographs of Ujala Ehtisham and her lawyer-sister, Faisah.

Nafeesa is excited. These aunties she is seeking—they were beautiful young women. Baji's thick dark hair falls to her shoulders. Her lips are parted, revealing a small gap between her front teeth–like her own! She wants to run to the librarian, to someone, to anyone to show what she has found and at the same time she wants to stay put to read.

RAWALPINDI

September 21, 1996

Yesterday at approximately 4:30 pm, Ujala Ehtisham, women's rights activist widely known by the nickname Baji, escaped from Adiala Jail where she has been held without bail for six months in pre-trial detention. Jail spokesperson Rahmal Gul stated that the prisoner's escape occurred during a changing of the guards during the visiting period. An unidentified male assisted Ehtisham's escape. The two culprits were last seen riding in a dark Nissan, heading south on Adiala Road. Police and military units have been placed on alert to recapture them.

Ehtisham was on trial in Lahore High Court on charges of kidnapping a young woman and brandishing a weapon. Recently the Court transferred jurisdiction to Islamabad Shariah Court to examine religious issues implicated by the defense. Regular sit-ins and protests have been occurring for months outside of the prison, as human rights workers and teachers have voiced their support for Ehtisham's efforts to help many girls who were abused by husbands, fathers, and other family members. She has been particularly outspoken in opposition to honor killings, a brutal practice that continues in some locales.

"Baji was a model prisoner," said Rahima Mai, Women's Jail Supervisor. "I am investigating now how our corrections staff and our penal practices could have prevented this escape from occurring. We will leave no stone unturned in our investigation."

The escape of Ethisham amounts to more egg on the face of the justice system and draws attention to the sisters some call "The She-Lions of Punjab," for their fierce opposition to what they call Pakistan's "other PPP": patriarchy, poverty, and parochialism. Others criticize the "she-lions" for their aggressive stances and public behavior as unmarried women.

Faisah Ehtisham, the defendant's sister, has mounted an aggressive defense at trial. She could not be reached for comment. Ehtisham's third sister, Reshma Mohammad, an Islamist scholar, testified as court-appointed jurisconsult. She resides in Karachi along with her husband and two sons. The fourth sister, Meena Shaheed, was assassinated on July 11 on a speakers' platform during a public rally at the Faisal Mosque in Islamabad. Supporters from the Women's Resource Center called her "a martyr for all the women of Pakistan." Her killer has not been identified and the case remains unsolved.

The Shariah Court has taken its decision under advisement and Court's deliberations are suspended pending Ehtisham's capture. A warrant has been issued for her arrest.

Nafeesa is breathless. Her mother—a martyr for women's rights—assassinated on the day she was born? She sits back, her eyes resting on the wall of books in front of her, in silence she absorbs what she has found in the library and in herself. She recalls the night before, while dancing at the studio—that woman watching, comforting her, if only for a step or two, a note or two, a beat of the drum. Suddenly there is a tap on her shoulder and she turns, expecting to see Meena standing there. Instead, it is the librarian with a small sheaf of paper in her hand and sympathy in her eyes.

"I'm so sorry," she says, acknowledging Nafeesa's tears and digging into the pocket of her navy blue shalwar kameez for a tissue. Before Nafeesa can say anything, the librarian spreads papers out on the table. "Apparently you found something. And so did I." She pauses. "Have you ever seen your birth certificate?" She lays before Nafeesa a cream-colored paper with green ink. In the blank marked *"Walida,"* it reads: *Meena Shaheed.* "And here is your maternal grandparents' marriage certificate. I had to trace it online back to London, England, 1958." In the blank marked "Husband," it reads: *Kulraj Singh of Karachi, Pakistan.* And in the blank marked "Wife," it reads: *Nafeesa Ahmed of Malakwal, Pakistan.*

Nafeesa cannot make sense of it. She looks to the librarian to explain. "It means your maternal family names are Ahmed and Singh— very unusual for a Sikh to marry a Muslim—very unusual indeed. That will be the knot for you to untie." Then she lays an oversized, yellowing volume on the table, beneath the lamplight. She points to particular pages she has marked with yellow sticky notes. "You may want to look here, too," she says. "It seems Nafeesa Ahmed, your maternal grandmother, may have had close ties with the Ahmed dynasty around Malakwal."

"Dynasty?"

"Well, it's hard to know," the librarian says. "This is just a place to begin. But if your grandmother's name was Ahmed from Malakwal—" She purses her lips. "Well, the Ahmeds pretty much own that entire rural area." She pushes another book at Nafeesa. "Here. Check this one out and you can read about that area's history—it's in central Punjab."

Nafeesa is overwhelmed. Her mother, assassinated. Possibly she comes from a feudal family. Nanaa told her that Babba converted to Islam in order to marry his Nafeesa. She knew that he had used the Muslim name Ehtisham, which explains why Mamou and his sisters have Arabic, not Sikh names.

Suddenly Nafeesa notices the time—she is late for her meeting with Rufina. She picks up the book and the papers. At the checkout desk the librarian runs Nafeesa's card through the reading machine several times.

"The machine does not recognize your card," she says.

"That can't be." Now Nafeesa is frustrated—she is late and this mistake is delaying her further.

"I'll speak with an administrator," says the librarian with determination. "Be right back." Nafeesa pages through the book about the Ahmeds, wanting to dive into it, wishing she had not made plans to meet up with Rufina at all.

The librarian returns, looking worried. "Sorry. But your library privileges have been revoked," she whispers as if to avoid embarrassment.

"Revoked!" Nafeesa shouts, "But why?"

"The administrator said it was on the request of Mr. Zeshan Shaheed, who says he is your father. Sorry," she says, walking away.

Nafeesa slips the newspaper story and the book about the Ahmeds into her khaki backpack and races down the stairs, skipping to the exit from the dim interior into the shocking daylight. Why should I be surprised? She asks herself. It's the old one-two punch. First, the actual slap in the face, followed by this metaphorical slap in the face. But my father won't stop me now. Does he believe he can cut off all of my access to information about my life? Does he plan to run my life? Why doesn't he help me? Why does he want to prevent me from finding out who I am?

Chapter 3

Like a Fish Without a Bicycle

Nankana Sahib, Pakistan, 2014

Kulraj Singh's mind is clearest in the dark. Before dawn, when the only sound is the cooing of turtledoves, he sits cross-legged and straight-backed before the shrine. His gray hair covers his shoulders like a living shawl. First, he whispers a greeting to the Guru: *Waheguru. I praise the Guru's name. Waheguru.* Then the delirious chatter of his mind stops and rests on the presence of his departed-yet-ever-present wife, Nafeesa. He speaks to her still.

It is autumn now, my Beloved, and the jacaranda is ablaze, all red and orange and yellow. They say it is dying and I scoff! How can that be when it flames in the sun! You are my particle of ash, the one I still long for, with whom I laugh alone in my bed at night where I am chained like a dog to this world. I pay one more breath to the angel of death to buy my ticket home to You.

Remember when we thought you were dying and we trembled in the starlight that summer on our rooftop in Karachi, when we gazed together into the face of the Sindhu Sea? That rattle you heard from the sea frightened you. Its wheezing is in my body now. My windpipe closes its valve against the rising tide. Bubbles of breath are clogged in the sodden branches of a trunk that grows in my throat. Death's van is parked outside my door, my Beloved, and there you are, watching all this under time's sky. When I wash, I whisper Your name into the water. I dress and I rest my mind on You. I comb the uncut hair of my body and I think of You, an elegant skeleton sitting tall in a boat, your shapely bones, so smooth and thick from carrying the weight of five children in the bowl of your pelvis. Oh, our children, Nafeesa! We preserve your name in our young granddaughter. I could see her face before she was born.

Yesterday a package arrived—bubble wrap, brown paper, tape, string, all bruised with wrinkles from the rubber stamps inked all over it. Quite a thing it was—and I tore into it like a youngster at a birthday party. Its energy was such it almost unwrapped itself. Inside was a manuscript. Yusuf has written about Ujala's escape from Adiala with him. They found their way to a small town in Kashmir and made a life for themselves there. And he enclosed a letter. Listen!

> *My dear Sora, the father of my wife,*
>
> *I hope you are in good health and that the entire family is well. I write to reassure you that Uji and I are alive. We are married and living under assumed names in Kashmir on the India side. We have not contacted you directly for fear of wiretaps, corrupt postal officials, and the rest. But now a dear friend agreed to mail this to you from inside Pakistan. I trust it has reached you safely.*
>
> *I enclose my story, "The She-lion of Punjab," for you to read before you hear about it in the media. I want to reassure you that although the manuscript will say otherwise, Ujala is alive and well. I wrote the story to raise awareness in Pakistan of her case again with the hope that the courts will dismiss it at last. Once we know when the story will be published, she and I intend to leave Kashmir for an urban area, perhaps near Delhi, until the Shariah Court's warrants have*

been quashed. Then we will return to Nankana Sahib. My wife's greatest wish is to kiss your face again.

I look forward to the day when we see you looking outside your window at this graying, middle-aged couple who will arrive at your door with their arms full of love for you and the entire family.

Your faithful son-in-law,

Yusuf Salman

Uji may be coming home at last, my love! Have we ever had better news? Amir and I are making a plan to help our Nafeesa. She has lost a mother and another grandmother. The child is a headstrong girl, frustrated and deeply sad. But she is not lost; she just doesn't know it yet.

O my Jaan, so long ago I promised you never to tell our children about your ancestors in Malakwal, so there would be no way either our children or your family could trace one another, so your brother Ali's wish for vengeance because of our marriage could do no more harm. But now you must release me from that promise. Our granddaughter has begun her own research which is leading to questions and more questions. Your younger brother spent a lifetime repenting his teenage confusion that almost led to your death. And your parents have passed away. But Ali Ahmed has enormous power in Malakwal and, as we both know, a feudal lord's fist of danger reaches everywhere. And there are crimes everywhere—the bombing of Zeshan's house, the murder of his grandfather and his mother. There is war everywhere and I have to wonder if it isn't time to let your granddaughter know which side she is on. This terrible inheritance is hers, too.

This Nafeesa wants to know all about this family she is just now discovering. Her father never told her, nor would he allow his mother to tell her, about Meena's assassination. Nor about Uji's imprisonment and the acid attack on Faisah. Not even about Reshma, lost to us again in the Islamist world. Please release me from the promise, my Jaan. I will watch for a sign from you.

Last night I placed the first half of Yusuf's story under our granddaughter's pillow to give her a taste of the legacy of courageous females that she has inherited. But she has been raised as a conservative girl so I wonder about her reaction. I have withheld Part Two until I know what her response is to Part One.

I will have to return to bed to rest before long, perhaps to sleep and dream of You. Sometimes, like You, I fear death—but then my mind lies down in that space between your beautiful bones within the sacred skeleton of You. Now I listen for the sounds of Nafeesa's waking, her door creaking, her footsteps.

***

Nafeesa wakes to the biting aroma of onions and spices. She hugs the manuscript she spent the night reading, and hurries to Amir in the kitchen. He is salting chickpeas and tossing them with chopped vegetables and roasted cumin seeds. She smiles with pleasure.

"Channa masala!"

"*Assalam Aleikum,*" he welcomes her and wipes his hands on a clean cloth. She sets Yusuf's story on a shelf and puts a pan under the water pump to rinse the rice. In the field behind the courtyard, a flock of crows crosses. Their beaks shatter the sunflowers' rough reddish-brown centers, breaking open the seeds of last season. A few tulips have survived in the dirty flower box outside the women's quarter. Nafeesa vows again to remember to water them.

Amir props open the kitchen window to watch the morning sunlight play with the shadows of broccoli and spinach, dark green leaves that pale to white. He lights the propane burner with a stick match. They can hear the soft constant chords of Punjabi songs Kulraj Singh plays as he pumps the harmonium and coughs.

Nafeesa is glad that, like her, Amir is not a strict Muslim, but she is especially glad that he is not a Sikh. Once he told her, "I am a skeptical Muslim, who relies on facts, reason and logic, evidence, trial and error." She wonders if Amir is using trial and error to spice the masala as he mixes seeds and tears spinach with his hands. He stops to pour her a cup of spiced milk tea. She warms her hands on the ceramic mug.

"*Shukriah*, Mamou," she says, leaning on her elbows, keeping him in her view. With a cotton ribbon, she ties her wavy hair away from the food he is preparing. "And thank you for putting Yusuf's story under my pillow, too. Do you think the *She-lion* story is true? It answers so many questions, but raises so many others."

"Ah, Nafeesa, thank your grandfather, not me. He is the one who slipped into your room to leave the manuscript. I wrote the note for him but I wasn't so sure he was doing the right thing."

"Oh, I know it was you, Mamou. Babba never bothers with me. You are the one who notices me, who takes me shopping, drives me to Lahore, feeds me. Babba is just so...Babba, occupied with his prayers." Mamou turns to her with a teacher's look on his face.

"Nafeesa, he is the one who insisted we share the manuscript with you. Yesterday we read the entire manuscript, rejoicing that Baji and Yusuf are alive and that there is hope we will be together again."

"Alive? Baji is alive? But in the story Yusuf tells the journalist that she is not."

Amir leaves the room and returns with Yusuf's letter. "Here. Read this. It came with the manuscript." As he returns to mixing and chopping, she reads the letter and looks up at him with a new understanding. "I pray you will meet her soon," he says sadly. "I only wish Baji had included a note to us, too." He pauses. "The day I helped you shop for women's things proved to me just how flawed the plan is for you to remain at Nankana Sahib, in a house of men. But it might not be safe for you to live in Lahore, either, with the Taliban threat and your father's family targeted. Now that we know where Baji is, Nafeesa, we wonder if she might come home here to help you, to be a kind of mother to you the way she was to Faisah, to Meena and to me." His voice is dreamy. "Maybe both Faisah and Baji will come home!" Amir's face flushes as he tries to control the longing in his voice. He laughs. "It hurts my heart to think of them. My sisters' liveliness would fill the entire house. And, yes, I believe the family will re-unite someday. *Allahu akbar!* Allah be praised!"

He returns to his task and begins slicing goat cheese. "So let me ask you, Nafeesa. Is the *She-lion* story true?"

"Yes!" she smiles. "I believe it is true."

"Then tell that to Abbu. He is eager to know your reaction to the story."

"*Achaa* . . . but may I ask you something first, Mamou? I found out yesterday that my father rescinded my library privileges! Now I can't research or even borrow a book."

Kulraj Singh appears at the kitchen door. "*Peace be with you,*" he says, leaning against the door frame.

"*Waleikum salaam,*" replies Nafeesa, reassuring him. "And peace be with you."

Amir leads his father to the plastic chair near the stove, but Kulraj Singh raises his palm to stop him. "Let's take our meal outside," he says in a craggy voice. "Let's sit at the bamboo table again, like a family. We have much to discuss and that would be the proper place to do it."

While Kulraj Singh leans against his son, Nafeesa brings him his sweater and returns to the kitchen to carry small trays with dal, rice, chutney, chopped cucumbers, carrots, and yogurt. Amir helps his father into a wicker chair and begins to sweep leaves away from the table. Kulraj Singh sits between his only son and his only granddaughter. A few visiting sparrows fly up into the leaves of the neem tree to listen to Kulraj Singh tell the story of the table once again.

"Many years ago, during my student days, I rescued this table from fire wreckage at Karachi's Architectural Library." He runs his hand over the tawny wooden surface. "It is a sole survivor."

"Sole survivor," Nafeesa whispers, thinking of herself that way. And for the first time she wants to speak to them from the privacy of her own sadness, which in her mind is right next to the door of her anger. She wants her grandfather to know what happened at the Punjab Library. "Babba, may I ask you something?" She takes a deep breath when he nods. "Did you know that my father has revoked my privileges at the Punjab Library?"

At that moment, the back gate unlatches and into the courtyard steps Zeshan. He begins interrogating her. "And what do you need the provincial library for, Nafeesa? When you have your school library and the city library?" His accusatory tone stuns them.

Amir's face is disapproving. "Since when do we monitor each other's library behavior, Zeshan?" he asks.

Babba's eyes close. "*Assalam aleikum*, my friend," he interrupts. "Join us for an early lunch. Amir, prepare a plate of food. Nafeesa, a cup of tea for your father, please."

She jumps up as Zeshan approaches the chair next to her. He tries to take her hand, but she pulls it away. "With all due respect, Father, what business is it of yours which paths of interest my mind travels?" She leaves the table before he can answer, but she listens through the kitchen window while she prepares tea.

"Nafeesa's question is my own," says Kulraj Singh. "Freedom of the mind is a fundamental value in this family."

Zeshan is irritated and his voice is gruff. "It is not the path of her mind, but the path of her character that troubles me. I learned that Nafeesa has been dancing in Lahore, walking the streets unescorted, staying with a family we do not know."

Nafeesa returns carrying a small tray. She stops and glares. "You have been spying on me!"

"Then you don't deny it. As your father, I have a right to know what you are doing and with whom."

Amir returns, setting the cracked blue ceramic pot in the center of the dispute. Nafeesa glances his way. He says, "I know the family she was staying with. They are good people."

Zeshan gulps a mouthful of tea and ignores Amir. In that moment, something in Nafeesa's rebellious manner changes. Her voice softens. "I feel sorry for you, Father. You can spy on me; you can abuse your authority; you can forbid me all you want." She stands between her father and her grandfather. "Are you welcome at our table? Yes. And will I serve you a meal to please you? Yes. But I am the landlord of my own mind and I will decide what resides there and what must get out." She has never spoken to her father so boldly and her clarity makes it apparent to her and to all of them that her words are earnest, that something inside her is changing.

"Let's enjoy this meal together," suggests Zeshan, chuckling, glancing at Kulraj Singh, "before I am the one you say must get out." The men grin at the little joke, but mealtime is tense. No one speaks about the library card, or the *She-lion* manuscript, or anything that matters to them. One sparrow dares to claim its spot beneath the table, to peck a few lentils that fall there, but it doesn't stay long.

Later Amir's chair grates against the patio bricks when he stands to collect the dishes. Nafeesa covers her head with the white gauze dupatta that rests over her shoulder and follows him inside. Zeshan does not remain after the meal. At the front gate a colorful row of hollyhocks fills in the cracks along the wall. The white dome of the Gurdwara, the sacred Sikh temple, reflects the sun.

"Sometimes it is not wise to rein in a young horse," Kulraj Singh says softly to Zeshan, and Nafeesa, who has chased after the men, can hear every word. "Better to let her head be free. Be her guide, not her master."

Nafeesa feels invisible. It seems not to matter to them that she is standing right there.

"And sometimes the whip works better," says Zeshan loudly, fully aware Nafeesa is nearby. He sighs, shocked by his own words, the shameful memory of slapping her. "Forgive me. I do not understand this girl." He turns to Nafeesa, who stares back defiantly. "I love her deeply, but see how she defies me? She is a stubborn creature."

"She is more like her grandmother than her mother," Babba says. "More like Nafeesa than Meena. Their natures were so different."

"Their natures, and perhaps their parents' ways were different, too," says Kulraj Singh. "My beloved was kept under her father's thumb and she rebelled. On the other hand, Meena was a free spirit whom we watched over and protected. But we never tried to control her."

"Yes, you have more experience as a parent, but the only way I know to protect her is to confine her." He stops and turns again. "So, Nafeesa, pack your things. I will return Friday after next to move you to my neighbor's house in Lahore where they can keep closer watch over you. You may continue your schooling, but the women there are confined in *purdah*, and they will teach you how to behave."

Amir's eyes widen. Nafeesa is stunned. Would Babba agree to this? *Purdah*!

"She will be ready," Kulraj Singh replies calmly. "Please call to tell us the time when you will arrive so we can share a farewell meal together."

Nafeesa begins to shake uncontrollably as the taillights on the SUV disappear. Kulraj Singh turns to hold her arm, but she is running away in tears. He faces Amir. "Now you know what to do with the second half of the *She-lion* story. Give it to Nafeesa now."

***

That evening Nafeesa keeps silence in the kitchen as Kulraj Singh pre-pares, in his slow, intentional way, a tray of small, shiny bowls, filled with clear water. His hands shake as he measures the water, polishes a mango and slices sweet cake. Out in the courtyard garden, Nafeesa sees two tiny, lime-colored parrots fly by. She clips a few marigolds, carries the tray he prepared into the shrine room, where Kulraj Singh lays them before Guru Nanak's image. She examines the photograph of the first Nafeesa, a framed formal portrait in sepia with her deep eyes and an open, unsmiling face. Nafeesa wishes she had known this grandmother—so different from her Nanaa. She wonders how Nanaa would have reacted to her father's plan to seclude her in *purdah*. She leaves Babba alone with his saints and his songs.

Later Kulraj Singh, Amir and Nafeesa sit under the neem tree again. The sun has warmed the brick patio but still they wear wool. Amir reheats biryani from yesterday's meal, but Nafeesa does not touch the food.

"It is time for another she-lion to escape," says Kulraj Singh and Amir swallows hard. No! He cries inside. Not Nafeesa, too.

"Living in *purdah* in Lahore is no escape," Nafeesa mumbles bitterly. "My father must hate me."

Kulraj Singh reaches out to her. "No no no, it is not hate. It is fear. It must seem like punishment to you, but to him, sadly, the only way he knows to love you is to control you. His fear of something hurting you, of losing you is so large, it eats him up sometimes."

Nafeesa looks away from him. "I will not live in *purdah*!" she declares.

"Yes! *This* she-lion," Kulraj Singh says, nodding at her and smiling, "will not be living in *purdah*. This she-lion will carry Yusuf's manuscript and letter to India, to Mumbai, to Faisah and Lia, and she will bring her aunties back home to us. I will see my daughters once again before I die."

"Die?" asks Nafeesa. She looks at Amir, who smirks to indicate that Kulraj Singh is exaggerating. "But is this serious?" she asks Amir. "I am going to Mumbai?"

"Yes, Nafeesa. Let's talk about Mumbai," Amir replies, and Nafeesa listens but has trouble absorbing what they are saying.

"But how will I get a visa for Mumbai?"

Her grandfather shrugs. "God will provide." He beams, enjoying how happy he is making her.

"Actually, the Indian High Commission will provide," Amir explains, passing his smart phone to Nafeesa. There on the screen she sees her name on an official document. "We do a little business with India. I have a friend in the government. And Babba has a friend—a Sikh of course . . ." Mamou finishes his sentence by extending his hand and rubbing his fingertips with his thumb.

Nafeesa is speechless. No *purdah* for her! Never before has she felt so loved, so understood. Plus, she will finally meet the women of her mother's family! And Babba called her a she-lion!

***

The next morning, as Amir prepares breakfast, he hears Nafeesa in the shower. Her singing tears open his longing to hear the laughter of his sisters– the old wound—that ache that survives everything. Nafeesa's departure will protect her from the plan her father has for her, and he is happy she is escaping that. But it hurts that she is leaving.

He shakes flour onto the table and mixes it with water to form a firm ball of dough. *Purdah*, he scoffs and balls the dough into a snake, winding it into a bun. *Ammi*, he exhales, twirling the mixture in the air and laying it flat on the spitting grill. He spoons butter along the folds of the dough. *Reshma*, he whispers, recalling the last time he saw his oldest sister, Reshma—shortly after Meena's funeral. *Baji*, he inhales the memory of her eyes, the day the police took her away. Each time the yeast tries to rise out of its circle, he smacks the bubble with the back of a spoon. *Meena, their common DNA, their twin understandings.* He flips the dough with tongs, and watches it fry. *Faisah*, flew to India with Lia. He hasn't seen her in eighteen years. He folds the paratha in half, spoons more butter, folds it again until the dough is quartered and sizzling. *And now Nafeesa is leaving.* Something begins to burn.

"How do I look?" Nafeesa asks the next day, trolling for a compliment. She is standing outside the door with her luggage. Amir reaches for her bag. She has lined her eyes with kajal and is wearing her slimmest jeans. A colorful headscarf frames her face. She carries large sunglasses.

"Like a religious hipster," he says and he waits for her giggle.

"You'll come visit Mumbai, Mamou?" He loves her wide smile, so like Meena's, like Baji's. "And, Mamou ...." She begins again. Her voice is strong, but seems unable to go on, as if it has gone in search of words it is confident it will find in time, but hasn't yet. He waits. "Forgive me for criticizing Babba. I didn't understand him. Now I do feel his love, and yours. Never have I felt so free to be myself."

"That's how real love feels, Nafeesa. Remember that feeling." They turn toward the scuffle of Kulraj Singh's slippers as he pads down the path. He hands her small boxes he wrapped in newsprint. "Food for the trip, and small gifts for the girls." She holds the packages against her body. "And remember, Nafeesa, you don't have to search for answers in dark libraries anymore. Now you can ask your questions in the light."

"What are you going to tell my father?" she asks. Her throat catches on the word, "father". Amir recognizes the loss of her father that she feels, the kind that floods the mind and the body with its unexpected visits. She whispers, "I wish I could say goodbye to my father."

He recalled the time when the two of them were driving home from Lahore, and Nafeesa confided to him. "Oh no, I forgot about Nanaa today, Mamou! My own grandmother!" Nafeesa had cried out like a repentant sinner.

Amir could no longer recall the day when he first forgot to remember his own mother.

"It is a completely normal thing," he said to her then, but he knew that the forgetting leaves a stain of shame and confusion, a stain that refuses to accept it is normal to forget someone you have loved.

"I'm not telling Rufina I'm leaving," she says. "It might get back to my father somehow." There is a fire in her voice. Amir will miss that, too.

Then Babba takes her plump hands into his own his rough skin and bones. "You are a grown woman now, and this is your moment." He speaks in his definitive way. "Think of this journey as a new nest you must live in, but you can decorate it any way you wish."

Then the three come close and breathe together for one last moment. Nafeesa looks up at Amir. "Do you think I can do it?" He listens to her from his own dark place. "I can't get your twin back, Mamou, but maybe I can bring Auntie Faisah, and Baji, too—if I can find her." Then they kiss each other's faces, rubbing their familiness all over one another the way cats do. "I'll be back," she says, her eyes focusing directly and jumping between the two of them to be sure they understand her promise. "It won't be like it was with the others. I will not disappear." Nafeesa pledges her foolish promise with all the earnestness of the young.

***

In 1996, after Ujala's escape from Adiala, her lawyer and sister, Faisah, proclaims to Lia Chee, U.S. journalist and friend, that the prison break itself was a brilliant sleight of hand, as it drew the eyes of Pakistani law enforcement south, simply because that is the direction the Nissan was heading as it sped away from the prison doors, even though roundabouts and back alleys always allow for a change in direction, and cars can be exchanged for buses, buses for airplanes, and anyone can hide in a cave. The official search for Baji Ujala, the famous escapee, is bungled and comes to naught and a warrant is issued for Faisah Ehtisham on suspicion of her aiding and abetting the prisoner's escape. Meanwhile, at the Islamabad airport, an ordinary plane departs for Dubai, followed by a regularly-scheduled transfer to another plane that eventually lands in India. Faisah Ehtisham and Lia Chee are on those planes and for the next eighteen years Mumbai becomes their home. They do not realize, until their escape from Pakistan, that their hearts are two old friends hidden inside distinctly dissimilar shells.

Months before her arrest, Ujala had introduced Faisah to Lia, whom she'd met on a bus ride from Punjab to the North West Frontier Province. Lia, a Chinese-American writer from South Carolina—a kindred, if different spirit—had helped Ujala rescue a Pathan girl from her brutal father. Lia's people were suburbanites, great-grandchildren of Chinese Christian converts who moved to Charleston in the early 1800s, who kept to themselves during generations of slavery and Jim Crow, but eventually mixed with white Southern Baptists—such as Lia's grandma, who met her Chinese husband-to-be over egg rolls at the Red Poppy Diner. They had to travel to a northern state to be married.

Like her grandmother, Lia was audacious and adventuresome, a freelance globe-trotter who scavenged the world for other people's stories. For a while, Ujala's efforts to rescue women who were destined to die was the story Lia loved to write, and her editors loved to read, too. Later, Baji Ujala brought Lia home with her to Nankana Sahib, where Lia became one more character in their extended family of Muslim misfits and Sikh saints.

On the patio in Nankana Sahib, Ujala had introduced Faisah to Lia. "Superb human rights organizer, extraordinary lawyer, and consummate know-it-all." Right away Faisah recognized Lia's spark and put her to work. Soon Lia developed the idea of a women's radio station—or was it Faisah's idea first? They never could recall which ideas were whose first, but they didn't care about that. They just throve on working together. Faisah provided legal strategy for Ujala's trial on charges for kidnapping the Pathan girl and taking her to the North West, and Lia took charge of press relations for the defense team. Lia and Faisah understood each other from the start. Faisah said that Lia was mouthy but smart. Lia said that Faisah was cunning but cool. Lia made decisions quickly and definitively. Faisah thought broadly, brooded and took her time. They became sidekicks, organizers and inseparable friends.

At the time everyone realized that Ujala's jailbreak was a high-risk operation, so due to the fact that Faisah was her barrister and an officer of the court, she was not allowed to play a direct role in the escape. Instead, Yusuf Salman arrived from the U.S. after many years abroad, and stepped up to do the job with a little help from inside the prison. Everyone knew what to expect if the escape failed—criminal charges and long prison terms. And if the escape was successful, government officials would feel humiliated by a jailbreak occurring right under their noses. They would be looking for targets to blame. As Ujala's closest known collaborators, Faisah and Lia expected that they would be arrested next. They debated what to do.

Who knows how long we might be detained?

We will be interrogated.

We will be separated.

When Faisah and Lia heard themselves speak aloud the word "separated," as in, we will be separated from each other, and the word "detained," as in we will be detained from our life together, their eyes locked, words stopped, and a new, pulsing awareness flashed between them. Neither wanted ever to be separated from the other. What had been unspoken became inevitable. Their common mind knew that life meant for them to be together. They pushed headlong into another plan.

Where to go?

Delhi or Mumbai?

Mumbai.

I'll call the airlines.

I'll find the passports.

I'll have money wired to a bank in Mumbai.

I'll call the lawyers' guild there.

I'll call the women's center.

I'll call Amir and Abbu.

"Abbu!" Faisah collapsed, thinking of her father, and Lia held her close. "How can I leave my father?"

"I don't know," cried Lia. "I love him, too."

At the airport in Lahore, goodbyes were whispered, the Guru's blessings were invoked, salaams were exchanged, and on the same day as Ujala's prison escape, Faisah and Lia ducked into an airport shuttle bus. They would not be truly free to return to Pakistan from India—a warrant was quickly issued against Faisah—so they planned to postpone their return until all was forgotten and they felt safe again. Might a return visit or a letter from them to Nankana Sahib expose them to danger? They dared not risk it. One year led to another: Ujala was still at large, and her case was still pending, paused somewhere in a Shariah Court that could not proceed without her. Amir and Kulraj Singh believed they were being watched. The ISI, Pakistan's intelligence police, could be anywhere it wanted to be.

Amir and Faisah have not seen each other in eighteen years. Because of Baji's escape, the Pakistani government will never give Amir an exit visa to visit Mumbai, and although Faisah has an Indian passport and after these many years might be able to get a visa to enter Pakistan, it could still be very risky. They just don't know. They do know that the ISI tapped the phone in Nankana Sahib for several years after Baji, Faisah, and Lia disappeared. Still, Amir now phones Faisah and Lia from time to time, reporting that life remains the same there—the garden, their father's prayers, the donkey trail to the gurdwara, the commute to Lahore, multiple computer screens, everyday shopping.

But for Faisah and Lia, life cannot be more different. Mumbai is a metropolis with a population larger than Karachi, twice the population of New York City in half the space. At first, they stay with colleagues in the human rights movement, sleeping three or four to a bed. Or they carry string beds to rooftops where they can be alone, to safely hold hands until they fall asleep side by side under the city's blanched-out starlight.

By noon Mumbai's air smolders with the odor of fish. To Faisah it is a delicious mix, *redolent, verdant,* she says; but Lia says *sweaty, stinky.* Lia hates the heat. "Worse than Carolina," she complains. Still, the city is exhilarating, a seaside of filthy beaches and mangroves, whiskey served openly in hotels, pink and yellow neon lights flashing at night, pigeons aflutter, streets full of scooters, bicycles wobbling, crates stacked, police everywhere, men carrying plastic grocery bags and boys playing cricket with homemade bats. The two of them are welcomed to meetings with their Indian counterparts— up grimy staircases and down unlit hallways, behind metal gates and into back offices and tiny apartments. They become part of the men and women in the vanguard of social change, people who are happy to help political refugees from Pakistan, and to put them to work for the cause of human rights. The way the others see it, Faisah is a lawyer, Lia is a writer, and the people march on. Eventually, except for the absence of family, they are relieved never to return to Pakistan.

Lia finds a day job with the *Mumbai Times* and Faisah joins a lawyers' collective. They lease a flat above a line of shops in lower Parel West, where they share a balcony with their next-door neighbor, a heroin addict who smokes his pipe and rolls his cigarettes alone on the balcony day and night.

Across the narrow street is a one-room factory, one of fifteen thousand such operations in the city, where women stitch baseball caps with emblems of various U.S. teams. The odor of grilled meat rises from the street vendors below. A month after arriving from such unlikely circumstances as a bus ride, a sister with a gun, a jailbreak and a last-minute flight, they settle in their own place—a small flat, one bed to share, a life ahead.

Yes.

Faisah lies awake one spring morning watching the light cross the saffron- painted wall while Lia sleeps in their tangle of cotton dhurries, snoring and squirming in a dream. Faisah's fingers run through her cropped hair as she watches Lia's breathing cause her belly to pulse between her pelvic bones. A sliver of sunlight outlines Lia's bare torso and Faisah is drawn to touch it, to feel the warmth of Lia's skin, but she restrains herself, fingering the scar that crosses her cheek and melds her eyelid to its socket. She reaches for her eye patch. Outside, police sirens wail and next door that BBC voice summarizes the news.

If she wakes, Faisah thinks, negotiating with herself, I could say I was just pulling the dhurrie up to cover her. But when Faisah's finger crosses the divide between them and touches Lia's exposed torso, they both cross that line of pleasure together. Lia awakens. She turns onto her back and draws Faisah into the crook of her arm. She holds her there—not like the playful puppies they were on the other side of that border, but with the tenderness of adult women full of love and passion for one another.

Lia's Journal Entry 1997

What could be stranger yet more natural, than to fall into the arms of your best friend and discover yourself? This morning Faisah reached for me. Hours later, when I looked in the mirror, I almost didn't

*recognize the woman I saw– eyes bright like she glowed from within.
She had a sultry quality about her, like a movie star, but without the
makeup. It was me, Lia, and before me in the mirror stood a bare-
breasted, loved woman. I loved myself in a new way, a deeper way,
the way I love my Faisah. I love everything she loves and I always
will. Maybe both of us had to become strangers in another country
to find this. Every cell in my body is where it belongs.*

Faisah's Journal Entry 1997

*Well, finally I got the guts to do it, and she liked it and I liked it and
it's the best thing in the world and that's that and I don't have any
more words for it.*

In Mumbai, their professional, social, and political lives become all one
thing; meetings mix with dinners, rallies, and more meetings, but their personal life is theirs alone. As in Pakistan, sex is a forbidden topic, and homo-
sexuality is even more taboo.

Ten years later, Mumbai changes. After India's first openly gay royal
prince comes out of the closet, he is disinherited publicly and appears on
television to begin a public discussion. Next follows Mumbai's first gay pride
march. Faisah and Lia's faces appear on the cover of the *Times*, wearing
bright lavender tee shirts with words printed across their chests: "A woman
without a man is like a fish without a bicycle." In the photo Faisah's long
wavy hair is flying. She has a smile across her eye-patched, scarred face
and a fist in the air. Lia's face flashes a wink at the camera. They become
instant celebrities, in-demand by the media. Of course, others in India's

women's movement are also lesbians, but even among political colleagues, the admission of intimacy between two women can be risky. And Lia and Faisah together are a peculiar case, too. Being Punjabi, Faisah can pass as Indian, but Lia looks like she'd be more comfortable in Beijing than in Mumbai, and her English sounds (to Indians anyway) like a Texan on a *Dallas* television rerun. People are drawn to their looks, including the eye patch. Too, as a Pakistani and as a Chinese Yankee, they have to suffer criticism for their respective governments' foreign policies, regardless of the fact that they, too, oppose the policies. Being on the defensive so often causes them to retreat into their domestic life whenever they can. Rarely do they invite others into their world. This is the world of Mumbai that Nafeesa enters in 2014.

***

The night before Nafeesa flies to Mumbai, Amir calls to tell Faisah and Lia about Yusuf's letter to Kulraj Singh. "Baji and Yusuf are alive in Kashmir!" he announces. They rejoice like children with their squeals and giggles. They always said they assumed she was still alive and safe, but truly they had their doubts.

"Where in Kashmir?" Lia wants to know. Faisah shakes her head as Amir explains that oddly the letter doesn't say where.

"Probably Yusuf didn't want to give away their location," says Amir. "In case the police intercepted the letter," says Amir. Then he is silent, slowly adding, "And Abbu is sending Meena's daughter, Nafeesa, to you. I warn you, she's a handful," he jokes, then hesitates. His voice drops. "She's extraordinary, Faisah. Abbu is sending her on a mission to bring Baji and you back home."

Faisah scoffs. "Sure thing, brother. Just hop on over to Kashmir, grab Baji and zip back to Pakistan. Don't worry that Kashmir is a war zone, passports and visas are required, there's an outstanding warrant for Baji's arrest and possibly mine, too, plus we have no idea about Baji's life now— eighteen years have passed. And to put a protected Muslim girl like Nafeesa on a mission like this—whatever is Abbu thinking?"

"Since when have we ever known what Abbu is thinking? What I can tell you is she arrives in Mumbai tomorrow."

Faisah's and Lia's eyes lock. Tomorrow?

Faisah and Lia have had good times and bad times over the years, but recently, they have been living on auto-pilot, without the relaxed and easy humor they once shared. There are stubborn silences between them, tense, polite interactions and occasional snide comments. Tenderness and love-making are rare. Their relationship has endured over the years, but something inside is wrong.

Lia's Journal Entry

She never turns to me anymore. She keeps everything to herself. Just being around her depresses me, a kind of contagion that makes us both miserable. I don't know what to do. If I coddle her, she cringes. If I tell her to snap out of it, she acts like I've slapped her face. If I offer to listen, she clams up. If I remind her to take her antidepressants, she gets indignant. I can't win. We can't win. Maybe the love has gone away. Maybe I should go away, too.

Faisah's Journal Entry

I think I've never needed Lia more than I do now, but I can feel she is ready to flee. I know I get on her nerves. She tiptoes around me and

I want to shout, "Stop! you don't need to tiptoe," but another part of
me wants to yell, "Could you tiptoe more quietly, please?" Really, I
am impossible. When was the last time I really made her feel loved?
When will be the next time?

Lia feels Faisah's despair. "Get a grip. Try yoga," she suggests. "At leastit's something we could share." But whatever she says sounds cold, evento her. And Faisah has nothing but contempt for yoga, or anything withouta political dimension. "Downward facing doing nothing," she calls it. Liaplops down on the patchwork cushion, crosses her legs and straightens herspine to begin her yoga routine.

Faisah commences her questioning. "How will Nafeesa deal with us?And with a city like Mumbai? She's only eighteen."

"Eighteen. Shit! The marrying age." Lia groans. "Well, I'm glad she'llbe with us and not in Pakistan with all those mothers appraising whether ornot she is perfect enough for their perfect sons."

"Your American is showing, Lia," Faisah mumbles, irritated. "You don'tknow what you are talking about." Lia holds the yoga pose in silence, extending her legs and bending forward, her nose to her knees. To Faisah thisyoga fad is nothing more than a distraction for Lia from her political work,where Lia worries about everything. Lia likes to believe she has a live-and-let-live attitude toward life, but Faisah knows better. She continues. "Thereare no women there to manage a marriage proposal for her. Really, withReshma possibly in the Taliban by now and Uji hiding who knows where,she has no women in the family other than the two of us."

"I'm sure the girl will find something to do in Mumbai. Imagine beingyoung in a city of eighteen million people, a film capital on the banks of theArabian Sea. It's like twenty San Franciscos rolled into one. She'll be fine."

Faisah dares not say what she thinks. "You're right. I guess first we needto get to know her."

Lia turns her head in downward dog to look at Faisah. "And she'll have to get to know us—the way we are. How is that gonna fly?"

Faisah sighs. Pondering Nafeesa's response to them as lesbians gives her a stomachache. "I imagine Nafeesa is a fairly traditional girl, so it may be a while before we can get through to her," she says. "She'll get the idea. Let's not rush her."

"Whatever," says Lia, releasing the pose and sitting back on her heels "Whatever."

Faisah fingers the scar across her face, petting it. Even after all these years she still hates meeting someone new and dealing with their reaction to "the face," as she calls it. The dread is smaller now, and she pretends it doesn't bother her, but it still sends a wave of nausea through her insides. Who could ever become accustomed to the stares on the street or the sudden reflection in a random glass window, or a mirror that does not lie? She is glad Lia will not accompany her to the airport. She wants to meet her niece alone, Pakistani to Pakistani, without the complications of American Lia. Chinese Lia. Lesbian Lia.

Faisah rises to finish cooking the curry as fumes wash the room with the aroma of mango powder and cumin and the sting of cayenne. Lia stretches out on the floor, perfectly still, and Faisah longs for her long, lean, enticing body. She decides to lie next to her for *savasana*. "Corpse pose," she laughs, "A depressive's favorite." The rough woven rug bores into the skin of her back. She keeps silent for only a moment.

"Do you think Nafeesa's even heard of lesbians, of gay people?" Faisah asks. Lia's eyes are open, unfocused, and her body unmoving.

"No," she responds without comment and Faisah feels Lia's irritation. Still, she persists.

"How will we explain?"

"Hush! It's still yoga, remember?" Immediately Lia regrets the sting of her words. She sees a tear glisten along the dark rim of Faisah's beautiful eye. Lia vows *ahimsa*, non-harming, and rolls to her side and stands. She bows *namaste* to the mat, slap dash and half-hearted.

Faisah makes a friendly smirk. "Is the light in you as hungry as the light in me?"

"Frickin' starving," Lia says, taking Faisah's hand and pulling her in for a full-frontal hug. She kisses Faisah's "good eye," as they call it, and then she kisses her eye patch. "So neither side of your split personality will forget you are loved," she says with certainty.

Lia and Faisah spend the rest of the day dragging boxes and bags from "Nafeesa's Nook," as they are already naming it. Their apartment is really one large room. They are creating a space for Nafeesa in an area they use for storage and laundry. The nook's walls are light gray, scratched and soiled. It has a small window, but no closet. They stack laundry baskets on the balcony outside the sliding glass door where their neighbor is asleep on his string bed.

"Looks pretty shitty," Lia says. "But it's okay. We can paint it. Nafeesa can choose the color." In the bottom of a box, Faisah finds a cobalt blue curtain patterned with white birds with wide, open wingspans. Lia presses out the creases in the cloth with the flat of her hand.

"Let's use it to hang it over the doorway for privacy," Faisah says, spreading it out on the floor. "We'll have to make do with what we have."

Lia laughs. "Growing up, to my mama 'making do' was an artform. Every mobile home, cheap tract house or flimsy apartment building we lived in, she always managed to make something new out of something old."

"In Pakistan, doing without is how we strengthen our muscles of ingenuity," says Faisah with pride.

"Doing without sucks," says Lia definitively. She lifts one end of Nafeesa's cot while Faisah pushes the other into the nook. They find clean sheets, pillows, and a dark patterned dhurrie. They stack a heap of heavy books to make a table and add a reading lamp, a crate for a shelf, and a small woolen mat. They stand back to admire what they have done. Not much, Lia thinks, but it shows effort. It's enough.

Against the orange wall behind their bed hangs the magazine photo of the two of them in a gay rights demonstration. They had it enlarged and framed into a poster. They beam confidence and happiness in the crooked frame. Faisah reaches out to take it down, but Lia wants to leave it up where Nafeesa can see for herself who and what they are.

"I don't want to hide in my own home," Lia says quietly, directly.

"I understand," says Faisah, "but, for Nafeesa's comfort, maybe we should take it down." Deciding about the poster is the last step before Faisah leaves to get Nafeesa from the airport. They stand back admiring the black and white proof of their youthful joy, when something between them subtly shifts.

"Maybe we should take it down," Lia agrees softly, raising her brows, gesturing in its direction, as Faisah moves toward the wall.

"Oh, we definitely have to change that poster," Faisah announces. "Let's re-hang it so it is straight." She jabs Lia's ribs. "Unlike the two of us, huh?"

Lia grins and wraps her arms around Faisah, lifting her off the floor. Faisah nuzzles into the crook of Lia's arm and stays there until it is time to leave. "One moment, rain, one moment, sunshine," they say in unison, as they have hundreds of times before.

***

The plane lands in a thunderstorm, rocking wildly, lurching, vibrating. Lightning flashes over the sea and rain sprays the cargo workers as they unload the plane's belly. Descending the jet's stairs, Nafeesa swears that the weather is so hot and swampy she thinks she can see snakes on the tarmac. Inside, the airport is a candy delight of newness—glass and steel, with lines of people everywhere. She follows other passengers through customs and immigration and baggage claims. She stands back, eyeing the bags that circle the carousel, thinking about Lahore. She always feared she would have a dull, meaningless life there, but now her life will not be like that—it will have color and passion and meaning. She loads her bags on a bright yellow cart pushed by a porter into the parking garage, and waits by the mural of a multi-armed goddess, where Faisah said she would meet her. Nafeesa is surrounded by concrete walls, overhead parking ramps, a broken roadway, traffic noise, pop music, lines of vehicles and a sea of people around the terminal. Still, she can hear her mobile phone ringing.

"Nafeesa? Is that you, Nafeesa? It's Faisah. Is that you over there … in those tight jeans? Is that you?"

Uh oh. Nafeesa immediately wishes she'd worn a shalwar kameez instead of jeans. She is anxious now when she turns around to see her auntie waving her mobile phone in the air and striding across the parking lane in her own tight jeans. A chubby middle-aged woman in large sunglasses, with cropped black hair streaked with gray and purple, she removes her sunglasses and grabs Nafeesa for a hug.

"You look so much like Amir," Faisah says, "—how is that brother of mine?" She holds Nafeesa's shoulders and kisses both cheeks. Then Faisah pushes Nafeesa back so they can exchange longer looks. Faisah watches Nafeesa absorb the reality of her black eye patch and below it the wide, pocked, patterned scar covering half of one entire cheek.

"I could say the same thing to you, Auntie. You look like Amir."

"Call me Faisah, will you? Auntie makes me feel old, just seems wrong." She grabs Nafeesa's hand to pull her along. Nafeesa laughs again. She tries not to stare at her auntie's face. "And don't worry about the face," Faisah says with a crooked smile. "It happened a long time ago. Acid attack." For a moment Nafeesa thinks Faisah is winking at her from behind the patch. "Usually I have a glass eye," Faisah explains. "It's in the shop, being fixed."

She laughs at how absurd she sounds. "You'll get used to it," she says, but Nafeesa looks away. "Everybody gets used to the face. Eventually."

Through the drizzle and distant thunder, they drive into old Bombay, past lakes of sewage and rutted roads, the red turrets and fancy facades of historic buildings, the skyscrapers, the twinkling strings of lights—necklaces of plenty that make every day a potential festival. The Arabian Sea is a party to the life of Mumbai, with all the little bridges and causeways, the irregular edges and moveable sands of the sea everywhere. In the distance, Nafeesa sees a flamingo stalking shrimp and algae. She has read about the famous slums of Mumbai, and now she is in them as they drive past huts with roofs constructed of corrugated metal. People and poverty look and smell the same as in Pakistan, but the energy she feels is definitely amped up, more hip hop than folk dance. The West Parel area is packed with police and tourists and tall green leafy patches of bamboo. Faisah drives at a walking pace, creeping along the crowded streets. Nafeesa lets herself feel as tired and hungry as she is.

At last, Faisah pulls the little Honda Civic into an underground security garage where, standing in the middle of an assigned parking space is a tall, lean East Asian woman. Her waist-length hair is straight, parted in the middle, and she wears serious, black-rimmed glasses. She opens Nafeesa's door as the car slows down.

"Hi," she says loudly, sticking out her hand in Nafeesa's direction. "I'm Lia." Her accent is American and her tone is friendly, but her eyes laser into Nafeesa.

Amir had mentioned Lia, but did not tell Nafeesa anything about her. Nafeesa hesitates just a moment at Lia's forthrightness, then replies, climbing out of the car, and giving and receiving the obligatory cheek kisses.

"Bet you're hungry. Let's go upstairs. I've got us a treat– McVeggies and fries warming in the oven." Lia holds up a large, white paper bag with the golden arches logo.

After they drag Nafeesa's blue suitcase upstairs, they sit at their one small table and Lia serves the re-heated dinner. Faisah is itching to read Yusuf's story. "You have the manuscript?" she asks Nafeesa. "We're dying to read it."

Nafeesa hesitates, feeling a slight pushback in herself. She didn't expect her auntie to want to talk about Yusuf's manuscript right away. She wants to talk about her new life in Mumbai. Nafeesa aims one end of a fried potato at her mouth and doesn't answer. She doesn't know what to say. How can she say no to an auntie?

"Never mind, Nafeesa. We can read it later."

After eating, they show Nafeesa her nook. "I truly love this flat, and my own room you made for me. I really do. *Shukriah.*" Nafeesa especially loves her key to the flat, which they hand her ceremoniously. She has never had her own key to any place she has lived. She notes the poster on the wall announcing that they are gay and feels a little shy about that. She has heard of lesbians, of course, but it is never something openly discussed. It is weird, very strange, she thinks, realizing then why Amir did not tell her anything about Lia. He would not know how to begin to talk about it. She compares Auntie Faisah's short-cropped hair to Lia's long, flowing locks. She wonders if that means something. Lia is in the kitchen and Auntie is the one who drove to the airport. Is Faisah the boy and Lia the girl? She doesn't know just how to think about it. All she knows is that she wants them to like her.

"Forgive us if we sound like the secret police or something," says Lia, "but we've lots of questions. We're trying to fill in the blanks."

"I've a lot of blanks I'll want you to fill in for me, too."

Faisah tilts her head and grins at her niece. "Frankly, I thought you'd be more of a child. You are brave to make this trip alone."

Nafeesa is unaccustomed to being considered anything close to brave. "I am eager to get on with my life.

"We have only a few rules," Faisah explains "You will have to call your father every week."

Nafeesa pauses, smirks. "Of course," she says. Lia and Faisah exchange glances. "And my best friend, Rufina, is in Lahore. May I call her too?"

"If you have the minutes," Faisah hesitates. "I imagine my brother filled your phone and will be generous in paying for your expenses." Then she sits down next to Nafeesa and takes her hand. "Amir said that he expects that your father may not visit Nankana Sahib once he learns that you have gone."

"Yes," says Nafeesa. "He will be furious that Babba and Mamou let me go. But please understand, I was eager to get away."

"Nafeesa, here in India you are free. At your age, you are legally emancipated. You have to answer to us only as family, not legally. You are an adult. You have a visa. A residence. A means of support," she adds, squeezing the envelope which Amir handed Nafeesa at the Lahore airport and which, out of respect, Nafeesa had given to Faisah. "At least until you finish your schooling."

"I almost finished twelfth grade, but not quite," she says. "I am committed to completing higher secondary school. Maybe continuing to university," she adds, revealing something she has never expressed out loud before.

"What else?" Lia asks. "What else do you want in your life here?"

Nafeesa straddles the stool at the counter. She stares out the window at the laundry hanging on the lines, still wet from the day's rain. What else? What else am I supposed to want? Do they think I want them to find me a husband? "Dancing," she says softly, looking up for their reaction. "I've been studying dance for many years."

"Dancing! I'm surprised," says Lia, "not that there's anything wrong with dancing. I just haven't known many Muslim girls who dance."

"My grandmother...my father's mother taught me the classical style when I was quite young—you know, telling old stories with your feet—toes in, toes out, mostly arms and hands, bells around the ankles, the drum, the bright clothes and the jewelry. How I loved the jewelry." Nafeesa stops talking, wonders if she was talking too much.

"Personally, I love to dance," says Lia. "Not very good at it, I'm afraid."

"Nanaa put me in studio classes just as soon as I was old enough, and we had a teacher who was not traditional. I mean she could do the traditional dances, but she wanted us to really move all of our bodies. 'The body reveals the body's way,' she would say and urge us to be wild and joyful, to use our hips and let our legs fly." Nafeesa exhales, relaxes. "I feel good just thinking of all she taught us. And I'd like to learn more here in Mumbai, if I may." She looks at Faisah.

"We will find a dance studio for you," promises Faisah, fiddling with the elastic on her eye patch. "But there are some pretty wild arts programs here in Mumbai. We'll look for something . . . appropriate."

"Aunties," Nafeesa says, twisting the edge of her dupatta, "or Faisah and Lia...what should I call you? Mrs. and Mrs. ... or what?" Nafeesa wants to let them know that she can see that there is something between them that one does not feel between roommates or even best friends. There is an awkward silence.

"Call me Lia. But, Faisah, what should Nafeesa call you?"

"I said at the airport to call me Faisah, but now I believe I like Auntie after all. There are lots of young aunties, are there not?"

"Yes, Auntie, there are." And Nafeesa laughs again. Outside there are the familiar sounds of traffic and shouts from the street. They have been talking for a long time and fatigue settles into their bodies from all the busyness that brought Nafeesa to them and all the preparations they made for the day. Nafeesa does not want the conversation to end. These women make her feel at home. She notices that they are staring at her carry-on bag. "Oh—the manuscript. Did Mamou tell you what is in it?"

"Well, he told us about it," Faisah says, "but didn't give many details about—"

"—all he said was that Yusuf and Baji are together in Jammu & Kashmir somewhere," Lia interrupts, "that they are safe and alive. I can't believe she's been in India all this time!"

"Well, Kashmir is not exactly India, Lia," Faisah comments.

"You know what I mean. Amir said Yusuf wrote their escape story, and in it he falsely reports that Baji died—so the old kidnapping case against her in Pakistan can be dismissed. I think that is a terrific strategy," adds Lia. "A writer's plan. A journalist's dream—that one's written words will change lives." She stops. "You've read the whole manuscript, Nafeesa?"

She nods and digs inside the carry-on to pull out a manila envelope stuffed with pages.

"It is quite thick!" says Faisah with delight.

"Yes, the story is long." Nafeesa moves to a chair and relaxes back with the papers on her lap. She takes her time. "He entitles it "The She-lion of Punjab," referring to Auntie Ujala. I mean, Baji is the she-lion." Nafeesa is almost swooning. "It is kind of a love story, if I may say so. Yusuf, the poet-journalist arriving all the way from New York to reunite with his long lost love and then becoming an accomplice to her prison escape! And it's a travelogue, too—transporting the reader over the mountains and valleys of Kashmir near the Line of Control. I learned a lot about the Conflict that I hadn't understood. It is a great escape story. He hides their car. They wear disguises and travel back roads and on buses. Baji cuts her hair to look like a boy. It's an adventure story, too. They find a very strange old woman, a shaman maybe, who guides them over the mountains and then disappears. They manage to evade both the Pakistani police and Indian patrols along the border and settle in a border town up there."

Lia interrupts her. "Maybe we could just read it for ourselves. We've waited almost half a lifetime to hear the story."

Nafeesa feels impatient, and afraid that if they read the story, they won't want to go to Jammu & Kashmir with her, or they will go on their own and leave her behind in Mumbai like a child. "And for me, it's been an entire lifetime to hear the story of my mother, and Baji and my aunties. And I want us to visit Baji and Yusuf. I feel like I know them already."

"Of course, you do," says Faisah. "We will all go as soon as possible, as soon as we can learn exactly where they are. Jammu & Kashmir is a vast and complicated place."

Nafeesa has one more question. She turns to Faisah, "Auntie, have you ever heard about our family having an estate in Malakwal?"

"Yes, I've heard of Malakwal, but not as a family place. Ammi never talked much about her family. She always said they perished in the Partition. Maybe Baji knows more."

"Can we go to Baji soon, please?" asks Nafeesa. "I promised Babba that I'd bring all three of you back to him."

"Uh... Nafeesa," Faisah says, "Even if we can find Baji, she can't return to Pakistan until her case is dismissed. You understand that, right? She would be arrested if she tried to cross the border."

"But once Yusuf's story is published, won't the case be dismissed like Yusuf planned? You're a lawyer! It could happen any day now. Correct?"

"I am, and the case should be dismissed, but courts move very slowly and unexpected things happen. Our lawyers can file motions requesting dismissal, but we don't want to draw too much attention—she had help escaping, you know."

"You mean, accomplices? Like Yusuf?"

"Exactly," says Faisah. "We must protect the others, too. But we will find her. I just can't predict how long it will be, if ever, before she can return to Nankana Sahib."

Nafeesa brings to mind Kulraj Singh's bony face and hacking cough. "I am not sure just how to say this, Auntie Faisah, but we do not have a lot of time. Babba is old and not that well. His last wish is to be with all his daughters before he . . . dies." She can feel her auntie's heart sinking.

"We will find a way soon," says Faisah in a soft, loving voice.

"And there it is, ladies and ladies," announces Lia. "Faisah's loving sunshine! Shine a little of that on me, if you please." Faisah kisses Lia quickly, right on her lips. Nafeesa is not even shocked. Then Faisah kisses Nafeesa in the very same way.

***

The next week, a letter arrives from Baji:

My dearest Faisah,

After all these years I was overjoyed to find your address on the internet. And Lia is with you! I am so pleased. I hope you receive this letter in good health and spirits.

How does one begin to cross two decades? I think about you often, but you are always twenty-five years old in my mind. I cannot imagine you middle-aged. Oh, how I have missed you. I pray to Allah to keep you happy. I pray Abbu is alive and well but I dare not write to him. I crave information about everyone, but especially him. He is elderly now, if he is—dare I write the word—alive.

I began this desperate search for you after I learned that Yusuf sent a letter to Abbu along with his manuscript telling his version of the story of our escape from Pakistan. We have been living in Akram, in Jammu & Kashmir, just a few hours from Srinagar. After the last time all of us were together, we had adventures that led us to this town where we made a modest home. I am still in my former occupation and he is what he is—which is another way of saying I do not want to write here what kind of work we do, but I must tell you that my husband is not what I believed he was or what he used to be.

My sister, I am living with a monster. I need your help desperately. I will try to describe what has happened in a way that is truthful and fair, and in the order that events have unfolded. Sadly, we have no children. Often we have wished for noisy, intrusive relatives living in the next room, or a cousin's wedding to attend. A life without children was not by our design, but by Allah's—and it took many years for me to accept— hard years of hope and disappointment, of miscarriages and emergencies, of pain and blood and exhaustion. My sister, once I held in the palm of my hand twin embryos smeared with red and yellow fluids from my body. One might have had the soul of our martyred sister. My grief at that moment was so profound I could not draw a breath. The bleeding caused me to pass into blessed unconsciousness for many days, but I lived—although life was never the same after that.

The hardest part of living here is the confinement required by weather and altitude and the militarized life and economy. During our first years, we survived on my small salary while he chopped wood, performed minor repairs, and submitted articles for which he was paid little. Mostly he stared out the window at the landscape's bare trees and barren meadows. That first May after the long winter, tourists began to arrive, mostly weekenders from Srinagar, and he spent days at the teahouse to pick up some news, to practice English, to find hikers who wanted to hire a local guide. He knew nothing about the area, of course, so at first he just had to pretend he knew where he was leading his clients into the hills. Before long he had learned enough to lead short backpacking expeditions. Eventually his body became strong. Then, a few years ago, he became very dissatisfied.

"I used to be somebody," he would say, referring to his years in New York and all the friends he had there, the accolades for his writing, the lecture circuit he created. Every fall he would insist that we should move to Delhi or perhaps Mumbai. He dreamed of landscapes with jacaranda and hibiscus, high rises and subways. I never wanted a life somewhere else. I simply felt safer staying where we were, but I didn't object to his planning because it never came to anything. He was as frozen and immobile as the mountains around us.

I could predict every year what would happen. He would start to plan our move to a city—collecting maps, making lists, saving money. He would talk about nothing else. He was obsessed. "Life will be so good then," he would say. "I will have my life back." I would pretend to listen. Then each year on a perfect fall day, when the sudden yellow brilliance of sunshine on the valley floor mesmerized the town, something deep inside of him surrendered to it, his restlessness died, and the wish to be anywhere else but in that glorious season, shriveled up and blew away. There was something about the air, the climate and the silence that grabbed us. It was as real as the aroma of tea, and as intangible. Then we longed for the return of the first snowfall, the way a child longs for the sound of a father's footfall when he comes home from a trip at long last. I knew it to be one of Allah's tricks—the return of awe that overwhelms a puny, even silly, desire to find a big city and a tiny apartment to live in. "Why would I want to do that?" he said. And he couldn't recall.

Time passed. I loved him and showed it. We learned to forgive each other's shortcomings time after time, renewed our decision to be to-gether in this life. I found satisfaction in life's ordinary repetitions. I studied the traditional culture of the region that had once had been common to all—before the Conflict hardened and polarized the peo-ple's religious and ethnic identities.

As always, women in trouble were drawn to me. The first I helped was a young teacher who had been my student. Her husband was ty-ing her to a tree every night and leaving her out in the cold for hours. My husband and I helped her and others, too, onto a train, or a bus, or once into a car with tourists returning to Srinagar. The women would be out of immediate harm from their families, but facing all the dangers of a lone girl in a big city.

Recently he and I argued over a manuscript he has been working on for the past few months—a long story about how we traveled here. I believed it was just a private journal and I was enjoying reading it. But then I found his correspondence with the magazine editor at The Convoy. My husband thinks it's a new and brilliant idea to end our legal troubles by killing me off (saying I died in childbirth) but he is distorting some of the real events of our escape, and is putting in jeopardy some of those who helped us—using their real names. He has assured me he would protect them by changing the names of everybody, but I believe he is betraying the one who actually walked me to the door and showed us the way out of the country! We ar-gued and argued about it. He said that using real names would draw interest and add credibility. He also entirely fabricated one section of the story to suit himself. I can explain about it later, but suffice it to say here that we argued and argued. I cried, he yelled. I yelled and he cried. It was the worst thing I'd ever endured.

Then one night I said I would contact the publisher to inform him I am alive. When I said that, he shoved me to the floor and kicked my legs. It wasn't the first time he had done that, but what was new was his threat to kill me. To kill me! Oh, my sister, he may make the fiction of my death into a true tale. The simplest way for me to escape is to take a bus to Srinagar and fly somewhere, but we are living under assumed names, and without a passport or a visa, where would I go? He has begun to track my movements, insists on walking me to work and back home again, insists on doing all the shopping, so that it's now impossible for me to leave the house alone.

Last week a friend at work helped me to find your address on the internet, but meanwhile the worst thing happened. During one of his rages, he pulled me down into our root cellar and locked me in—for an entire weekend—in a space not much larger than a public toilet stall. It was truly hell. No matter how I cried, he ignored me. He left the house and returned only at night, giving me no food or water. It was only on Monday morning when I had to dress for work that he released me. No apology. He acted as if nothing had happened. I was soiled and starving, dehydrated and shaking, but I had to clean up and go to work as if nothing were wrong.

Since then, I've pretended to be the compliant wife he wants. I considered leaving him in the past, but could not imagine life without him, and I couldn't return to Pakistan, and what woman can travel alone safely anymore? I understood his feeling like a failure as a writer, and the wound of not having your talent recognized, but, like so many men in our culture, in the world itself, he took his entitlements for granted. But no more! Faisah, it stops here.

I am planning my escape—and I need you desperately. First, you must delay the publication. Or stop his publisher from using the name I am concerned about—you know which one. Talk to the editors, threaten a lawsuit, do whatever it takes to protect my dear friend. Then please come to Akram and get me. Avoid my husband at all costs. He is completely obsessed and dangerous. Anyone who helps me will also be in jeopardy. You can find my location by coming to my job—there are several workplaces of the type I always have, so you will find it with a little searching. Ask for Janna, my dear friend who mailed this letter for me. She will tell you the names we now use. She knows that there are troubles at home, but she does not realize the extent of it. So be very careful, very careful.

Forever your sister,

Baji

Chapter 4

Kashmir: A Hidden Slice of the World

Mumbai, India: 2014

Faisah's one eye stares at Lia. It is disturbed enough for two. Lia pulls Faisah up from the sofa, wraps her long arms around her, and they curl their faces into each other's neck. Then Lia starts to bawl as they stand together and completely fall apart. Nafeesa sees something new, something honest and intense, about the way they share the pain of reading what Baji has been going through. In one second, she is out of her chair and standing close to them, waiting at the door of their grief. They reach out to draw her in, and Nafeesa dares to hope that whatever happens next, they are in it together.

"Jammu & Kashmir," says Faisah, shaking her head. "I still can't get over the fact that we have both been in India all these years." Nafeesa thinks how only a week has passed since she arrived in Mumbai and already she is being guided to Baji Ujala. Her heart is racing. She moves to the kitchen area to give them privacy, but they seem not to notice. They sit on the sofa, under the reading lamp, passing pages of the letter back and forth. In the kitchen, Nafeesa pumps water into a saucepan, lights the stove and watches the water's slow, warming, bubbly edge. She looks around.

The flat is tiny and messy. She has never known sloppy women before. She thinks that maybe this is how she can help them. She would complain if it were someone else's house to keep orderly, but this is one thing she can do for them that they don't seem able to do very well for themselves. She realizes she can learn so much from them—professional women, traveled, independent; and, from being with them for the past week, she knows they have their differences, but they seem happy together. And since reading Baji's letter, she can sense that the two of them also feel her urgency to find Baji and return to Pakistan. Still, it is so hard to accept the Yusuf she describes in her letter. She turns to Faisah.

"Auntie, how can that be? That the loving man in the *She-lion* manuscript is the same man in Baji's letter?"

"Well, it's almost eighteen years later," Faisah says, not looking up from texting on her phone. "A person can change in eighteen years."

Lia walks over to the kitchen. "Nafeesa, you know Yusuf wrote that story himself and narrates it as well, so as a writer he is free to make himself the most loving, perceptive, amazing human being in the world. It's a writer's super power."

Nafeesa grins at her own naïveté but is still not satisfied. She wants to call Rufina to talk it over with her, but there is so much she cannot explain to Rufina—the manuscript itself and the escape story. After all, prison escapes are illegal. Lesbian aunties and what she's doing in Mumbai. What *am* I doing in Mumbai, she begins to wonder.

Faisah continues with her planning. "I'll call Mohammed in Delhi," she says, punching numbers on her phone. "You can't have too many lawyers in a situation like this." Lia opens her laptop and begins typing. Next Faisah calls an old Lahori friend and lawyer, Mumtaz Chaudry, who agrees to handle the dismissal of Ujala's case in Shariah Court. "We've already received a draft of the article," she tells him in a sad voice. "Yes, it confirms her death. . . Yes, in childbirth. The piece will be published in the coming days or weeks. We're not sure exactly when." Later Faisah tells Nafeesa, "I had to lie to him. Best that he not know that Baji is alive. Mumtaz is an officer of the court and ethically committed to not presenting falsehoods."

Among the dirty dishes, old tins and empty jars, Nafeesa finds a glass container brimming with tea leaves. She opens it and sniffs–they are fresh. Soon the pan sashays as it simmers, then the water boils, and the correct measure of tea and sugar is stirred in, blending with cinnamon, coriander, cumin. Soon the tea leaves boil as sugar becomes syrup and spices mix mysteriously. When the right amount of time has passed, Nafeesa strains the leaves and adds thick white milk from a tin can until the concoction turns to the right tone of milky bronze.

Nafeesa offers tea to the two aunties in their old retro mugs with slogans printed on them: *Power to the People!* shouts one—dark fist in the air, a background of fading psychedelic colors. *Love Is All We Need!* sings out a worn outline of the early Beatles across the side of a blue mug with an old crack. *Love Is Not Enough!* argues a third mug in a full upper case black and white. She pours the tea confidently. She cannot fix Baji's situation, or how it makes everybody feel, but she does know how to make a proper cup of tea. Nanaa taught me, she thinks, her heart tightening, *O Nanaa.*

"Do not worry for a moment," announces Faisah. "We know what to do."

"We do?" Lia laughs. They sit back, tea steaming in the light streaming through the sliding glass door. "Of course, we do. We are women who thrive on exerting ourselves in the world of power and ideas."

With their cups in hand, Faisah outlines a plan. "Number one," she begins, pulling back the index finger of her left hand with her right.

"Good Lord, here she goes." Lia rolls her eyes and blows across the surface of the cup. She turns to Nafeesa. "Watch out when Faisah starts counting off tasks—some of them will be coming your way." Their eyes dart directly to the first finger.

"Number one," Faisah repeats, and her voice sparkles with details and analysis. "We contact the publisher by phone, explain that we represent an unnamed client who will contest certain material facts of the *She-Lion* manuscript, without stating directly what they are."

"The publisher won't care about a few facts being off," Lia says, smirking. "Trust me. I understand editors."

"That's ok, we don't want them to care too much right away," continues Faisah. "We don't want them contacting Yusuf and putting Baji in danger. But the call will introduce some unease into the editorial process, slow it down. We say we will come to Delhi to discuss it —that we believe the matter can be easily resolved." She pauses. "Number two, we find a death certificate to file in the Pakistani court. That should take care of the dismissal."

"And how do we manage to obtain a death certificate in India?" Lia asks. "Without a death? Hmm?" Nafeesa wonders the same thing.

"Not sure. I'll look into it in Kashmir. Baji may have some ideas. Maybe ask the Delhi lawyers. But tell no one she is alive! We just probe about how the death certification process works and whether there may be a way."

"Ok," agrees Lia. The bribery thumb on her right hand rubs the two fingertips she raises in front of her face. "It's bound to cost money." She finishes her tea and rises, stretching, waving to their neighbor on the porch. He is in his underwear, smoking and staring at a pelican that has landed on a nearby railing in the lemon light of the setting sun.

Lia sits cross-legged on the floor with her long hair framing her entire torso. She and Faisah begin arguing about what to do, not fighting really, but to each idea, the other adds the strategic question, *but what if?* They are picking it all apart. Nafeesa watches as Lia convinces Faisah of her position. "We must split up," she says, "one of us goes to Akram and one goes to Delhi to deal with the publisher." Seeing Faisah's objection, she adds, "I don't want to do it either, but we do not have much time." She pours more tea into *Love Is All We Need*.

Nafeesa holds her breath. *What about me? Don't forget about me.*

Faisah sips from *Love Is Not Enough*. "OK. But I go to Akram and you go to Delhi."

Nafeesa is anxious that they have not assigned her a task. *I want to go too! What about me?* She interrupts. "Number three," Nafeesa says, putting *Power to the People* on the floor. She bends back her ring finger just as Faisah did. "I make travel arrangements, do laundry, pack bags . . ." They look up at her. "I go to Akram with you, Auntie, and I do whatever needs doing to free Baji."

Lia releases her yoga twist and Faisah's eyes light up. "You called her Baji."

"You said she was everybody's baji, so she's mine, too. Shall we free her together or not?" asks Nafeesa, as if she's known Baji Ujala her entire life.

***

Later the seabirds stop their squawking and find night perches on rooftops, balconies and palm trees along the beaches of Mumbai. The sky darkens and city lights glow. The three women sit on pillows on the balcony. They use up all their phone card minutes that night with calls to Nankana Sahib.

"Mamou, guess what! Auntie Faisah received a letter from Baji! Wait! Let me put Auntie on speaker." Faisah tells him about Baji's situation, and there is silence as they wait for Amir to absorb the meaning of what she has described.

"Okay," is all his sad and angry voice says. "I'll leave the strategizing to you. But what about Nafeesa?" Her eyes widen. At last, someone is asking about her.

"I'll be with Auntie Faisah in Jammu & Kashmir, Mamou," she shouts into the phone's speaker and she hears his gasp. From studying the online road maps, the bus and plane schedules, as she did earlier in the day, plus knowing about the dangers of the Himalayas, the changeable weather, a nearby war zone, and Yusuf, too, Nafeesa really wonders what lies ahead. Kashmir is a dangerous place. Quickly, she changes the subject. "And how is Babba?"

"He sleeps quite a lot now. Doesn't eat much. The other day he tripped and twisted his knee. So now a neighbor comes to help him while I'm at work. And of course, he chants and prays but for much shorter periods."

Faisah's voice softens. "Oh." Her heartbeat skips, the way it does when one receives bad news and for just a moment, the heart doesn't know how to go on. Now Faisah appreciates what Nafeesa was trying to tell her about the seriousness of Kulraj Singh's condition. "We will be home soon, Amir. Tell Abbu we are on our way."

"I'll recharge this phone card to the max and wire more funds! Be sure to call me along the way. And, Faisah, promise me you will keep Nafeesa safe and away from Yusuf."

"Promise, brother."

"Mamou, don't tell my father what we are doing. Okay?"

"Faisah?" Mamou asks his sister for advice about this.

"I agree with her, Amir, Nafeesa has good instincts. At least wait until we have located Baji."

"Nafeesa, we have not yet told your father that you have left. He has been traveling on business," replies Amir. "But the last time we spoke, he did mention that a girl your age should not be living with fathers and uncles and grandfathers. Perhaps he will understand and feel relieved that you are with Faisah. He comes for lunch later this week—expecting to move you back to Lahore. Babba says he will ask Zeshan for his forgiveness, and he is confident that it will all work out as God's plan."

The room goes quiet. Nafeesa can tell they are about to end the call, and she still has something to say. In a way she does want her father to worry, to care enough about her to worry, even a little, but also she does not. "Mamou, tell my father that I am safe here and tell him I said not to worry. And tell Babba I am bringing everybody home to him, as I promised."

***

The day arrives when Zeshan rides to Nankana Sahib for lunch with Kulraj Singh and Amir, intending to bring Nafeesa back to Lahore to live in purdah with his friend's wife and daughters. "Stop here," he orders his driver when they are still at some distance from the house. "I'd like to walk from here." He wants to get his thoughts in order before facing Nafeesa and her teenage rage. He wanders along a road, thinking how brown the landscape is this year, despite the monsoons of summer. Still the men and women work their patches with rakes and hoes, and children carry baskets of potatoes to the many handcarts. At a distance are mud brick quarters, where three young women are rocking babies. The girls will age quickly, bearing child after child, bearing food shortages, and continual sickness. Always the last to eat, the last to be taken to a clinic, they are wrapped first in their dupattas, later their shawls, and finally their shrouds.

Still, there is a colorful beauty that comes from living wrapped inside cloth you make from the seed you collect from the ground, plant into the earth you till, water and nurture until it grows, and you pick at the peak of its fullness before the seeds fall again. Then you separate the white balls of fiber from the seeds and later wash and spin it into thread and weave it into cloth and dye it with all the colors the vegetables of the earth provide—indigo and saffron, sepia and crimson—then you press, cut and sew each piece into the shapes of human bodies, decorate them with beads and shards of glass, contrasting threads, embroidery, glitter. You slip the shirt over your head and glance in a mirror. You step into billowy pants—a new suit of clothes. How happy it makes you.

There I go again, idealizing the poor, when I've had a life of such privilege! Zeshan admonishes himself as he approaches Kulraj Singh's house.

The whitewashed wall by the road is discolored by mud and peeling from the perennial effects of heat and cold, but there are lovely magenta flowers growing in abundance by the gate. Amir planted a garden of lavender that scents the air and there is a new pen with a wooden shelter he built for a mother goat and her kid. Across the road is an enormous crop of spent sunflowers. Some stand with their heads bowed. Sparrows flit among the flowers on the ground where seeds litter the garden.

Wearing a white shalwar kameez, Amir comes to the road to greet Zeshan. It is cool in the shade of the yard, and Amir offers a light shawl for Zeshan's shoulders, and invites the driver in for a drink. The driver declines the invitation, as he's been trained to do and as Amir expects. Amir hands him a flask of tea and a wrapped paratha. Zeshan and Amir walk to the courtyard together.

Zeshan knows that Kulraj Singh's thyroid is quickening and his generous heart is slowing. "How is your father today?" he asks, looking around for Nafeesa.

"It's a good day. Abbu is sitting under the neem tree, but isn't eating much. May I get you something?" Amir's exquisite manners put Zeshan at ease. Sunlight filters through the fronds of the mighty neem tree that rules the interior courtyard. Amir leaves the two men alone and goes into the house.

"Hello," Zeshan calls out to Kulraj Singh. His heart hurts when he sees his father-in-law lying on a string bed, where reflections of leaves dance across his white cotton shirt. He is propped on pillows, with closed eyes, and a light blanket over his leg. How he has aged, thinks Zeshan, his skin so pale and dry, his long beard as white as his turban. His slippers are aligned just so, as Amir arranged them, no doubt.

Kulraj Singh squints. "God does not want me back yet. I have a little time left. Don't give up."

Zeshan unfolds a plastic chair and sits nearby. Amir returns with the tray of sweets and mango slices, and Zeshan selects a coconut biscuit. "And where is Nafeesa?" he asks.

Kulraj Singh's blue eyes are clear, but his voice is strained when he speaks. "I sent my granddaughter on a sacred mission—to bring my daughters home." He points his finger at Zeshan. "You must not interfere. Nafeesa is with Faisah. They will look after each other and together they will bring Uji home." He takes a raspy breath. "Like all the young women of this family, Nafeesa has taken on a challenge to her soul that will determine what she is made of. We will help her, but we will not interfere with her mission." Again he eyes Zeshan. "Agreed?"

Zeshan's jaw stiffens and his eyes widen. "She is in Mumbai?" he asks.

"Uh, not exactly," says Amir and he explains the latest developments with Nafeesa and Faisah going to Kashmir to get Baji.

"They found her?"

"Not exactly," says Kulraj Singh. "They are going to her town near the LoC."

"Tell me everything," Zeshan insists. "I know people in that area." He picks up his phone. His fury that Nafeesa has left without his permission is overridden by his joy that Ujala and Faisah might be returning to Pakistan—aunties to find a husband for Nafeesa.

Kulraj Singh tries to rise from the string bed while Zeshan begins punching numbers into his mobile phone. Little by little he pushes himself up from his seat to his full height. "Put down the phone a moment," he whispers, and Zeshan does. He respects Kulraj Singh, a man who never asks him for anything in a world where he feels everyone always wants something from him, and Kulraj Singh is the man who has forgiven him even when he was unable to protect Meena from the assassin's bullet. Zeshan was not even there when it happened.

Kulraj Singh sways a bit as he stands, signaling with his finger that it is his wish to do it by himself, so Zeshan resists the urge to take him by the arm. They attend the silence between them. Crows call from the rows of a recently cleared field behind the courtyard, and Kulraj Singh pads his way toward the bamboo table. Zeshan helps him ease into the chair and Kulraj Singh leans back against the pillows.

"We know nothing," he says. "We are here by accident. Only God knows." He points to the sky. A little wind flutters the leaves. Two sparrows fly from a high branch and nibble at coconut crumbs on the brick floor. "But Kulraj Singh?" he continues speaking of himself as if he is not present, "he has been trying to know the mind of God all his life. Now at the end he knows almost nothing, except he knows when love is in his presence. That is what I feel, dear Zeshan. Your love for your daughter, for this family, for all of us."

Zeshan's heart is full. No one has ever recognized the depth of his love, not even Meena, or himself. In his invisible way, Amir has entered and filled his teacup to the brim.

"Now Amir will give you the details of their plan to bring Ujala back. Then you can use that powerful mobile of yours," says Kulraj Singh, "and use it quickly to help those girls with their mission. But, please, only if they need you. Do not overreach."

***

Lia is a woman who goes for what she wants. From Mumbai she phones *The Convoy*'s publisher directly. "Mr. Govinder," she says, "I'll expect a call from your solicitor. Then we can schedule an appointment with ours, Mohammed Farrah. I'm sure this is something we can easily resolve."

Nafeesa is listening as she chops carrots at the table. Faisah waits until Lia finishes the call. "Well, what did you learn?"

"He says that he doesn't need a solicitor. In addition to being the editor and publisher, he has a law degree. He would not reveal the publication date for *She-Lion*." Lia spreads her green yoga mat on the floor. "Anyway, I'll fly there as soon as an appointment can be coordinated with your solicitor-friend."

Faisah opens the sliding glass door to let in some air. "Mo can be very persuasive," she smiles. "Part pit-bull, part Doberman," she growls.

Lia adjusts her shoulders in downward dog. "Ha! Can't wait to walk that low-down dog into Govinder's office. Publishers run from lawyers," says Lia. "Just the threat of a lawsuit made by a credible lawyer should be enough to convince them to back off."

"And Zeshan?" asks Faisah. "Will they be certain not to use his name in the story?"

"My father was involved?" asks Nafeesa. "My father?"

"Zeshan obtained false IDs for Baji and Yusuf—not a key factor, but enough for criminal charges. Keeping his name out of the story should be no problem."

"My father helped with a prison escape?" Nafeesa asks in disbelief.

"Yes! He risked his reputation and his life to help Baji," says Lia.

Faisah's good eye peers at Nafeesa. "Now what about the laundry and the packing and the travel arrangements? Hmmm?"

Nafeesa gathers piles of unwashed clothes. So many jeans—light summer blues, gray winter corduroys, black, black, black. Seems like black is Lia's favorite color. Even her underwear is black. "Where is the soap powder?" she asks.

"No idea," Lia replies. "We hardly ever do laundry. Laundrymen from the Dhobi Ghat pick it up. But sometimes we do our own wash in the sink. You can take a quick walk up by High Street Phoenix to find a place that sells soap. Might take you twenty or thirty minutes." Nafeesa grabs her purse and the street map.

"Stay on the main streets and call us if you are lost," Faisah shouts, and with that, Nafeesa is free. She is an adult on an adult task. No brother, no father, no uncle, no auntie or grandmother to accompany her on a walk very much in public, only a bevy of birds that fly among the flowering trees along the flowing streets of Mumbai.

***

The day Nafeesa and Faisah fly to Srinagar, Lia flies to New Delhi. She meets their solicitor, Mohammed Farrah, in the lobby of *The Convoy's* office on the tenth floor of a skyscraper. The office is quite different from what she had imagined. Given the politically progressive slant of the magazine, she expected to find a hole-in-the-wall office with lots of posters and cigarette smoke. Instead, there is an expansive waiting area and a glamorous receptionist with bright red lipstick that bears an uncertain relationship with her lips. The receptionist directs them to one side of a long empty conference room. They realize that Desi Govinder, the magazine editor-publisher-lawyer, is making them wait there alone, "just like any corporate lackey," whispers Mo.

Govinder doesn't enter the room until they have been seated and served an unrequested, tepid and entirely unsatisfactory cup of tea–all orchestrated to elevate his position in the negotiation. Govinder himself is right out of central casting—a short, untrimmed beard, oozing greasy charm and full of B.S. He keeps one-upping them with frequent literary references and political name-dropping. Arundhati Roy this and Tariq Ali that. Salman Rushdie this and Basharat Peer that. In contrast, Mo is a tall, muscular man with an impressive moustache and a devilish goatee. He knows how to project meanness without opening his mouth, so when Govinder begins offering his apologies for being too busy to be on time for their appointment, Mo returns the flim-flam with a simultaneously warm and icy stare.

For his first move, Mo plays his easy card. "Libel," he says. "It's pure libel to accuse our client, Zeshan Shaheed, of conspiring in Baji Ujala's prison escape."

"We are making no accusations, just reporting facts," Govinder argues. "And Yusuf Salman was there at the time, after all, so he would know who did what. The story is quite a scoop."

"Can you confirm the article is his?" Mo asks. "Where is Yusuf Salman anyway?"

"Irrelevant," Govinder shoots right back at him. "The story is newsworthy with a lot of human interest in both India and Pakistan. And, after all, sad as Ujala Ethisham's passing may be, its effect is sympathetic to your . . ." Govinder stares directly at Lia . . . "interests." And so it goes. Govinder and Mo bark back and forth over the fence like big dogs.

Lia interrupts them quietly, staying in her role as one of Mo's group of clients, as he advised. "But why not use pseudonyms until facts are confirmed. We all do that sometimes. To protect our sources," she adds. Govinder does not speak to Lia, just looks at her condescendingly, as if she has not been a professional journalist for more than twenty years.

Mo jumps in. "At least delay publication," he begs, but Govinder explains that he wants to re-ignite Pakistan's public interest in Baji's story, plus renew interest in Meena's assassination. "We will start the story in Pakistan, then add to it in India. It's all about marketing. The online clicks."

Blah blah blah. Progressive, my ass, Lia thinks, reading the nauseated look on Mo's face. It's just corporate journalism!

Then Mo puts on his meanest, most moralistic face. "And you claim to be a progressive!" Mo stands to his full six and a half foot stature, the size of which is only amplified by the solid black kurta and jacket he wears. "But you won't protect the very people who are in the streets working, while you sit back in your big office and reap profit from their dedication. I recall the old days, Govinder. Are you completely co-opted now? Shame on you!"

Lia is alarmed, thinking Mo is taking the wrong tack. She wishes Faisah were there. She would know how to handle Govinder. Still, Lia stands up next to Mo across the table from Govinder in her five-foot ten-inch show of support. Govinder dares not stand. They are two beanpoles and he is a seedling wondering which one of them fate will require him to climb. They are all silent, reconsidering their positions.

Then Mo nods, and they take their seats and sip their cold Darjeeling in silence. Mo's face softens. His scary moustache droops. "Govinder, my friend. Let's not be this way. In the big picture, we are on the same side. Please help us. It's in the People's best interest to remove those names. Keep the rest."

Govinder sighs. "Yes, I will do as you ask," he concedes an inch. Within minutes, Mo and Lia are bowing their namastes in his direction. Then Govinder speaks again. "Just to be clear. I will not delay publication. I have a magazine to run, after all."

Mo throws Lia a glance that says: Do not say a word. But she speaks anyway. "Sir, what would be the date of publication then?"

Govinder stands. He is starting to flip the light switch on the wall and leave the room. Without thinking about it, Lia reaches for his hand to stop him, and he recoils. "Stop that. I do not touch women," he says haughtily in Mo's direction. Oh, right, thinks Lia, girl cooties. Seeing she is offended, Govinder backtracks pompously, "I am sorry, Madam. I may be progressive politically but I am also devout, a devoted husband. And as for the date of publication, Madam, I can't tell you when, but I can tell you this. First, I must notify Yusuf Salman. After that, publication will proceed forthwith."

Lia is breathless. She has to let Faisah know she must hurry to find Baji before Yusuf learns they had tried to delay publication of his article. Then he'd realize that she and Faisah are in India with access to Akram. They could be putting Baji in even more danger.

***

On Wednesday the Mumbai sky clouds over and the Srinagar flight is delayed. Nafeesa's Pakistani passport, with its immediately suspect green cover, is confiscated and scrutinized by airport security. Faisah steps up in lawyerly fashion to explain that her Pakistani niece is traveling with her Indian auntie to visit another auntie in Jammu and Kashmir. The official in her tight khaki uniform stamps the passport and waves Nafeesa through. She takes a quick, second look at Faisah's eye patch, but barely glances at her Indian passport, safe in its black cover embossed with shiny gold script. Faisah gave up her Pakistani citizenship years earlier as part of her formal application for the Mumbai bar. Not having her passport over-scrutinized was the first of many ways that being a citizen of India made life better for her.

They spend the afternoon at the Srinagar gate in Mumbai. "This delay means we will miss the last bus to Akram, but I don't really mind, do you?" asks Faisah. "We can stay overnight in Srinagar and take the bus tomorrow. Plus, this will give us time to slow down and get to know each other better."

Suddenly Nafeesa feels shy. Flying worries her—this is only her second time in an airplane and the first ride was bumpy. Srinagar worries her. Girls back home whose brothers served in the Pakistani army told horrific tales about Kashmir—grenades tossed into markets, a hotel set on fire, eyes intentionally blinded, girls raped in the streets. She can feel herself slipping back into her cloak of fear. "Is it not dangerous there?"

"Well, tourists no longer flock to Srinagar the way they used to," says Faisah, "unless, like us, they are on a special mission." She smiles, but Nafeesa does not smile back. "Nafeesa, it's not Sringar I'm worried about. It's the town where Baji lives, Akram. It is very close to the Line of Control, a locked-down, locked-up militarized place, they say." She takes a breath. "But that is where we must go to get our Baji back."

Nafeesa understands and nods her agreement.

The Srinagar flight, when it finally takes off, is only an hour long. Their view of Kashmir from the air fills with beiges and grays, then on their slow descent, brightens to evergreen with patches of spring moss, white clouds and sparkling lakes. The taxi drops them at a cheap guesthouse in Lal Chowak, in central Srinagar. The tiny room with one bed and a shared toilet is on the ground floor. The room has a rack for hanging clothes, a night table and lamp. A sign tacked onto the inside of the door says that electricity is not available between four and ten p.m. Both the table and the rack are chained to the floor so no one can remove them.

Nafeesa is repulsed by the conditions. She is not used to deprivation of this sort. She knows that she is, as Nanaa sometimes called her, a spoiled, hothouse flower.

Later they walk along the edge of Dal Lake, the enormous body of fresh water across from Shalimar Garden. The closer they are to the boat rental area, the more crowded everything becomes. It is as if, on cue, a crowd of actors walked onto their stage, barking at them to buy their flowers, to touch their pashminas, to taste their curries. They choose a bright purple-painted *shikara*, one of the lake's many multicolored gondolas, and sit beneath its striped canopy. When the boatman pushes off, a colony of gulls takes flight. There are fish moving through the shallows in a kind of underwater chore-ography.

Faisah sniffs the air and looks at Nafeesa with laughing eyes. "The water stinks," she says, pinching her nostrils. Nafeesa giggles.

Soon the lake becomes a marketplace, as other boats with their wares sidle up to theirs. "Would you like an overpriced hat?" Nafeesa asks Faisah, acting the role of one of the nearby hawkers. "Or perhaps a set of ugly plastic bangles?" They turn away from one boat and another appears on the other side. Their boatman is no help. These are obviously his relatives or friends.

Faisah puts on her arrogant lawyer tone, offering him only two options. "Pull us away from these other boats or take us back," she insists. The salesmen continue pushing their wares. "Now!" she shouts, but again the boatman ignores her.

This is when Faisah discovers how fast and inventive Nafeesa can be and what an asset to their rescue team. Nafeesa sticks her finger down her throat to force herself to vomit mutton balls, curds and rice all over the pile of pashmina shawls someone pushed onto her lap. The regurgitated odors of ginger, cumin and garlic overwhelm even the sewer smell of the lake. Quickly, the commercial boats draw away, taking the pile of soiled pashminas with them. Their *shiraka*'s boatman pulls back on his long oar over and over, and with a dozen sure strokes they are back at the edge of the lake. Nafeesa wipes away all traces of her last meal. In the bottom of the *shiraka* is a sopping cotton cloth full of sunflowers and vomit.

She and Faisah can hardly stop giggling in the taxi, holding hands the whole way back to the guesthouse. In their room Faisah flips the light switch to no avail. They undress in the dark and climb into the bed. Both set the alarms on their mobiles and plug them in, hoping the power will return in the night to recharge them for the day that lies ahead.

In the morning, Faisah suggests they take a walk in the Moghul Garden. "Maybe stop for tea? The bus doesn't leave for a few hours." They change from urban clothes into simple shalwar kameezes. They wrap their heads and necks in dupattas, and strap their purses and clench them across their bodies. A porter outside of the guesthouse hails a taxi and they settle in the back seat.

Shalimar Garden has many arched, gated entrances that open to wide, grassy areas hemmed with thick hedges that have been pruned into geometric patterns. It is reminiscent of Lahore's Shalimar Gardens —except for the picturesque mountain backdrop of the Karakoram Range, always snow-covered, even in summer. There are tall trees and abundant red flowers shaped like tall flames, and there are fountains, walkways, pools of water, canals leading to small pink houses with blue-green roofs. But unlike Lahore, where the gardens always teem with visitors, here there are few.

Faisah and Nafeesa have the garden almost entirely to themselves. It is eerie to feel alone in such a place of heavenly delight, as the tourist brochures describe it. There are multitudes of pigeons on the ground and cranes in the treetops. After a while, Faisah spreads her dupatta on the grass with care, and unwraps the aromatic Kashmiri rista, street food they purchased outside the gate. The garlicky meatballs compete with the fennel and the mint for their tongues' attention, but it is the red chili sauce that wins. They are both panting and sweating, their plastic forks fighting in the box of rice for the grain that can quench the delicious burn. Soon tree squirrels approach, but the two women have nothing left to share.

"How are you, Nafeesa?" Faisah asks and Nafeesa looks into her lap.

"Fine," she replies, but she sees the disbelief on Faisah's face. Nafeesa's shoulders slump against the peach tree. At last, she has a female relative to talk to, but the first thing she does is tell a lie—that she is fine.

Faisah touches Nafeesa's hand and speaks in a low voice. "You and I are a team and must understand each other." She waits for her niece's response.

Nafeesa lifts her eyes to the sky. "For so long my life has been a slow, unhappy procession, Auntie. Now it seems I must race to keep up with it." She feels guilty, wondering how she can complain about her life while her auntie lives with a part of her face missing.

"Yes, you have suffered a kiloton of losses," says Faisah. "First, your mother—dear, dear Meena. I miss her still. We worked together at the women's radio station, you know." Nafeesa perks up. No, she never knew her mother worked at a radio station or anywhere else. "Your grandmother is gone now, your great-grandfather, your home in Lahore, and now you are separated from your father, away from your friends and Nankana Sahib. It must be confusing and frightening to wonder what the next loss might be." Faisah tries to comfort Nafeesa with a verse from the Qur'an. "Whatever we have is not really ours. Everything belongs to Allah."

But Nafeesa stopped listening since Faisah spoke the word "grandmother." O Nanaa! My Nanaa! She wants to cry.

"Go ahead, Nafeesa. It's worth crying about."

And Nafeesa feels the relief of flooding tears and she sniffs as she speaks. "I miss Nanaa, and moving fast the way you do is frightening, but in a way I like it. It's like a twirling, whirling dance, something Sufi." She blushes. "I don't know. I can't explain it."

"You explain it very well. And I think your Nanaa would understand. Go on. Is there more?"

"Honestly? Yes, but . . ." Nafeesa hesitates. She can't continue. It hurts to be so open after being so closed for so long. If she starts to talk to Auntie about Nanaa, she might never stop crying.

Faisah takes her hand. "There is plenty of time for us. I just want you to know that having you here is almost like having my little sister back." Recalling Meena, Faisah's tears burn along the corner of her good eye. "You look so much like your mother." She takes the edge of her cotton dupatta, with its yellow and orange sunflowers and a deep purple background, and pats the spot where the tears are forming. Nafeesa touches her auntie's face.

"Will you tell me about my mother, please?" she begs. "Oh, tell me about Meena." And for the next two hours, Faisah does.

Later in the afternoon rain, Faisah and Nafeesa walk to the city's train and bus depot, passing military vehicles and soldiers among the city's sopping, flowering bushes. The two o'clock bus to Akram has room for about twenty passengers—it is new and clean and they take their seats near the front. Overcrowded, honking minivans speed by their bus. The tension of being strangers to each other has disappeared. Now they can talk easily or simply be silent together.

Soon the bus enters the part of Kashmir that the travel book calls paradise, and they agree that indeed it is. The Kashmir Valley is a hidden slice of the world, one of those places where human beings have been left in peace long enough for a range of cultures to deepen, to widen, to soar like crazy in all directions. But politically Kashmir continues to be a contradiction—like Dal Lake was the night before. On the one hand it is a militarized hell zone full of burned-out vehicles and youth blinded by rifle-fired pellets. Gunfire cracks at night and sirens wail in the day. On the other hand, there is paradise— the Lolab Valley they travel through, past the Sufi shrine of Shah Walli, a saint who is said to have had the power to raise the dead. It is no wonder the dead would choose to return to these cedar-forested mountainsides, the wet, green meadows fresh and full of rivulets and grazing cattle, goats, a few horses. Tidy orchards along the river are filled with walnut, apple, apricot and cherry trees. A light rain continues to fall. Over the clatter of tires on a bumpy road, they cannot hear the birds that fly through the fruit trees, but Faisah tries to imagine their songs.

Nafeesa, however, is distracted by passengers. "I don't like how men look at me," she says. "They stare and stare. Isn't it rude?"

"Oh, yes." Faisah sighs. "Women traveling without a man, especially young women, have to put up with a lot." She changes the subject. "What are your thoughts about Akram?"

"To do whatever you tell me to do?" asks Nafeesa and Faisah laughs.

"Great answer, but do you understand our plan?"

"We are going to find Baji and take her back to Babba?"

"Yes, that's right. And one issue is language. In Srinagar we could speak Urdu or Hindi and we were understood, but I wonder how we'll get by in Akram."

"I speak a little Kashmiri," Nafeesa says. "My friend, Rufina, has family from Kashmir and some of them live with her. I've picked up a few words."

Faisah is excited. "That could be very helpful. We do not know where Baji lives, but we know she used to teach mostly in secondary schools. I did a little online research and located the most likely one. We should be able to walk there from the bus depot." Faisah comes alive with feeling.

"Today may be the day of our reunion. . . after all these years. My *baji*, my lifelong friend." Then she reverts to her planning voice. "We will have a good chance to find her at school. But we will have to always be on the lookout for Yusuf. She said he walks with her everywhere."

"What does he look like?"

"Who knows? It's been so many years. People change."

"What if she's not there?"

"If it's not her school, then we try the next one."

"I mean what if it is her school, but she's not there?"

"Good question." Faisah can see that Nafeesa was picking up on the *what if?* habit. "Then we talk with her teacher friend, Janna, the one who mailed Baji's letter to me. We will have to be inventive, to figure out who to trust and what to do next."

"Where will we stay?" Nafeesa asked, more curious than anxious.

"Like I said, we'll be inventive and figure out who to trust and what to do next. We know we can ask Janna."

Nafeesa breaks the pace of their back and forth. She speaks quietly. "Auntie, you can count on me. I may be young, but I have experience with being inventive, figuring out who to trust and what to do next. Isn't that how I found you?"

"That's how the women in our family have always been, Nafeesa—doing risky things in dangerous places." Nafeesa reaches for her hand and Faisah squeezes back. "And for the right reasons."

"I'm not worried," Nafeesa says with confidence. "Are you?"

With the comforting presence of Auntie Faisah sitting beside her, Nafeesa allows herself to think about Nanaa—about the day in her room in Nankana Sahib months ago when she received a text from her father informing her that the hospital reported to him that Nanaa had died during the night of a festering wound, an overwhelming infection. For weeks Nafeesa could think of little else, but gradually the compulsion to remember her grandmother subsided. Today, realizing that there doesn't have to be a reason for it and with the rhythm of the bus to ease her, her mind mixes with vivid memories of the woman who raised her.

Her grandmother used to complain about Nafeesa's late nights with her light on, but Nafeesa would pretty much ignore her. Nanaa would fall asleep at a normal time and never know how late Nafeesa stayed awake, but when she tried to wake Nafeesa in the morning, of course—chatty and busy, asking questions, invading her room and her consciousness, before she had even used the toilet, then Nafeesa would be grouchy. "I'm not a morning person," Nafeesa would say, but Nanaa had no respect for that. She'd say, "If it's morning and you're a person, then you are a morning person, Nafeesa. Now get up and prepare for school." Or get ready to go shopping. Or get ready for whatever Nanaa had in mind. Really, Nanaa liked Nafeesa to accompany her on her errands, someone to listen to her incessant chatter. Still, recalling those mornings with Nanaa now, she couldn't help but wish for just one more.

Nafeesa recalls the short tour she and Faisah took the day before, where their driver pointed out Durga's temple on a hill overlooking Srinagar. As a child, Nanaa had read her stories about Hindu goddesses in the little storybooks, and Nafeesa was fascinated by them then, as she still is. As a teenager, she would wander into the library's children's section, drawn to the books with pictures of dark-eyed women swinging mighty swords over their heads, multi-armed figures with wild hair and sexy clothes. She wished then that Islam had something to match that. Her childhood favorite was Durga, the mountain goddess, the mother of the Universe, the one whose energy provides all life its very existence. Durga was a fighter who never gave up. She rode into battle to challenge demons; entire armies attacked her, but Durga showed no mercy and slew them all. One demon attacked Durga in the guise of a buffalo, but Durga tied it up with ropes of her own making. When a buffalo demon turned into a lion, Durga drew her sword to behead it before it could jump her. One thing after another came at Durga, and she drove each one away. Once, while Durga was enjoying a sip of wine from her cup, a raging elephant started to charge her, so she just flung her trident and slayed the demon once and for all. Even while Durga was a little inebriated, she was all-powerful for the sake of ridding the world of evil. Their driver told them that Durga is worshipped in Kashmir, and is a well-known symbol for the Indian independence movement. In Pakistan Durga had made no sense to her, but now that she is in Kashmir, Nafeesa wonders if she could ever cultivate such powers herself—such courage, strength and the will to never give up a righteous fight. Maybe now, arriving in Akram, she will find out.

***

In Akram, the ground is soaked and muddy. Sewage and trash are strewn all over the transit stand. It is early fall, and the morning air is icy fresh. Faisah and Nafeesa are wrapped up in their woolen shawls. Passengers slosh through a disgusting pond to a checkpoint where soldiers line both sides of the Srinagar road and block the path to the adjacent market that is little more than a double line of wooden food and clothing stands. Sunbeams shine from behind a cumulus cloud, causing everything to sparkle–hell and heaven alike. The women scrape their slimy shoes and wash down the filthy ankles of their shalwars with cups of gutter water.

Indian security officers in their tan uniforms check each bus passenger's ID. As expected, they are questioned about their visit to Akram, and in light of Nafeesa's Pakistani passport, calls have to be made. Officers have to approve. Rupees have to be paid. At last, they are allowed to pass.

Faisah approaches locals to ask in Hindi for directions to the school. At every encounter, people withdraw, to one extent or the other, from the unmistakable horror that mars her face. Some people actually do not stop staring. Some take an awkward second glance when they think doing so will not be noticed. Still others only blink, pegging Faisah as pitiful. Nafeesa is amazed that, through it all, her auntie just carries on. She seems to forgive them all their ignorance before she is even slighted, as if she is a royal divinity granting a blanket clemency to those who, after all, are only human. For a moment Nafeesa wonders if perhaps she should do the asking—to save her auntie the humiliation, and to use her bit of Kashmiri. Faisah is reading her niece's mind. She is not humiliated and tells Nafeesa so. "It's simply what I have," she says. "That's all."

At the market a woman behind the counter responds to Nafeesa's inquiries about the school with a twist of her lips. She points to the sign across the road: "Akram: The Crown of Kashmir," it reads, "Tourist Information." Brochures describe day trips and mountain climbing, but there are no maps in them. "A map of the village, please," Nafeesa asks the vendor.

The man gestures with his chin toward an olive-green truck surrounded by Indian soldiers, standing with their arms folded across their khaki vests. "There are no maps of Akram," he replies, "and this is no village. Akram is a real town, but they don't want anyone to know where things are." He points to the soldiers with his thumb. "We are too close to the LoC here. Less than five kilometers that way, but ask me anything and I'll direct you."

"Girls' Secondary School in the town?"

"Of course, Madam, which one? We have several."

"A government school? Where a teacher named Janna works?"

"No idea," he says, pausing, asking suspiciously, "Where are your husbands?"

They walk away and begin to climb the road in the direction the tourist agent pointed. Nafeesa races up the hill, swinging her arms and hips again. Faisah takes it step by step.

"I should not have used Janna's name," Faisah says, angry with herself.

"Questions can reveal more than answers." Nafeesa understands that the less the local people know about them, the better; and Faisah has revealed the name of Baji's friend. "I won't make that mistake again," she sighs. It is a strain for her to hike up the hill. Nafeesa offers to carry her bag and Faisah lets her do it.

Soon they hear the mid-day call to prayer and head in the direction of the mosque. Faisah hopes to find some old women there to ask where the school is located. And so it goes for a couple of hours—a mosque, then a market, then a secondary school, the wrong secondary school, until eventually they locate the last school. The building looks new, clean, painted a pleasant yellow with white trim. There are shadows moving around inside the classrooms behind the drawn window shades.

Nafeesa thinks they must look ridiculously out of place—hiding in a cluster of aspen trees, chewing on meat rolls, wearing city shoes all wrong for muddy Akram. But no one is looking at them. Passersby are busy with their donkeys, their machinery, their own lives.

Faisah hands her the water bottle. "Here, have a drink. Then let's go."

Nafeesa follows behind, feeling like a hungry dog that doesn't know what it is looking for exactly, but is excited by the scent. As they approach the door, they see colorful artwork taped on the inside of the windows and the orderly, quiet classes inside. "Where is Madam Janna's classroom, Sir?" Nafeesa asks the uniformed security guard in Kashmiri.

He hesitates, inspecting Faisah's scar and eyepatch. "Second floor toward the back. Room 202," he answers in a kind of robotic, but not unfriendly voice. "But remain in the Headmistress's office," he instructs in Kashmiri. "They will get her for you." They nod to him politely, but as soon as they are out of his sight, they climb the back stairs and find Room 202. Peeking through the small window in the classroom door, they see perhaps forty girls, wearing navy blue uniforms with pale blue dupattas, seated in four rows of desks. A lovely, pudgy woman walks gracefully among them.

The students are taking turns reading aloud from books they share. The teacher is turning pages of her book in unison with the students. The girl seated closest to the door stares at Faisah and Nafeesa through the window. She rises and opens the door, curtsies and asks if she can help. Seeing visitors, the other girls automatically begin to rise from their desks to greet them, while the teacher and Faisah exchange quick glances.

"Remain seated, girls," the teacher directs. "Samina, draw the curtains, please. It is so bright in here. Amna, you may continue with the lesson, page 55." She comes to the door and steps into the hall.

"Janna—?" begins Faisah.

"Shh! Not here. Meet me at my house after school. Two p.m." She hands a small piece of paper to Faisah from deep in the pocket of her pheran, the long, loose cloak worn by Kashmiri women. Janna holds on to Faisah's hand when she tries to pull it away. "And do not come to the school again," she says intensely. They hurry down the stairs without making a sound, and slip out the back door.

Janna lives on a narrow back street where, the note says, they will find a house with a large metal flower pot full of orange geraniums in front of its gate. Nafeesa scans the view of each street at every turn they take. She has come to realize that part of her job is to be her auntie's missing eye, to complete her half-vision. Although Faisah has vision in her good eye, it tires from doing the work of two, especially when the sun is bright, like on this day.

"Aha!" says Nafeesa, pointing down a dirt passage at a happy burst of orange flowers baking against a blue stucco wall. Goats graze next to a patch of green. Across the street a solid metal fence encloses what a fading sign says once was the Akram Ice Factory. The street is quiet. A distant dove coos and another responds. Sunlight strobes through the shadowy mountain peaks and warms their faces and dries the spindly geraniums.

The two women lean against the wooden gate to wait for Janna. Faisah is tired. They rose very early that morning, took the long bus ride and hiked uphill and all around the town. She stopped along the way several times and now needs to sit down. She is panting, but there is no place to rest. Nafeesa looks at the old knocker on the gate. "Perhaps we should knock. Maybe Janna has a husband or children or someone who might let us rest inside?" Faisah bends over at the waist with the back of her legs supported by the wall.

"Are you dizzy?" asks Nafeesa.

Faisah's reply is forced. "Yes, quite dizzy." She points to the door. "Knock. Knock hard."

Nafeesa pounds the heavy ring three times, as hard as she can, and the thud resounds. Then they hear rustling cloth and scuffling shoes and a key turn in the lock. A dark eye peers through the peephole, then a woman opens the door, just a crack. "Yes," she says. "May I help you?" Nafeesa sees a woman in a rose and gray embroidered dress with a folded triangle of cloth over her head, tied in back like a gypsy.

Faisah straightens up and looks toward the door. Her face freezes for a second. The two women rush into each other's arms. "Baji!"

"Faisah!"

Nafeesa's throat tightens. Baji is here!

***

What must it be like to have a sister, to be close to a sister, to share everything, then to lose her, to not want to believe that she is dead, to be separated so long that you might pass each other on the street and never notice? To lose her so long ago you only wonder occasionally if she is in good health, if she still lives. You forget what her voice sounds like, or believe you have forgotten because you cannot bring it to mind. What did she sound like? But then a miracle happens and years later when you are no longer young, no longer full of the possibilities of youth, but instead you are coasting on the remains of a lifetime of experience, and you hear a stranger's voice ask, "May I help you?" and you know at once whose voice it is. You know the shape of the face, the dimple, the particular smile of those particular lips. And you recognize the light in the eyes of your sister.

All of these things Nafeesa, who has no sister herself, feels in the mystery of that moment as the sisters wrap themselves in each other's arms. The moment changes, Faisah lets go, but Baji continues to hold on for a moment longer. Then she raises her head from the place where it rested on Faisah's neck. She turns and smiles. "You must be Nafeesa. I would recognize you anywhere." Nafeesa sees an aged, ghostly reflection of herself—the small gap between her teeth, and a familiar mannerism, the way Baji shakes her dark brown and gray hair loose from the scarf. She is a smaller woman than Nafeesa expected her to be. They are exactly the same height. "You are the image of your mother, Nafeesa. And of ours," she says, glancing again at Faisah whose good eye still brims with tears.

Faisah pats her eye, folds her handkerchief and watches Baji as she speaks to their niece. "It is strange to use my mother's name in address-ing you, Nafeesa, and to hear her name spoken by me, as if I were hearing my father's voice calling to her from the bottom of the staircase of our child-hood." She looks down the path. "Come inside," she says urgently.

Baji talks nonstop, holding Faisah's hands, letting them go, then grasping at them again, like an anxious, lonely woman. "There is not much time. Soon I must return to school. Yusuf will be looking for me." She picks up a multi-colored shawl. "Janna will be home soon to take care of you. I will return tomorrow after school begins. Yusuf thinks I am at school working. School thinks I am at home sick. I have been doing this for many days hoping for you to arrive. I love you both. _Allah hafiz._" Baji kisses them one more time, grabs her book bag and rushes out the gate.

Faisah rests on a narrow bed in one corner of the room alone in her thoughts. Nafeesa wanders the room, examining posters and the eyes in photographs, touching books, tapestries, canned food on the shelf. Janna's house is two rooms constructed of half-plastered brick. It is a house determined to keep warm. Rugs are everywhere—on the floor, rugs on top of rugs, overlapping rugs and rugs on the walls. There is a camp stove on the floor and pots and pans on shelves, drawings and photos of people marked "missing," and colorful protest posters suspended on wire. She has three chairs—two wooden ones and one stuffed armchair, plus a hanging light bulb and two kerosene lamps. In the back room are bags of rice and corn, a water pump, and a toilet.

The books and drawings reveal Janna is an artist. From the posters it is obvious she is politically active. Apparently, she lives alone. Very unusual. There is a glimmering mountain view from the back window. Nafeesa realizes she is memorizing it, planning for contingencies, in case they have to escape quickly or disappear in the back—should Yusuf pound pound pound on the front knocker.

"My head is pound-pound-pounding," Faisah groans. Nafeesa grabs the bottle of aspirin from a shelf above the stove and pumps fresh water. She sits next to Faisah to help her take the pills and drink them down. Faisah swallows noisily and catches her breath, while Nafeesa moves to a chair. Faisah is having difficulty taking deep breaths. "I can still feel Baji holding me against her body," she says in a halted, other-worldly way. "I can still taste her tears in my mouth." Nafeesa has not heard hyperrational Faisah talk in this way before. "I am feeling dreamy," she says and pulls a pile of blankets up to her chin, extends her legs and rolls to her side. "Here you are, my dead sister's baby daughter, grown and traveling with me through this time warp. I promised Amir I would protect you, but look at me lying here, useless and babbling."

"Not useless. Remember, Auntie, it's only illness. It will pass."

"Lovely and so young," Faisah murmurs, "but so loud and so stupid, like me, but she learns quickly, and—after all, I was loud and stupid once myself." Faisah speaks as if Nafeesa is not present. Nafeesa leans closer to hear every unedited word. "And Baji—old, thin, angles and edges. Who would recognize her?"

The door moves and Janna steps inside. Light shines in her tawny eyes that she has lined with pale green kohl. She is plump, which adds to her beauty, rounding her face and filling its lovely lines. She wears a loose V-neck blouse and a traditional pheran, pants with layers of cloth and a crotch that falls to the knees. Her hair is a mass of thick dark curls constantly escaping the pins and cloth she uses to hold them up. Janna lights the stove and puts on water for rice. Faisah stops mumbling in her half-sleep.

"Sleep if you like, Faisah. You two will stay with me." Her every movement is deliberate and graceful. She hands Faisah warm tea. "You must drink a lot in the mountains. I am afraid the altitude is affecting you." She feels Faisah's forehead with her palm and looks worried. "Watch her," Janna says, turning to Nafeesa. "Tell me if she has trouble breathing."

Faisah sips tea. "I have so many questions for you," she says half-heartedly, and Nafeesa interrupts her.

"Auntie, please, will you let me ask the questions? You need to rest."

Faisah lies back and inhales. "Yes, of course. For the last two days you have been my eyes. Now you will be my voice as well."

Janna settles into the faded armchair with her second cup of tea. Nafeesa sits cross-legged on the floor next to her and asks Janna a question. "Would you tell us about yourself, Madam Janna?"

"Good start," Faisah comments. She is pleased by Nafeesa's approach and says so. "An open-ended question. The best way to begin an investigation is to understand your informant."

Janna rests comfortably on bolsters and begins. "I grew up in a nearby village. My parents died a long time ago but I have sisters and brothers who still live here and in other places, too. I am forty years old. My children are married and live nearby. I am a half-widow. My husband is one of the disappeared loved ones of Kashmir. One morning fifteen years ago, on his way to work he was arrested by Indian security forces and disappeared." She delivers this summary like testimony she has given many times before. "Half-wife, half-widow," she says. "There are thousands of us in this part of Kashmir. We are married, but our husbands are missing. We cannot prove they are dead but we cannot find them or their bodies either. I could fill a book with stories of all the efforts to find them. Not one has ever been found. Not one." Her voice has a bitter, inflammatory tone. "Until recently, the mullahs said we could not re-marry—not that I want to do that. No, I decided a long time ago that being Bashir's half-wife was better than not being his wife at all. Thanks to Baji, I can earn a living while many half-widows cannot. And we cannot inherit for the same reasons. Some families—not mine, but some—are hostile toward the half-widows. Sometimes we live together to do what we can to help each other, or work with the NGOs to get compensation, or information, or some response from the government."

She stares at nothing. In the silence a goat bleats in the yard next door, and outside a dove lands on the windowsill. Nafeesa looks to Faisah for a sign, unsure if she should probe any more. Such a painful subject. *Move on*, gestures Faisah.

"How did you meet Baji?" Nafeesa asks and Auntie Faisah nods approval with closed eyes. Janna laughs.

"You mean Asma Mohan? That's what we call her here. And her husband is Mohan Ali, not Yusuf. Those are the names they used when they arrived eighteen years ago. She hesitates. "But let me call them Baji and Yusuf, as you do. I like that. Baji was a friend of my husband, Bashir. They both taught in secondary schools—he at the boys' and she at the girls'. After Bashir disappeared, she became my best friend, tutoring me through the teaching certificate program, mentoring me as an apprentice teacher, and helping me get my current position."

Nafeesa is patient, watching for whether Janna has finished before toss-ing her another question. "And how did you learn Baji's true story?"

"Well, it didn't take long to realize that your baji is the kind of person who pretends to be much less than she is. A remarkable teacher and first-class teacher trainer, as well. A wonderful friend, but she never talked about her past. It's unusual for people who have been friends for so long not to share those things, don't you agree? But I respected that she had her reasons. She and Yusuf were Pakistani, after all, a single fact that can raise suspicions with the authorities around here—keep that in mind, by the way— good reason for you to keep a low profile yourselves.

"Then, some years ago she told me about a girl in her class here who was threatened by her father—basically, he was selling her for a small orchard and some goats. The girl refused to go and the father threatened her life. This was the first of several cases where she and I—and Yusuf, too, he was a big help—rescued girls in trouble. We got them out of Akram, and doing that kind of work really brought us closer." She pauses. "It is so ironic that now she is in a similar situation —needing to be rescued from her husband. And the fact that it is Yusuf is quite a shock."

Faisah exhales sharply. She, too, feels the burn of Yusuf's betrayal.

Janna continues. "Eventually, Baji confided things about her marriage. They were trying to conceive a child. Once I took care of her during a mis-carriage that occurred while she was at school." Janna stops, distracted, staring at Faisah who is lying on the bed. "Actually, the miscarriage oc-curred right there. I brought her here to recover. Sorry, but that's how it happened."

"No, do not apologize, Madam Janna. Please go on."

"Baji was in a great deal of pain and fortunately I had pain medication in the house. While she was also under the influence of those narcotics, she began calling for her mother and for you, Faisah, and Meena, too. It was the first time I heard your names. She never once asked for Yusuf. And I guess that's not so unusual. In such a state, don't we all crave to return to the first comforts we ever knew? But as she improved and I raised the subject of phoning Yusuf to come and get her, she became agitated, begging me not to call him, to let her stay, not to make her go home. She did not want to return to him, she said. Ever.

In the waning light Nafeesa can see the shock on Faisah's face as she listens to a complete stranger confirming details of the horror Baji described in her letter.

"Eventually I explained to Yusuf that she had miscarried. I lied and said she had developed a fever and that the doctor I called advised she not be moved. He agreed and she stayed with me for almost a week. He never visited. We were alone the entire time. By then my daughter had married and moved out. I took off work to stay home with Baji. That was when she told me how she and Yusuf had escaped from your horrible father."

Nafeesa turns to Faisah and their eyes lock. *Your horrible father.* A string of three words that they never ever expected to hear. Nafeesa thinks it must be Baji's way of telling Janna why they had to escape Pakistan—leaving out the criminal aspects—the trial, the prison break, and the rest of it. "She said that she had to escape an abusive father?" Faisah asks and Janna nods.

"And now," she continues, "Baji must escape her horrible husband. And I am determined to help. Were it not for her, I would be a beggar with a bowl."

"Exactly what did she say about Yusuf?" asks Faisah. "About why she needs to get away from him?"

Blue shades of evening streak the room as mountain peaks block the setting sun. Jana rises and lights kerosene lamps around the room. "Please. I need to stop. Let me use the toilet and put dinner on the stove."

Nafeesa jumps up from the floor to help. "Yes, yes, sorry, yes, we can come back to this later. Please let me help. I'd love to learn to cook Kashmiri style." Nafeesa knows how to charm a teacher: be the hardest-working student.

Janna gathers wrapped scraps from the kitchen, while Nafeesa peels potatoes and tosses the skins outside for the goats, as Janna gently directs. Faisah seems to be nodding off to sleep while they cook. The aromas of fenugreek and fennel, cardamom and mutton fat fill the room. Janna spices the yogurt and Nafeesa stirs the mix. She can understand why Baji would choose to recover in this place with this nurturing woman. Something about Janna reminds her of Amir. She cooks like he does, she thought, except for the meat.

Janna inserts a CD into an old player and the music begins. Nafeesa does not know the tune but she recognizes the rhythm, and her body absorbs the sound. Subtle sensations arise from nowhere and the mind gets out of the way. Janna turns toward the stove, her pelvis circles and her arms extend. Nafeesa takes tiny steps with great intention and remains where she stands, the ball of one foot pushing her as she sinks and pivots, all the while alert, visualizing the musicians. There is an ease between the two of them as each enters her own routine near the other, but not dancing together. They create variations of each other's movements, the same, but different. Nafeesa rotates her body, watching while Janna's hair falls at last from its clips and she bends forward flinging her hair with power over and over until the music starts to slow, the mood changes, and they return to a full stillness, relaxed and happy now that something has opened up. They smile at the surprising recognition.

Faisah groans. Janna places a steaming plate of grilled mutton with cooked potatoes and yogurt underneath Faisah's nose to entice her to eat, but her stomach convulses and she retches. Janna helps her up by the arm and leads her through the dim back room to the toilet. Nafeesa backs away to give them a path. Soon Faisah returns to the bed, spent and exhausted. "My mouth tastes like a sour old spoon."

"You are sick," Janna calls from across the room.

"I'm fine," Faisah insists.

"You are sick," Janna repeats, "and if it's altitude sickness, as I think it is, it can be fatal." Nafeesa's breathing stops at the mention of the word, "fatal."

"Let's see how I feel in an hour."

Nafeesa sets the alarm on her mobile phone and speaks to Janna. "Can we talk again about Baji and Yusuf?" Janna looks reluctant. "You know, she wrote to us about the cellar."

"Yes," Jana replies. "Being buried in the cellar was the worst. Worse than being pushed, or hit, it was the hell of close confinement. The only positive thing is that in the cellar she became determined to leave Yusuf or die trying."

"I can't imagine what that must have been like. Buried alive," Faisah whispers.

"We will never let her experience that again," says Janna.

"Never again," Nafeesa pledges.

The last light of day creates tree shadows that play in constant motion on the far wall. Nafeesa feels a pang of pleasure that she is alive in the world, and of pain that Nanaa is not and Babba will soon pass on, and that Baji lives in terror in her own home. The timer on her mobile phone rings.

"I feel dizzy," Faisah whines. She rolls over and grabs her lurching stomach.

Janna is fast with the bucket, while Nafeesa poses another question for Janna. "And our plan for Baji's escape is...?" She looks at Janna. Janna looks at Faisah.

"I thought you two would be the ones with ideas," says Janna. Nafeesa gawks for a moment. Janna isn't joking. They have no escape plan—they are completely unprepared.

"We will discuss it with Baji tomorrow," says Faisah, clearing her throat.

"She'll come here in the morning, right?"

"After she is certain Yusuf has left. There is a hidden cellar at school where she stays out of sight of the other teachers and students."

"A cellar," says Faisah, recoiling. None of them can stop thinking about the cellar at Baji's house.

That night Faisah and Janna share the bed under a single maroon fleece, while Nafeesa finds some pillows and a plaid blanket and makes a bed on the floor. Faisah is restless during the night and is awake for the roosters and the lavender sky at daybreak, finally falling asleep just when an alarm clock goes off. That is when she finally surrenders to her illness. "I have a headache and fever. I'm exhausted and nauseous. Useless to anyone."

"It's altitude sickness," Janna explains. "You came up from Srinagar too quickly."

"But the elevation is not so high here. And Nafeesa doesn't have it."

"Everyone responds differently," Janna says. "You have three of the four main symptoms of serious altitude sickness and only one thing helps."

Faisah groans. "Let's do it!"

"You must return to a lower altitude. Go to Srinagar on the next bus."

"Srinagar? No. I can't leave. We have to get Baji out of here."

Hearing Faisah's insistence, Nafeesa begins punching buttons on the mobile phone. She calls Lia. "I've been trying to get through to you two," Lia says, "about our meeting with the publisher in Delhi." Nafeesa interrupts.

"Listen, Lia. We found Baji. Faisah is very sick. We need your help. Here, talk with Janna. She is Baji's friend." After Janna explains the situation to Lia, Nafeesa hands Faisah the phone and Lia tells her what to do.

"I'm still at the Delhi airport, Faisah. Janna will put you on the bus this morning. I'll arrange for a medicab at the Srinagar bus station to take you to the hospital. You rest there until I arrive later today. Nafeesa will meet with Baji to make their escape plan, which they will tell Janna, who will pass the information on to Amir and to you and me, so we can track their progress. We will stay in Srinagar until Baji and Nafeesa meet up with us, and then we will have a big reunion dinner—on me!"

Faisah groans. "Don't mention food."

"Agreed?" Lia inquires as if she is negotiating with a willful child.

"OK," Faisah surrenders, just like Nafeesa knows she will–Auntie Faisah will not deny Lia anything she really wants. But now that she is leaving me alone in Akram, Nafeesa wonders, whatever do I do with Baji?

Chapter 5

Forever Your Sister

Akram, Jammu & Kashmir, India, 2015

The rising sun fingers the icy dawn. Little birds on wires are puffing feathers, tucking and sunning to keep warm. Janna's neighbor's car chokes on the cold as he drives the shivering women to the bus station. Janna pulls her hair back and covers it with a light blue scarf wrapped casually around her neck. Nafeesa feels genuine fondness for this woman who has given them her home and her comfort, and who is such a good friend to Baji. Faisah absorbs the chill greedily, and leans against Nafeesa's shoulder as they pat one another's hands. By the time they reach the depot, the car has become uncomfortably stuffy.

Faisah taps the driver on the shoulder of his bulky green coat. "Thank you for the ride, brother," she says and he nods. Janna buys Faisah's ticket and takes her hand, helping her onto the bus. Once seated inside, Faisah covers her head, leans against the dirty bus window, and listlessly waves goodbye. The bus driver coaxes the vehicle's tires out of the mud and up onto the Srinagar road.

Janna's neighbor clears his throat politely, but pointedly. "Will you be late for work?" he asks Janna, breathing into his gloved hands to warm them.

She tightens her scarf. "Yes, we must not be late."

The schoolyard is full of teenage girls, some not much younger than Nafeesa, standing, chatting in small groups, clutching their schoolbooks to their chests, colorful plastic bags and backpacks at their feet. Nafeesa feels a tug in their direction, a curiosity about their lives, their styles, their dreams. But it is only a tug. The stronger pull is toward her own future, and for today that means finally getting to know Baji and safely boarding a bus to Srinagar.

At the gate of the schoolyard, Janna starts to step out of the car, but stops. Her eyes shift toward the road where Baji stands next to a man Nafeesa assumes is Yusuf. She has to admit to herself that she is surprised. She expected Yusuf to be an old henna-haired *Hajji*, but truly he is handsome, breathtaking, right out of Bollywood—a slightly graying Shah Rukh Khan. Next to him, she thinks, Baji is way past her prime.

Janna hurries toward the school. If Janna is almost late, then Baji is late as well. Yusuf is a step or two ahead of Baji, both of them practically jogging toward the door. Baji rushes past Janna without even a glance of recognition and the car speeds away, with Nafeesa still in the back seat, holding the key to Janna's house tightly in her fist. When the neighbor parks the car, she hurries past the petals of the orange geraniums that have frozen onto the ground beside the bold blue-painted walls. Inside she busies herself preparing tea and toast for Baji, who should arrive once Yusuf has left the area of the school. When Nafeesa hears footsteps crunching on the frosty gravel outside, she pulls open the heavy door and nervously thrusts a cup of tea in Baji's face.

"My goodness," Baji says, backing away. Nafeesa almost spills the drink.

"Oh, so sorry, Baji!" She grabs Baji's purse, and Baji grabs it right back. Nafeesa is surprised by her insistence, her strength.

"I can carry it," Baji says in a calm voice. "Here, take this one." She hands Nafeesa her heavy book bag. Once inside Nafeesa locks the door, as Janna instructed, then places a teapot and fresh cups on a paisley cloth.

For a few moments they sit together in silence at the small square table. The morning sun brightens the room. There are mountain shadows in the distant field and a few horses cross the landscape. Baji stares at them with an intensity that makes Nafeesa want to turn away.

Then Baji's eyes soften and she leans across the table to reach for Nafeesa's hands. "I must hear all about your life, Nafeesa. But first you must listen to me." Baji points out the window as she watches Nafeesa's face. "See that mountain over there?" Her eyes follow her finger to the ghostly slice of the Karakoram peaks where the slanted rays of early light are revealing their depths and complexities. "My life has been like that," Baji says. She speaks in the low, insistent, intimate tone of a teacher reading aloud poetry or an ancient story. "It has been a place where wild things grow in the heat and where the cold accumulates until it quakes from an unexpected fire colliding inside itself. My mountains breathe in and around and within the house of God." Baji spreads a thin golden fleece across her lap. "Which do I miss more—my father, my mother, or the self I used to be? The joy of holding my dearest Faisah yesterday unwrapped an old heartache–today I look around for her and already she has been taken from me.

"Oh, we will see her soon, Baj—" Then Baji interrupts.

"There is no way to predict how the wheel will turn, Nafeesa, so it's best not to expect anything. Anything at all." Nafeesa tries to focus on what Ujala is saying and not the strange way in which she is saying it. She wants to remember her every word so she can repeat it all to Faisah later over the phone. "I remember the day Yusuf and I crossed into India." Ujala lifts the steaming teacup to her lips and then sets it back down. "It was late afternoon when a carload of Indian soldiers came winding down the road toward us. I turned back to the edge of the forest to help Beezah, who had stripped down to her skin, naked in the cooling afternoon. Indeed, what Yusuf wrote in that part of his story is true and Faisah told me you have read it."

Nafeesa nods, says nothing, and Baji continues. "There was something about Beezah that was irresistible. She said that she wanted to show me the proper way to enter a forest. You will come to understand about Beezah, Nafeesa. To her, where we were standing was the edge between this world and midnight. It was sacred ground. She kept circling a tall cedar at the entrance to the woodland, while Yusuf waved to me wildly from the road, perhaps half a kilometer away. I asked myself, should I run to him or hide in the forest with Beezah and join him later? Should I bring Beezah along with us? Or leave her there, to make her way back to Pakistan by herself? My mind mulled the dilemma, weighing the options, letting them ripen without thought." Baji seems to rest her eyes somewhere in the past as she speaks.

"I wrapped Beezah in her woolen shawl and stretched open the waist of her trousers so she could step into them to dress herself again. At that time, Beezah was in her mid-fifties. She seemed to me to be an old woman, but fit and familiar with the forest, more than you can imagine. Still, she was struggling to breathe, to stand up. The climb had worn her out. She was like a strong pack mule at day's end.

"'You go on,' Beezah insisted, asking me, 'Isn't that your life waiting for you out there?' I remember how Beezah raised her brow, tilted her head and threw her sightline in Yusuf's direction. From that distance he was indiscernible. Could have been anything—a pine tree, a fox, something discarded along the side of the road. At that moment he seemed unimportant. Fear was not drawing me to hide in the forest nor was longing leading me to him. There simply was not one molecule in my body that moved in his direction.

"Beezah's question baffled me: *Isn't that your life waiting for you out there?* It was deeper than the question of escaping Pakistan. 'I'll accompany you back to your home, Beezah,' I said. 'Now that I've hiked this donkey trail once—and by tomorrow—twice. It will be easy for me to return here alone.'

She smiled her easy grin, and the many folds of her face spread, the shine returned to her dark eyes when she spoke. I ran back to Yusuf, huffing and puffing, downhill and up. 'Wait for me in Akram,' I told him. 'I'll be back tomorrow or the next day.' He objected, of course, but we were exposed there on the open road and anxious to keep moving. He could have come with us, of course, but he didn't, and it's just as well. I kissed him goodbye and started up the hill again where Beezah was waiting in the brush. We turned from Yusuf and drew the cloak of darkness around us.

"I know now that to go with Yusuf at that moment would have meant following a path he was defining and that held its own risks, as did returning to Pakistan with Beezah. But there was something about meeting her that reminded me of who I was deep inside. Not the public hero, not the criminal, not even the second mother of my own family. It was something I cannot explain, something I had glimpsed in the silence of the snow in Chitral in the North West during the previous winter, and then again, sometimes while I was alone in prison. It was something holy, for which I have no words. My father always predicted that I would search one day and I might or might not ever find what I was seeking. He said that everyone has to be born and everyone has to die, but only some find their path to God. He called it 'a path as unique as your fingerprints, and as close as the stone in your shoe.'"

Ujala's hazel eyes are bright, and as she speaks, they move in a staccato fashion, as if scanning pages of a book out there in the air, or running through frames from a roll of film, searching for the right angle to explain her life to Nafeesa.

"But what Yusuf writes next in his story is pure fiction– that I walked into Akram with him that day. He would never want anyone to think his wife might have had second thoughts about him." Her voice is flat and low. "Honestly, I am still unsure if following Beezah was a wise or a foolish decision. I think she cast some kind of spell over me. It was weeks before I crossed over the Line of Control again, and of course, by the time I found him, he had worked himself up into a fit of worry, so that when I knocked on his door that day, his relief to see me was a stew of anger and betrayal that eventually worsened over time. He began to blame me for everything that went wrong in his life."

Ujala finishes her cup of tea and rests her back against the stuffed chair. Nafeesa stays in the silence and waits. She thinks her auntie is speaking like Babba—in this gentle, mysterious way that once repelled her. How little she has understood about anything! She offers Ujala a piece of cinnamon toast, holding it out by its crusty corner between her thumb and forefinger.

Ujala takes the toast and continues. "That moment on the mountain was a key decision in my life—to help Beezah return or to go forward with Yusuf. It's important to know how to make a decision, Nafeesa, and also how to keep hold of a decision once you've decided to follow your true self. One cannot take both the path one chooses and at the same moment also take the path one declines. And if you think you can just take a path later, then you are wrong. Because then it would be a different path, would it not? In this world we have to choose even when we know life also is choosing. Still, things seem to happen one at a time, so we must respond one at a time. In a way, we happen one at a time, too. We can't change that." Suddenly she faces Nafeesa directly, demanding a response. "Can we?"

"Why, no, of course not, Auntie."

"Call me Baji. Everyone does. Or they used to," she laughs. "When has one woman had so many names? Born Ujala, nickname Uji, alias Asma—but call me Baji—I'm everyone's elder sister."

Now she is sounding silly and Nafeesa is growing to appreciate her strangeness, but she also is seeking an opening in the story so they can make a plan to escape from Yusuf and return to Srinagar. Baji gives her none. Instead, she describes bit by bit the next eight hours of that day, eighteen years earlier, when she had watched Beezah's back hour after hour–her heavy trousers, her tan jacket, her green shawl, her boots, following, step by step over the foothills, just inside the border of the forest.

"We kept silence long after we passed the LoC. Eventually language became useless there. The night was calm, lit by a billion stars, a piece of creation itself. It was a night when the earth kept us company, humming in a voice as soft as a kitten. But, Nafeesa, in the nighttime, wild animals also dwell in the mountains, and they stalk and feed. Beezah and I met one that night. She saw it before I did, focused as I was on the back of her body and the next step ahead.

"At one point along a steep path, Beezah stopped and turned. She crept toward me like in a slow-motion film. One index finger was planted firmly over her lips; the other index finger was aimed from the tip of her outstretched arm to an outcropping of rock ahead of us. There was a shadowy silhouette of something that crawled into the stream of moonlight. It was a snow leopard! Dusky white and orange and black-spotted. I was both terrified and thrilled by its thick furry beauty, its enormous paws, its resting posture from which it could momentarily spring with its piercing teeth and claws ready, and race toward the jugular of any prey it wanted, including us. I was paralyzed. I feared even glancing at Beezah. The brim of her flat cap almost covered her eyes. She frothed a little at the corners of her mouth, like a beast herself in her thick jacket and furry scarf. Beezah was moving her hand, inching it bit by bit into the pocket of her pants. She held a sharp trident in her hand. Suddenly, it was Beezah who pounced, rising up in a flash and with such a horrendous roar from the depths of her that she seemed to expand before my eyes and fly into the air, flinging it, slicing the space between that magnificent cat and us. Instantly the trident met its mark and embedded itself into the leopard's front paw. The cat cried out then, whimpering as it limped back into the trees."

Baji takes a bite of toast and narrows her eyes. "Can you cook? I am hungry and I can keep talking while you prepare something to eat."

Nafeesa is breathless and happy to have something to do. She hunts through Janna's luke-warm icebox. As Baji talks, Nafeesa whips eggs and cheese with some chopped red chard and a few sage leaves. She squats to light the propane camp stove on the floor, listening.

"After the snow leopard, we doubled our pace. We felt energized, strong again. Hours later, once we entered the Neelam Valley, we finally rested on enormous glacial boulders. We gobbled up what was left of the cheese and cold tea." Baji's voice drops. "Then the day broke apart into lavender and yellow."

Nafeesa stops clattering the dishes and tries to imagine that sunrise.

"That was when Beezah broke the silence of the night time. 'The snow leopard is sacred to these mountains,' Beezah whispered. 'I pray she forgives the injury. . . but I believe she will. She would understand. After all, you are the cub I must protect.' I asked Beezah how she knew the leopard was a she, and Beezah just laughed in my face."

The eggs are ready, so tentatively Nafeesa asks Baji, "Shouldn't we make our Srinagar plan to get you out of here?"

Baji stands up. "But we *are* making our plan, and the first step is for you to understand the story I am telling you. Just be quiet and listen," she admonishes Nafeesa, the way Nanaa used to do. "I stayed with Beezah for a week or more," Baji continues. "I am not sure exactly how long because by the time Beezah and I dragged ourselves back to her hut—which, as Yusuf describes in his story, was 'something like a cabin, something like a cave'— we were exhausted and sick, too tired to cook. We slept long hours and ate very little—some boiled potatoes, goat milk and dried cheese squares that Beezah had strung up inside the corrugated tin roof. Beezah recovered first.

"I remember her lighting the stove and heating water," Baji says while Nafeesa clears the table. "Beezah was making tea and mixing rice and spices, frying the cheese. But even though I was quite hungry, I could not swallow any solids. I could only cough and cough until my insides were raw. 'You have Himalayan fever,' Beezah said. 'Don't worry. I know what to do.' For many days she continually heated cloths in water on the stove and wrapped them around my feet. Then she would lay icy cold cloths on my forehead. Soon she was cleaning her house, carrying in wood, feeding her goats and her pigeons, returning to her normal routines. She would wring a clean cloth to drip water into my mouth, cooling my lips, forcing fluids and warm honey into my body. In the early mornings, she filled me with the sweet nectar she spooned out and fresh yogurt from her herd. Then she would sit on the floor cross-legged, still and silent for hours. In the early evenings, she would leave me, even after I began to recover. 'I'll be back at moonrise,' she would say, and I would watch the horizon until the first glow appeared. Then I would see her distant silhouette climbing toward the hut."

Nafeesa goes back to the table and sits across from her. Baji reaches for her hand. "At some point," she says, squeezing Nafeesa's palm, "I was able to sit, then to stand, then to take a few steps. Sometimes Beezah recited poetry. I remember my favorite—it was one of Lalla's:

> *At the end of a crazy-moon night*
> *the love of God rose,*
> *I said, "It's me, Lalla."*
> *The Beloved woke. We became That*
> *and the lake is crystal clear.*

"I was so confused and asked Beezah what does that mean? Guess what Beezah said!" Baji laughs as she asks. "'Yes,' is what she said. Just yes. Beezah taught me strange prayers in Sanskrit and told me that the sound of Durga's mantra is what inspired her to use the trident to warn off the leopard. 'As precious as she is,' Beezah said, 'the cat cares not for us, any more than any other creature of the forest. Her job, like ours, is to survive, and then dissolve back into That. Surely she would have attacked us.'

"'When you return to Yusuf on the donkey trail,' she told me, 'I will give you that trident to take with you.'" Baji pauses, widening her eyes, quoting

Beezah's words: "'Assuming you do return. And I'll give you some herbs for the leopard's paw in case she approaches you for help.' By this time, Beezah's strange ways seemed quite natural to me.

"On the morning of my leaving, Beezah described her dream from the night before. 'Two queens of heaven met us at a gate. You were on the outside and I was on the inside. A horse pulled at the gate with ropes strapped across its flanks, and the snow leopard leapt from the sky and onto the horse's back. One queen called the horse to her and another one called the snow leopard. Then the gate opened by itself and we were re-united.' Beezah gazed into my eyes.

"'We will meet again, my dear.'

"'Yes,' I said, having learned from her that a yes is often a wiser response than questioning why. I thanked her for saving my life.

"At that Beezah laughed out loud. 'Not saving your life, my dear. Saving your soul! Remember—many lives. One soul.'

"On my return trip over the mountain, I faced no obstacles, no snow leopards, no soldiers, no hunger or thirst, no scraped skin or broken bones, not even sunburn. I believe that Beezah or one of her goddesses must have prepared the way. By sunset I was in the newspaper office at Akram, and asked there for Yusuf's whereabouts, using his new Indian name, Mohan Ali. By the time of the evening call to prayer, I was knocking on the door to a small house on Shahi Road.

"It opened to the face of my beloved," Baji says. "That's how I used to refer to my husband—as my beloved." A tear forms in the pool of her eyes. For a moment it is as if Baji is eighteen years younger, standing at his door, eager to be with him again. Her face brightens and Nafeesa's heart breaks a little.

"As for Yusuf and me, let's just say that our relationship was never the same. Something broke when I left him and returned with Beezah. I had lost a sense of time and stayed much longer than I should have. And Yusuf was so angry. He said I had left him out again. I was always rejecting him even after he sacrificed his preferred life in New York in order to save me from prison in Adiala. I knew he'd been afraid for me—that I would never find my way across again without him. And I felt guilty, of course, although I knew he was irrational and tried to explain. I was only helping an old woman who had helped us. I became ill. I had to stay. I explained it all to him many times, but he was bitter and I had to wonder where my supportive, loving partner had gone. Over time I concluded that the situation we were in and my so-called abandonment of him had caused irreparable damage to what was just beginning to be 'us.' Of course, it wasn't always like that. Later, he would soften and be like the old Yusuf, but then unexpectedly, he'd strike out and I'd try to avoid him as much as possible at those times. He would not speak to me for days, sometimes for weeks. It was pretty lonely.

"Still, life pressed on the way it does—through the forces of cells in our bodies, the DNA of fire and earth, the flow of water that moves according to the wind, the moon, the heat of the sun, the shape of the shore line. . .." She lifts her head to face Nafeesa again. "Talk about dithering. Whatever am I saying?" she laughs.

"Let's just say that over the years I became a simple teacher who lived under the thumb of her husband, as most wives do." Nafeesa senses that Baji is giving her a warning. "I felt I had made a serious mistake moving here with Yusuf. I began to question everything in my life. In the end, had I really helped that Pathan girl with the sliced nose who only wanted to dance? She ended up under the rule of her father's house after all, did she not? And Khanum, the woman I put on the train? Now she is lost in Karachi. Has she ever found a way to survive outside the mansion of her monstrous husband? And dear Faisah, my Faisah! Was it her report over the radio waves about my imprisonment that brought those men into the alleyway with their bottle of acid? Was she blinded and scarred for life because of me? Am I the reason your mother was killed?"

Nafeesa shakes her head. She wants to argue, but Baji ignores her.

"No, nothing appears the same from the perspective of life in Akram. I questioned everything. I became lonely. I longed for my sisters, my family. There were days I needed proof for myself that I was alive. I stared at the sheets of snow, the reams of winter that lay on the valley floor, as if they were paper on which my life was being written by someone else.

"First, I was hired as a teacher's aide. After I had proven myself, I could stand happily again at a chalkboard in front of children, and crowd around a table of tea and sweets with teacher-friends, and even have a little money in my pocket. I could pull on my boots to go shopping or trudge the streets of town in the early morning to prepare my classroom with peace of mind. The classroom was my quiet joy.

"And Yusuf. Yes, the prison break and running away together—they were necessary, of course, and also romantic, suggesting a happy ending for us. But after we arrived in Kashmir, when Yusuf changed his name to Mohan Ali, more than his identity card changed. He changed, too.

"It's an old story, Nafeesa. A husband hitting a wife. But still, I guess like all young girls, it was a story I never expected would describe my life. When I remember it now, I picture his hand—that hand I loved to stroke, I . . . Let's just say that when he laid his hand on me in that way, what broke was not just my nose. I felt an utter humiliation and betrayal by the very flesh I had cherished. I have never gotten over it. Even though it happened repeatedly, it was that first strike that I can never forget. Each push or shove or slap reopens that sore, that degraded state in which my hatred and fear began to fester."

Baji looks up, entirely dry-eyed. She runs her finger along the bump on her nose. In that moment Nafeesa feels like an old woman herself. She imagines Baji cupping her hands beneath her nose as they fill with blood. "Baji?" Nafeesa wants to reach out to her but doesn't know if she should touch her, or where.

"It's all right, Nafeesa." Baji clears her throat. She lifts her palms and shrugs. "Look on the bright side. I had only one nose to break." She smiles, breathes deeply and tries to speed up her story. "I began to feel I had traded one prison for another. Over the years Yusuf's demanding, jealous, possessive ways became worse and more frequent. He stopped asking my opinion on any topic, and criticized everything I did. He took my pay envelope and gave me a tiny allowance. He became less affectionate but more demanding at the same time. He blamed me for his situation. 'If it weren't for you,' he would say, 'I would be a leading journalist and could live anywhere in the world—New Delhi, or New York or London. But without my identity, I am nobody.' 'Then leave,' I shouted at him recently. 'No one is keeping you here.' But that did not satisfy him. He asked me, 'And if I return to that other world as Yusuf Salman, where do I say I have been all these years? If I've not been in hiding with you, where is my resume of publications? And if I have been with you, then everyone will ask: where is Baji Ujala now? Then what would I say? No, Uji. I will never be famous.'" She pauses. "His next words were chilling. 'My career is dead,' he said, 'as long as you are alive.'

"It was not just rhetoric. It was a death threat and he knew that I knew it. It would be easy for him to do away with me. Happens all the time. And that was when I wrote the letter to Faisah."

Baji stops and scoots her chair back from Janna's table. Faisah pumps water for the few dishes they have dirtied. She washes and Baji dries. Both of them are in tears. Nafeesa squeezes a cold dishcloth into a teacup. "It is a heartbreaking story, Baji. How could you bear it?" Baji places her hand on Nafeesa's forearm and leans against her.

Nafeesa looks into her face, closely for the first time. Finally, someone is explaining everything to her. Nafeesa whispers, "Baji?"

"Yes?"

"May I ask you something?"

"Yes."

"Even something out of the blue?"

"Blue. Red. Any color at all!"

"Do you know anything about the Ahmed family of Malakwal?"

"Of course. That was Ammi's family. They are powerful landlords in that area but we have nothing to do with them. It's a long story, Nafeesa, but let's just say that they disapproved of our parents' marriage, her brothers felt marrying a Sikh dishonored the family—even though Abbu converted to Islam to marry her– and they almost killed her. It was many years ago in Lahore in Shalimar Garden, but Abbu escaped with her. The Ahmeds are dangerous people with long memories who could still be searching for us. Who knows? That was Ammi's greatest fear and it was her last wish that we stay away from the Ahmeds and Malakwal to protect the family. We all honor it."

"Amir and Faisah, too?"

"Actually, they don't know about the Ahmeds and Malakwal. I only know about it because Abbu wanted me to understand the need to keep the children safe. Now so much time has passed, and everyone has grown up, moved, changed names. I'm sure none of it matters anymore. And now that you understand it all, you too will play an important role."

"What do you mean, Baji?

"We are not going to Srinagar, Nafeesa. You and I are going to return to Pakistan on that donkey trail. Beezah will help us. I am sure of it."

***

While Nafeesa is in Akram with Baji, Lia is in Srinagar, as a saline drip hydrates Faisah—*like a summer garden*, she thinks. Lia orchestrates an arrangement of orange marigolds and purple cosmos in an enormous vase. She devotes her attention to the floral task—distracting herself from Faisah's short breathing, cringing lips and the one closed eye that means she is in agony. Soon the saline bag is empty, and Lia goes to find a nurse to connect another.

"I don't need to be in a hospital," Faisah insists. "Disconnect this thing. Just get me some pain pills to go."

Hours later the two women huddle at a small table in a nearby restaurant. "You're just a lowlander, darlin'," teases Lia.

"A weakling," Faisah confesses.

"Oh, you just hate having any shortcomings."

"I do prefer them in other people." Faisah pauses. "Suddenly I'm starving. For something more than sugar water."

Lia scans the menu. "Yay! Punjabi food!"

"You Americans," scoffs Faisah. "You just want your sad saag paneer and your boring chicken tikka. Then you're happy."

"And the onion naan," whines Lia. "I want my onion naan!" Lia is relieved they are together again. One day apart seems too long. Even at home when Faisah is depressed and Lia can't take it for one minute more, she will walk out, saying she is going to a movie, and then call Faisah from the theater to see if she will come join her. Co-dependency Incorporated, that's us, Lia laughs to herself, thinking maybe they are just two different leaves on the same neem tree.

They sit by a curtained window where Srinagar's street traffic is visible, but they have privacy behind the printed cotton cloth. Lia reaches for the green chile sauce. "We have to get them out of Akram ASAP," she tells Faisah as she spreads sauce on a crispy pappadum. It splits apart under the pressure of the spoon. "How will Nafeesa manage without us?"

Faisah erupts with pride. "She's one of us, Lia! Her mother's daughter, even if she doesn't recognize it in herself yet. She and Baji can take the Srinagar bus tomorrow, leave Akram mid-day, while school is in session, when Yusuf won't be around. Should be simple. No problem. I just did it myself."

But Lia is not so sure it will be all that simple—didn't Baji describe in her letter how Yusuf is tracking her every move, never leaving her alone? The waiter brings small plates that crowd their little table. Faisah scoops curry into her dish, inhaling fresh ginger.

Lia passes her the hot sauce. "When do you think Nafeesa will call?" she asks and Faisah shrugs. "I warned them that the story could be published at any time. By now Yusuf may know about our meeting with Govinder."

Faisah grips her phone. "My God, what have I done? I've left Nafeesa in a truly dangerous situation."

Lia grabs her wrist. "Let's get some privacy first." They rush to the ladies' toilet, a small, untiled concrete room. They dial Nafeesa and Janna's numbers, but the phone recording repeats, "Circuits are busy. Try again later."

Faisah is almost in tears. She calls Amir. "How is Abbu?" she asks. "Oh." Her voice becomes a whisper. As Lia watches Faisah breathe, her heart swells. She knows it was not good news about Kulraj Singh. She takes the phone, which Faisah surrenders easily, and she explains their predicament to Amir, gives him Janna's phone number.

Amir responds in a definitive tone she has never heard him use. "Do not return to Akram—too dangerous. And do not leave Faisah alone in Srinagar. I have talked to Zeshan at great length. He is upset about Nafeesa leaving, but has promised to help."

"What can Zeshan do in Kashmir?" Lia asks, putting the phone on speaker so Faisah can hear Amir.

"Zeshan has contacts everywhere," he says. "And do not go back to Mumbai. Yusuf might be right behind you. Once he hears from that editor and he can't find Baji, he will assume she is with you."

"Yes, brother, we will stay here in Srinagar," says Faisah. "We still need an Indian death certificate for the dismissal of Baji's case. Then when Baji and Nafeesa arrive, we'll fly to Lahore. Meet us there."

Amir is full of questions. "How will Baji cross the border? Her Pakistan passport expired long ago. Might she have an Indian passport? She'll need a visa."

"We don't know," Lia says, her eyes asking Faisah, who is dazed, short of breath: What have we been thinking? Why didn't we remember there would be a visa problem for Baji? "We'll keep trying to reach Baji and Janna and let you know our next steps, but they may call you first. And give the phone numbers to Zeshan."

They wind their way back to their table and finish the meal without talking. Both are deep in thought. Soon the kheer is gone from its dish, the last drop of tea has been consumed, and the bill has been paid. Lia reaches for the door handle and pulls. They step outside.

Crossing the Jhelum River over an old bridge, they enter a crowded market lined with two and three-storied buildings—shops on the first floors, living quarters above. There are piles of apples and peaches for sale. Piles and piles of dead, unplucked chickens. Bored policemen in khaki berets watch the streets in an unremarkable way. Lia can see that Faisah is tiring as they walk. She checks the street for a taxi, but sees none. Up ahead of them there is a great deal of noise. A large crowd of demonstrators is shouting pro-Pakistan slogans and hurling rocks at a line of Indian paramilitary. Tanks and motorcycles are gunning their engines and lining up. There are four or five shots of gunfire, then all traffic stops.

Lia and Faisah hurry to a white building with an arched portico surrounded by iron fencing and a heavy gate. They lean against a granite wall to catch their breath, when a door opens and a young man motions them inside, then disappears through a calico curtain. A phone rings out and both women slap their pockets to check.

Faisah answers, whispering, "It's Janna." Lia leans in to listen.

Janna's voice sounds as if it is being forced through her throat. "They've gone," she says.

"On the afternoon bus?"

"No. Baji left a note, asking me to call you and your brother. They are crossing into Pakistan on their own the same way she came years ago. She couldn't risk the bus because Yusuf would find them there." Janna is crying, having difficulty speaking. She swallows hard. "They are going to Baji and Yusuf's house first, then will meet me at the Fort so I can drive them past the checkpoint. What is she thinking, Faisah? How will they pass the military? What if Yusuf is at the house? What if he follows them? He would know the way."

"Take a breath, Janna," Faisah says. "Take a breath." But Faisah can hardly breathe herself. "You are doing everything you can. We know where they are going—to Muzzafarabad on the other side– and Lia and I will leave right away and catch up with them in Pakistan. We will find help there." Lia remains silent, serious, nodding her assent to Faisah's plan. "We are grateful, Janna, but don't call Amir. We will do that. Come visit when this is over. Stay in touch. *Allah hafiz.*"

Outside the building, the military has cleared the street. The room seems more silent than silent and the world around them empty. The man who invited them inside is nowhere to be seen. At last, Faisah speaks.

"I do see some beauty in Baji's plan," she says, leaning her elbows into her knees, staring at the stone floor. "Mountains don't require passports or visas."

***

Zeshan devours every detail Amir discloses about Nafeesa and Ujala in Kashmir, ending the phone call and searching for *The She-lion of Punjab* on-line. True to his word, the publisher does not reveal him as the person who provided the false IDs for Ujala and Yusuf. But the published story exposes

Ujala's prison supervisor, Rahima Mai, as an accomplice to the escape! That single fact will become the lead for a news story and will spread through Pakistan's sensationalizing internet news sites. I must warn Rahima Mai, he thinks—it is the least I can do. But where is she?

"Very difficult to find such a person," he mutters, pacing the floor. On the ochre-painted office wall hang his humanitarian awards, an indulgence he allows his ego. How does one find a retired civil servant? Ah, pension records. Yes, he can call his friend at the retirement board. Zeshan can't help but enjoy the pleasure of pulling his weight to help those in need, confirming to himself each time he does it that he is a good man after all. He loves aligning all the pieces of a plan and watching them fall into place. His contact at the retirement board gives him the address for Rahima Mai. "In strictest confidence," his friend says, quoting the organization's marketing line, "Our pensioners are our people."

"Oh, I am sure they are," replies Zeshan, thinking of all the under-the-table deals those bureaucrats at the pension board pursue for "their" people. But he can warn Rahima Mai to go into hiding for a while now that Yusuf has revealed her role in the prison escape. Give her a few rupees to go stay with a friend, something like that. But first he must find a way to help Ujala and Nafeesa in Kashmir. If he can't wipe out the war zone they have to cross, or enkindle the cold night they must endure, at least he can reduce Yusuf's threat to them.

He hurries to his file drawer for his maps. There he finds Kotha, the border town in Pakistan where, according to Yusuf's story, he and Ujala crossed over years ago. And there is Akram, the town where they have been living in Kashmir. Somehow the name Akram is familiar. He rifles through closed files until he locates one marked "Akram." Yes! It is a place where, ten years earlier, he wired funds to a mosque for flood relief. As it turned out, the funds were diverted by locals to the insurgency and were used to buy explosives and Kalashnikovs instead of bandages and medicine. Still, it is a connection he can use. He calls the number in the file. "Try again later," the recording repeats and he flips his mobile phone shut.

Zeshan wonders if this is the kind of interference he promised Kulraj Singh he would not do. On the other hand, he thinks, Ujala and Nafeesa did ask for help. And who could be more in need than two unaccompanied women–one old and one still a girl, lost in the wilderness with a vengeful man stalking them through a militarized zone? No, Kulraj Singh would approve. He must find a way to delay Yusuf so Uji and Nafeesa can escape.

He finds an email address and sends a message, asking for the mosque's help in detaining Yusuf. He types on the subject line: "Foundation wants to send you funds." That should get someone's attention, he scoffs. He tries calling again and checks his email. No response in either place.

A slight glow from the west reminds Zeshan that he should leave for Rahima Mai's village on the far edge of the city. Out the window he can see the street filling with vehicles. He asks his driver to bring the car around and hears a knock at the door. Unusual. No one comes to his office without an invitation. Another knock at the door. What a bother. He turns off his phone and stands perfectly still, soundless. Perhaps they will go away, thinking no one is here. Then his computer pings the arrival of a new message and he returns to his desk. It is someone from the Akram mosque responding—they say they are aware who Mohan Ali is. Yes, they will find him in Akram and detain him, but for how long? Meanwhile, they ask, would Zeshan consider another donation?

Yes, he replies. Yes.

Suddenly the door opens. There stands an older woman with a face round as a mountain boulder and a body to match. She is overdressed for such a warm day, wearing both a maroon sweater and a blue jacket. A wisp of gray hair falls from beneath her dupatta. She holds a plastic suitcase and is out of breath, red-faced. A beggar? She probably wants a donation.

"Yes?" he asks kindly and she announces herself like a soldier.

"Rahima Mai, retired Major."

"You are Rahima Mai?"

"Yes, sir."

"Of Adiala Prison?"

"Formerly."

"Just the person I was looking for! I am sorry, I didn't recognize you. Please have a seat. May I offer you some tea?" Rahima Mai places the suitcase by the door and rubs the palms of her ruddy hands together, making a swishing sound. She says nothing.

"However did you find me?" he asks, thinking how Yusuf's story was only just published online–and while he's been dithering about finding Rahima Mai, she's magically appeared.

"You are easy to find," she replies vaguely. The rich are easy to find.

"It has been a long time," he says pleasantly.

"Eighteen years, three months, four days," she says automatically.

That kind of answer stops Zeshan's small talk—she is talking numbers, something he understands. He pours hot water into a porcelain pot painted with bluebirds and sets the cups and spoons on the tray. "How may I help you?"

She blinks her rheumy eyes and turns the table on his question. "I believe you said you were looking for me?"

"Oh, yes. Well, I have news."

"I saw the news. We must protect her." There is no question they both are referring to Ujala. The look on her face catches him like a fishhook. Then he wonders if she could be a government informant tricking him into a confession.

"But she died," he lies, "it was in the story."

She snaps her neck around to face him. "Died?" She shakes her head. "I don't think so. Of course, a report that she has died would lead to a dismissal of her case, would it not?" He nods and Rahima Mai presses on. "But where will she go? She cannot travel without a passport or visas. Perhaps she and Yusuf will return the same way they left."

"Yes, but she will be traveling without Yusuf Salman," he says, and Rahima Mai's already broad face broadens even more. He can see that she has gotten what she came for—the information that Baji is returning but Yusuf is not. She stands and straightens the sweater under her coat.

"*Shukriah,* but I cannot stay for tea. I must leave Lahore at once."

"That was going to be my recommendation to you—under the circumstances. But where will you go? And exactly where will Ujala go?"

Rahima Mai reaches for her suitcase and puts her index finger to her lips. "Need-to-know-only basis," she says. "Shh."

Zeshan is taken aback. Rahima Mai is the only person who can identify the exact path that Baji and Nafeesa would travel, since she drew the map that they followed over the LoC. He stands with a teapot in one hand and a cup and saucer in the other and watches the door close behind her. Then it re-opens, and Rahima Mai sticks her big head in. Her sparkly dupatta has fallen to her shoulders. "I will need a donation. For travel expenses, you understand."

He hurries to get the key to his cash drawer. "Of course," he says. "I understand completely."

***

By the guesthouse window in Srinagar, Lia is chewing her fingernails. Bedclothes and bags, papers and purses are strewn around the room. "Let's get the hell out of here," she yells at Faisah. "But how are we gonna do that?"

"Lia, it's okay," Faisah yells back. "We'll take the Peace Bus to Muzza-farabad, and get help there to find Baji and Nafeesa."

Lia makes a face and laughs. "Peace Bus? Is that like the Love Train?"

Faisah ignores the joke and tries to explain. "Both Pakistan and India have local buses that have been crossing the LoC for years. Through earthquakes and landslides, floods, political tensions, and minor criminal activity, the buses manage to go on. It's a way to encourage cooperation between businesses and contact among families along the border."

"You think Pakistan will give you a visa to enter?"

"I think so. I'm an Indian citizen now and they aren't likely to connect me to the prison escape after all these years. It's worth the risk."

Lia is not really listening to Faisah. "I don't want to go back to Pakistan. It's more dangerous there now than it was when we left, especially for Americans." She swings her head around so fast her long hair slaps her own face. "And Yusuf might be on the Peace Bus," Lia argues. "Ever consider that? Isn't that the quickest way into Pakistan from Kashmir—if you don't take a damn donkey trail, that is?" She stops. She can hear her own callousness and she doesn't like it. "Okay. I agree. We have to help Baji and Nafeesa, but let's think this thing through."

Faisah fingers the envelope that the desk clerk handed her. "Mo's colleague delivered the death certificate for Baji."

As Lia reaches for the envelope, she starts to cry. "It's all just too much, Faisah. You're just starting to recover from being deathly ill. Now we're forging a death certificate. And we could have been killed in the street back there."

Faisah draws her close and strokes her hair. "Lia," she whispers, "Baji and Nafeesa may be lost. Abbu is dying. Would we deny him being with his daughters one more time?"

Lia sighs. "Of course, we will find them," Lia whispers back, "but first, a moment of yoga." She lies down on the floor and Faisah hurries next to her.

"Ah," says Faisah, "corpse pose—my favorite."

Lia smirks. "And so appropriate," she says, closing her eyes and reaching for Faisah's hand.

The next day, with temporary travel permits in hand, they board the Peace Bus, a modern, well-kept bus in which every seat is occupied—men, women, children, boxes, baggage. Security police search everyone before they board. No government forces from either side are allowed to travel on board, although they patrol the depots along the way. The trip takes about four hours to cross over, allowing for stops along the way.

Faisah and Lia sit together in the fifth row, looking like two Hollywood starlets. Lia is wearing her biggest sunglasses to avoid any attention to what she calls "the Chinese side of her American self or the American side of her Chinese self." Faisah's knock-off Ray Bans cover her eye patch. Off and on the two women pretend to sleep and speak little, since Lia's spoken Urdu with its unique American accent always draws attention. "You do Urdu," Lia sings in a she-sells-sea-shells kind of way. "But my Urdu is doo-doo."

It is a rocky road alongside the Jhelum River. Sometimes it's a wide and rolling river where people walk, carry their plastic shopping bags, ride their bicycles, lead a few sheep. That is when it is a friendly river, a childhood memory that flows beneath bridges in Punjab, where men with long oars fish in small boats, cast their nets as they smoke cigarettes under their messy turbans. At other times the Jhelum becomes wild and narrow, cutting rock over the millennia, wearing away volcanic formations, shale, clay, limestone, embedded with seashells from the earth's ancestral seabed. Its narrow gorge is the only outlet that drains the Kashmir Valley, and the pressure of that passage is legendary. In anticipation of viewing it, the bus veers a bit to the left as passengers from the right side fill the aisle to photograph the river racing itself at high speed.

Faisah and Lia unwrap the paneer parathas and the grilled sandwiches they brought along. Soon, as others uncover their dishes, enticing aromas fill the bus–cardamom, cinnamon, cloves and saffron, goat meat, fennel, roasted potatoes and spicy greens. Ease settles in as Kashmir's divided families share what food they have. Faisah and Lia are delighted to offer their *baqerkhanis*, puff pastries stuffed with almonds and chutney, coated with sesame seeds.

They arrive at the Muzzafarabad depot in mid-afternoon. It is packed with buses, highly-decorated commercial trucks, tuk-tuks, and every kind of taxi, scooter and bicycle. There are soldiers everywhere, as in Srinagar and Akram. In many ways, Kashmir is the same on both sides.

"Seems shabbier than I remember," says Lia, and Faisah sighs, saddened, a bit hurt by Lia's comment, although she knows just what Lia means. After eighteen years, her country's condition seems no better. Maybe it is worse.

"Earthquakes and war do that," she says.

The bus pulls into its assigned stall equipped with special security devices the police use to scan passengers as they descend the front stairs of the vehicle. There is a delay while the police check baggage. Faisah looks around at the long line of disembarking passengers, gathering their coats and luggage, pulling wheeled carts, or hauling cartons on their backs or lifting by their handles every kind of bag in every color and material you could ever want—leather and raffia, plastic and cotton, prints with birds and stripes, decorations, embroidery and glitter. Her eye falls on an old woman's face—round and hidden like a nut inside the shell of her shawl. The woman drags a suitcase by the handle and clenches her purse against her body. She rocks back and forth as she walks, her eyes searching for a porter. Faisah wonders where she has seen her before.

As Lia joins her under the portico, Faisah points at the woman. "Who is...?"

Lia interrupts. "Shh!" she nudges Faisah. "Well, I'll be damned!" she whispers. "It's Rahima Mai! Baji's supervisor at Adiala. I wonder if she knows she's in Yusuf's story," Lia says. Then, like a good reporter, she walks right up to ask her.

Faisah gets ahead of Lia as she approaches the woman, and Rahima Mai steps back, unnerved. "Remember me?" Faisah extends her hand. "Baji's sister? The lawyer who would visit Adiala."

Then Rahima Mai comes alive, wrapping both of them in her big arms. "Faisah Ehtisham," she says. "*Assalam akeikum.* Yes, I remember you. And the eye patch," she winks. Then her face darkens. She reaches for their arms and draws them closer to her. "Have you read the latest issue of *The Convoy*? 'The She-Lion of Punjab'?" Faisah and Lia nod. "Worrisome. Very worrisome indeed. Now I'm on my way to my village where I have an auntie who will be glad to hide me until this whole thing passes."

"Baji and Nafeesa are on their way there right now!" Faisah blurts out.

"To Auntie Beezah? Then it's true what Mr. Shaheed told me." She scans their island of satchels, sacks, sweaters and coats. Her eyes land on Faisah's surprised face.

"You talked with Zeshan Shaheed?" Faisah asks.

"Yesterday. At his office." Rahima Mai pauses, rubbing her knees. "But first let's find a hotel and then we can sit and talk all night if we want to." She wraps her worn Kashmiri shawl around herself. "I know just the place." She reaches for her bag, but Lia picks it up, and Rahima Mai is happy to let her lug it. "A little trouble with my knees," she says, leading them single file through the crowd.

***

In their hotel room, Faisah, Lia and Rahima Mai sit at a small table, spreading out their remaining snacks and drinks. Through the window to the northeast, vees of geese undulate across the blue. There are layers of mesas, ridges and ranges, one behind the next, endlessly. And below them is the confluence of the Neelam and the Jhelum.

"It's the same river we saw in Akram," Faisah tells Lia. "The Kishen-ganga."

Rahima Mai nods with pride. "Yes, the Kishenganga, the Neelam, it is the river of life here in Kashmir. Its source lies up in the valley where I was raised."

"And where Baji and Nafeesa are now," Lia adds. She sucks on a potato chip from a small package the hotel provided. "At least we believe they are." She chews another chip. "Tasteless," she mumbles, wanting a real potato chip. Rahima Mai re-opens a bag of pappadum chips and shakes some onto the cloth she places over the table.

"I am lucky to have found you girls. Life is so dull now that I have retired. You young girls cheer me up again." Faisah and Lia smile. They like being called young girls, as they both are close to fifty. While Faisah drinks her orange soda and keeps an eye on the river traffic, Rahima Mai doles out the pappadum chips. "Who is this Nafeesa exactly? The one you said is with Baji?"

"My niece," replies Faisah. "The daughter of my sister, Meena." Rahima Mai seems not to remember. "Remember the young woman who was shot at the Faisal Mosque? You granted Baji release time to attend her funeral?"

Rahima Mai bows her head. "Ah, yes, so sad. Baji was so, so sad." She looks up. "Tsk tsk, me, too. What a tragedy." She pauses. "And she was pregnant, wasn't she? When she was killed?"

"And that child is Nafeesa," says Faisah.

Rahima Mai stops popping cookies into her mouth. "Nafeesa and Baji are together now? She puts a sticky hand over Faisah's. "So how do we help them?"

"Tomorrow I will file Baji's death certificate with the court here. They will send it on to Islamabad. Then we go find them on the donkey trail."

Rahima Mai tightens her lips together. "No. Tomorrow we must go to Kotha, to Auntie Beezah. Courts take forever. You could be standing in line all day. Remember, I am Kashmiri! I know what's what around here. Tomorrow we take the morning bus and by dinnertime we will find Auntie

Beezah." Her eyes flash. "The court filing can wait."

Faisah looks at Lia who has not taken her eyes off Rahima Mai since she opened up the pappadums. Faisah shrugs. "I agree. I can file it on the way back."

Rahima Mai becomes effusive. "Right you are! Wait until you meet Auntie Beezah—a completely unique human being, Kashmiri to her marrow, a saint. She will know exactly where Baji and Nafeesa are on her mountain."

In the morning they find an internet café where they learn that *The Convoy* has published another installment of "The She Lion of Punjab." Faisah sends one email to the lawyer Chaudry in Islamabad, advising him that she will file the death certificate within a few days, and another email to Amir, being deliberately vague: "We are where and when we said we would be, and today we leave to execute our plan." You never know if the government might be hacking or lurking.

The Neelam Valley bus is full of energetic climbers and their gear, along with locals who carry simple bags and watch the tourists. The three women opt to sit in the seats across the back of the bus, where they can protect both their belongings and their conversations.

"I feel like I've been on this ride before," says Faisah. "Yusuf described it well in his story. Maybe he does have a little Hemingway in him."

Looking unimpressed, Lia lowers her voice. "Yeah. Yeah. Yeah. He's still a fricking A-hole. They say Hemingway was, too, by the way."

Sitting between them, taking up enough space for two, Rahima Mai is happy to add her opinion of Yusuf. "I never understood what Baji saw in that man." She firmly pinches her nostrils, holding her nose.

Lia turns to her. "So tell me more about Beezah. She is a saint?"

"Auntie Beezah is a living crossroad, part Sufi, part Buddhist, a kind of Vedic practitioner. She is what we call a *Rishi*—people who live away from family life, who have pure hearts that incessantly seek God. They say *rishis* are responsible for creating the beauty of Kashmir, making it a heaven on earth. They never denounce different faiths, but cultivate simplicity, patience and love. They plant fruit-bearing trees to share with all, and they abstain from meat." As is her habit, Lia writes furiously in her little book.

"Auntie Beezah came from the area where Kashmir's most intense rishis live, southeast of Srinagar. Early in life she retreated to the hills, found her cave, and befriended some wandering Tibetans who taught her. In the Kashmiri way, she mixed it all up, seeing no contradiction, nothing to fear or fight, to defend or promote. She planted her fruit trees fifty years ago, and invited the people of Kotha to help themselves. Back then, there was no Indian Kashmir and Pakistan Kashmir; there was only one Kashmir." She smacks her lips and begins to nap, murmuring, "I can still recall the sweetness of those apples."

Sitting on the sofa next to Rahima Mai, Faisah's mind starts making its list. First, it sketches out what to do once they locate Baji and Nafeesa, then it shifts to legal options, and to returning to Nankana Sahib, to her father and brother. As she leans against Rahima Mai's soft, sleeping body, she lets herself feel how much she has missed them. She opens her good eye to Lia in a chair across from her, smiling, saying nothing. Our souls match, Faisah thinks. Neither one wants to be the first to look away.

***

Baji and Nafeesa tidy up Janna's house and prepare for their flight over the foothills. While Baji wipes the table and gathers her bags, Nafeesa fills plastic water bottles from the pump. She is excited. It is like Durga. No obstacle too great for the shower of arrows, the flying trident, the beheading sword. Not a murderous husband. Not an arrest warrant. Not a war zone. Not an old donkey trail. Not the dark of night.

"If Yusuf searches for us on the mountain road, we'll be gone," Baji says, but the lines across her forehead betray her anxiety. "But he won't go to the mountains. He'll be checking the four o'clock Srinagar bus instead."

"How long will it take us to cross over? All night?"

"Tonight, and most of tomorrow night. We'll sleep in the forest in the daytime if we need to, and if the moon isn't too bright, we might hike all night."

Nafeesa tries to sound casual. "Sleep in the forest? Never imagined doing that before." She notices that Baji seems oblivious to her own poor physical condition—both skinny and soft. Although Nafeesa is young and somewhat strong, she is not accustomed to mountain climbing. Just the altitude of Akram leaves her winded. But she keeps these worries to herself and listens to Baji.

"If it's cold, we can wrap up in sleeping bags. Plus, we will need new boots, of course."

"Won't the police arrest you once we arrive?" asks Nafeesa, wondering if Baji has thought of this since she apparently is unaware of the current phase of the moon or how hard it is to hike in new boots. "Won't the Pakistani police take you back to prison?"

Baji turns to face her. "I may look good for my age, but I doubt they'll recognize me from eighteen years ago. I can use my Asma Mohan alias. Or maybe my case will be dismissed by then—once Yusuf's story is published and they all believe I am dead–that should be any day now. We can hide out with Beezah in the Kotha hills until we are certain it's safe to leave."

"I hate to ask this, Baji, but do you think Beezah is still alive?"

"Oh, I'm sure she is," Baji insists as if the matter were an established fact.

"And what if the Indian army finds us?"

"Don't worry so much, Nafeesa." Baji's voice is dreamy. "We will be-come invisible to them. Anything can be anything at all inside the shawl of midnight."

Now Nafeesa really is worried. What kind of mountain guide talks like that? "We promised Auntie Faisah we would call her. Shall I?" Baji appears not to be listening. She is unfolding a dark shawl and checking herself in the mirror again. Nafeesa dials Faisah's number. "Try again later" the automatic message responds. She dials Lia's number. "Try again later," it says. She dials Mamou. "Try again later," the phone voice repeats in its robotic way.

When Nafeesa closes her mobile phone, there is Baji watching her patiently. "Internet connections are quite unreliable here. Most things in life are unpredictable, you know. You'll get used to it." Baji raises her eyebrow. "And if you don't now, you can always try again later."

By the time they lock Janna's door, Nafeesa feels like she is the last car on a runaway train. How has she come to this dangerous situation with no one to depend on except Baji? Could there be something wrong with Baji—in the head? Yesterday she'd have followed Baji's star right up to heaven, now she wonders if hers is a star at all. Baji seems disorganized, unprepared and unrealistic. Nafeesa's mind is flashing warning lights. Maybe Baji is a little crazy from all she'd been through. Or maybe it is just fear that is unsettling Nafeesa's own mind. She has to admit, she began to have second thoughts when Baji mentioned sleeping out in the forest where there are wild animals, trigger-happy soldiers, and possibly an enraged husband and . . . a naked Beezah.

For the first time, Nafeesa wishes her father were there to tell her what to do—to stop her or to urge her on. She pictures that giant mole on his forehead, the way it slips into the creases of his disapproval. The fury she felt about his canceling her library card and his planning to send her into *purdah*, has played itself out. It all seems inconsequential now. Instead of the autonomy she craved then, now she just wants to hand it back and crawl under the covers of her grandmother's empty bed, call Rufina on the phone and walk with her to the dance studio, where they could turn the music up loud. How simple it all had been before...before... before what? Before her Nanaa died. Sadness and fear begin to overtake her. She thinks she hears Nanaa's stern voice admonishing her: *Nafeesa, an adult woman steps into her own life. Now you must take a new kind of dance step. And what kind of dance will that be?*

***

Baji and Nafeesa walk single file down back roads of Akram, roads so narrow that only one person can pass, or one motorcycle, a single ox, or a bicycle. " Where are we going first?" Nafeesa asks.

"Home," says Baji, stepping aside for a man leading a donkey to pass by. "I need some things—Rahima Mai's old map and a few other things. You will come along, pretend to be my student. Yusuf will be on his best behavior if I have a student with me. We will get Yusuf out of the house long enough for me to retrieve the items I need." Baji had hidden the map and jewels Rahima Mai gave her when she escaped Adiala, along with a small pistol. She plans to use the jewels to buy groceries and some trekking equipment; then she and Nafeesa will rendezvous with Janna to cross the checkpoint and begin their climb around the Line of Control into Pakistan.

The two women wind their way across muddy Akram. The sky is covered by a blanket of clouds that lies across a bed of mountain peaks. There are Indian soldiers everywhere—on every corner, sometimes two or three to a block, always one close enough to be in view of the next. They are especially thick around government buildings—the courthouse, the municipal center, the schools. For her protection, Baji places herself between Nafeesa and any man they pass on the street. At the main checkpoint in the town center, Baji shows the officials their documents. "My niece, visiting from Islamabad," she explains and a lady soldier escorts them behind the sentry box where she pats them down. Baji makes small talk while the woman works. Nafeesa understands Kashmiri well enough to realize Baji once was the teacher of one of the woman's daughters. Soon she smiles and waves them through.

Next they pass the market, the mosque, the old fort and a vast military lot full of tanks. There are crowds of people—mostly men—shopping, pushing through the tension between the military occupation and the effort to maintain a normal, civilian life. The crowds thin as they approach the outskirts of town, close to the foothills. Ahead Nafeesa hears the distant calls of raptors. She imagines the frightening, wide expanse of their wings. Ahead a curving narrow highway cuts into the hilly mountainside. She stops scanning the expanse. Is that the highway that Yusuf describes in his story? The place where they left Beezah behind? Or where Baji left Yusuf behind?

"We're almost there now," Baji says when they are alone on a back street. "Look at me," she demands. When Nafeesa turns to face her, Baji swings her arm, smashing her fist into Nafeesa's left cheekbone. It is a searing pain and Nafeesa cries out. "Just follow my lead," orders Baji, walking up to a thick wooden door and turning her key in the heavy lock.

Nafeesa is stunned, blinded and in shock. She bends over and holds her hand to her cheek, her eye. Blood drips from the corner of her mouth and seeps down her throat. She recalls her father's slap and begins to cough, choking on her own saliva and blood. "Why did you hit me?" she demands, "Why?"

"Shh," signals Baji. She opens the door and they step inside.

Yusuf glances up from a small table covered with papers spread around a laptop computer. "You are home," he mumbles, standing as they enter the room. Then his eyes fall on Nafeesa's face. "Oh, and you are hurt." He speaks in a gentle voice. "Come over here to the pump. Let Asma wash it. What happened to you?"

Nafeesa begins to cry and does not know where to turn. She hides in Baji's arms.

"Iffat was my student, Mohan. Her husband did this. She needs our help." He nods. Nafeesa shakes her head, holding her jaw. The pain is as real as any she's ever felt.

"I understand. I'll go for ice."

"Yes, good idea. I'll wash her up—just as soon as she calms down." When the door slams shut behind Yusuf, Baji hurries to move aside a small rug and to open a trap door embedded in the floorboards.

"Help me," she demands.

Nafeesa takes her hand as Baji starts to descend the ladder, and looks down into the hole in the floor, thinking what it would be like to be imprisoned there, in a space the size of a large bed, without a window, with only dirt walls and floor. The ceiling is too low to allow an adult to stand. She imagines rats and spiders. She shivers. Baji is giving her instructions but she is not listening.

"Listen. We don't have much time. When Yusuf returns, you tell me that you've decided to go home and must leave right away or your husband will be very angry. He'll try to talk you out of it. Say you want me to walk you home—that your husband would be jealous if you were to walk with a strange man." Baji stops her fast talk and reaches up to touch Nafeesa's hand that steadies the ladder as she climbs. "I am sorry I had to hit you, Nafeesa. My coming home early from school had to be convincing, so your wound had to be convincing. If I had told you ahead of time that I was going to hit you hard, would you have come with me? Of course not. It was the only way."

"Yes, Baji!" Nafeesa shouts. She is angry about the slap, and somehow feels fooled, and yelled at and talked down to, and bossed around. Oh, yes, she is thinking, yes, I understand. I understand that I am taking orders from a crazy person, a desperate, unstable woman who is dragging me into her insane plan to climb the Himalayan foothills and cross a war zone in the dark of night. I understand that much. I think the punch knocked some sense into me, like the slap from my father. I will find some way to escape back to Janna's house. Maybe Yusuf will help me. Maybe Baji has been making up all these terrible things about him. He doesn't seem so bad.

Nafeesa pulls Baji up out of the cellar and they replace the rug over the trapdoor. Baji's eyes are pinkish and puffy and her face is bloodless from holding her breath. She gasps from her burst of exertion. Nafeesa starts to take the heavy bag Baji holds but Baji clutches it and won't let go. Baji brushes off her clothes and goes directly out the front door, leaving it ajar. Nafeesa leans against the wooden back of the wide sofa as a wave of nausea tosses in her gut. Her face is too tender for her to touch with her fingertips. She is afraid Baji has broken her cheekbone.

Once back inside, Baji busies herself at the computer. "I'm checking his email," she whispers loudly across the room. Her dirty fingers work the keys. "I want to see if he's had any messages from that publisher." Her voice is panicky. Nafeesa can see that Baji is scrolling much too quickly to read the messages. She seems unfamiliar with navigating the page.

"Would you like me to do it?" she asks. Baji spins around in the revolving office chair. "Gladly. And I'll listen for Yusuf." She stands by the door. "I know the sound of his truck's engine," she says, as Nafeesa begins scrolling.

"What's the name of the magazine again?" she asks.

"The Convoy."

"Yes! A message arrived today. Here it is."

"And here he is," Baji whispers from the window. "Close it out! Quick!"

Yusuf enters, squeezing the top of a plastic bag with his big fist. Nafeesa feels genuinely touched by his kindness in getting the ice for her injury. Baji tears into the package, wraps several pieces of ice in cloth, and places them against Nafeesa's face. She recoils. Her cheek and jaw ache. Exhausted, she sits on the old sofa in the far corner, with the ice pack over her face. Baji comes to sit next to her while Yusuf putters in the kitchen area. He does not check the computer.

"Say that you have to go back to your husband now," Baji nags in whispers, elbowing Nafeesa's side, cracking open her rage.

She hurt me again!

"I'm so tired," Nafeesa says aloud. "Perhaps I could take a little nap?" Baji does not respond.

"Of course you can, Iffat," Yusuf says. He brings her a soft blue pillow from the bed and a large woolen shawl. Baji puts the pillow under her head.

"I worry that your husband will be searching for you," she says, handing Nafeesa a few white pills. "Here. Just aspirin, but it should help."

Nafeesa swallows them without water. She is trying to make sense of it. She has to decide what to believe, and then she must make a plan based on that, but right now thinking seems impossible. She switches off the reading lamp, closes her eyes and turns an ear to the pillow. Nafeesa's head pounds as she puzzles out what is real. Here is one set of possibilities, she tells herself, trying to think strategically, like Auntie Faisah: Yusuf is the sane one. After all, he is the one being kind to her. Baji seems dangerous and unstable. She punched her without warning, and although she had an explanation, it was a serious assault, maybe a fracture. Baji's plan to cross the mountains in the dark on a path she has not walked in almost two decades seems risky, if not insane. They are not in any condition to hike, and the consequences of getting caught on either side of the Line of Control could be extreme, possibly fatal.

But there is another possible scenario: Nafeesa did not have time to erase the computer search history, so when Yusuf opens the search engine, he will see they have been reading his email from the publisher. Who knows if he has read it already? Yusuf is a dangerous, abusive man who is now putting on a big act for me, as Baji said he would. Baji has gotten the things we need for the journey and, if we are going to go, we should not delay leaving. The longer we stay, the greater the danger. Nafeesa looks over at the door, where the bright sun pierces the small window. Soon midday will grow to late afternoon. What should she do? She recalls Baji's words: "One cannot take both the path one chooses and at the same moment also take the path one declines." It is time to act.

She bursts into tears and looks up at Baji, each full faced to the other. "Oh, Madam Asma, I must be home before my husband finds out I did not return directly, as he ordered when I left him. There will be only more blood and broken bones. Will you walk me?"

"Are you sure?" Yusuf asks from the kitchen area. "Why not stay here and I'll put you on the Srinagar bus later. You can start your life over there. We know people who can help." For a moment Nafeesa is tempted to say yes and return alone to Faisah and Lia in Srinagar, but how can she break her promise to Babba—to bring his daughters home to him?

"Yes," says Baji, nodding, as if concurring with Yusuf, "Do whatever is best."

Nafeesa sits calmly in a warm sunbeam. "No, I should go home at once," she says.

"Yes, of course. I'll drive you," offers Yusuf.

"But I want to return to my husband. I am not allowed to ride with you."

"Then I'll walk with you," he insists.

"I'll take her, Mohan," Baji interrupts. "You know it's not right for her to walk with a stranger."

"No one will realize I'm a stranger."

"Excuse me, Sir, but my husband will," says Nafeesa. "And he will be jealous and angry." Why is Yusuf being so insistent?

"Then I will go with both of you. There can be no gossip and no jealousy if I am coming to accompany my wife back to our home." For a split-second Baji's eyes widen in terror. Does he know she is making her move to escape him? Is it written all over her blanched face? Is his thinking only a step behind theirs?

"I don't want to make matters worse," Nafeesa tells Yusuf. "My husband is an unreasonable man. Perhaps if you come later, thirty minutes or so after we leave. Then my husband will see that you are there for your wife—he is an unreasonable man." She takes her gray cardigan from the office chair.

"Then may I have directions to your house," he asks and Nafeesa's stomach clenches.

"I'm terrible with directions," she says. Quickly Baji invents directions to Iffat's imaginary house and they set a time to meet Yusuf there.

"My husband will want to invite Madam in for tea, since she was my teacher."

"So perhaps you should come an hour or so after we leave here, Mohan?" says Baji, but Nafeesa thinks Baji sounds ridiculous. Or maybe not. She cannot tell.

"Yes, I will drive there at some point." He leaves his intentions vague.

Baji glances at Nafeesa, and moves toward the door. There is a small mirror on the wall, and in it Nafeesa sees that the left side of her face is entirely black and blue and the eye is swollen and red. She looks like she's been in a boxing match. She pulls her dupatta across her face and the two women step out into the sunshine. Yusuf shuts the old door behind them, but Nafeesa thinks she hears it creak open again.

***

Once outside the gate, Baji reaches beneath a dark green juniper and pulls out the leather pouch she'd retrieved from the cellar. Then noiselessly she hoists herself onto the fender of Yusuf's truck, reaches inside the hood, and without looking, begins pulling wires loose. She closes the hood soundlessly and stashes wires inside her sleeves. They cross to the other side of the street.

"Keep up, Nafeesa!" Baji hisses over her shoulder. Baji is moving fast for an old woman. Once she gets going, she seems to float above the street. Nafeesa scoots along double-time to dodge the many bicycles and motorbikes traveling in both directions along the road. She adjusts her dupatta to cover the battered side of her face, as Baji repeats the plan. "This is how it will work and the only way it will work, Nafeesa"—she grabs her arm—"so pay attention. There is no time to waste before Yusuf discovers the publisher's email, or that your house does not exist, or that we did not take the bus to Srinagar. This is no game we are playing. Our lives are at stake. Do you understand? We have to take care of each other."

"Yes, Baji, I am listening."

Baji looks her up and down. "We will have to split up, but only briefly. Ten minutes. Do you understand?" She furrows her brow. "You will buy food and water for us. Here's the list." She hands Nafeesa a small paper and some cash. "I know I can exchange some of these stones for supplies at the mountain climbing shop, so I'll get us backpacks, boots, walking sticks, and other things we'll need. We will meet at the Fort, across from that checkpoint. Remember where that is?" Nafeesa points in the right direction. "Very good. Janna will meet us there to drive us out of town and get us past the next checkpoint." Nafeesa nods her understanding. "Now repeat it," instructs Baji.

"I get food and drinks. You get hiking supplies. We meet Janna who takes us to the mountains."

Baji is pleased. She smiles at Nafeesa for the first time since the slap. "I'll meet you at the Fort in ten minutes." She points across the street. "There's the food store. Here's the money. Ten minutes. No longer!" Baji marches off, leading with her chin.

The shopping list is short and it is not long before Nafeesa carries out of the store bottles of water, dried apples, crackers, a brick of yellow cheese and dried mutton. The bag in her hand swings lightly in a regular beat. She can feel the wind on one side of her face and her heart dances again. For a moment, the pain subsides. She turns the corner leading to the Fort and runs smack into Yusuf.

He grabs her arm, and stops her from fleeing, holding her shoulders tightly and bringing his face close to hers—closer than any man has ever come. Her dupatta falls onto her shoulders. She expects him to be angry, but instead he smiles. There is a little dimple in his cheek, a sparkle in his eye. He is so close she can smell his skin. Then he lets go.

"Where are you going in such a hurry, Iffat?" His tone is light-hearted. "And where is Madam Asma?"

Nafeesa's brain is scrambling. How to explain? "I was shopping. Madam went to get a few things. We will meet back at my house."

His friendly smile becomes an ugly one. "So you are not walking together after all?"

"Well, we did for a while, but then we realized, I mean, I realized I needed to get some food—for my husband. For tea." A cloud crosses in front of the sun and casts a shadow. Nafeesa feels the chill.

"Iffat, you realize that Madam is crazy, do you not? You saw what she did to my truck! You are lying! There was no plan for tea. I must find Madam. Tell me exactly where she is." He is yelling.

She tightens her shawl and scans the street for a friendly face. "I don't know, Sir. We are to meet at my house." No one on the street is paying any attention to them. No one stops. This is between a man and a woman and no one has any interest in interfering.

"I went to your house," he says in an ominous tone, "and there was no house where Madam said there would be one—just a vacant lot." Nafeesa is speechless, terrified. He grabs her arm and pulls her close, again. "Enough lies. We will look for her together. Where is she waiting for you?"

Nafeesa focuses on her shoes, praying that someone passing by might hear Yusuf's harsh tone and intervene to help her. She says nothing. With a painful grip on her arm, Yusuf pulls her along the street as bicycles and carts pass them by. Should she lead him away from Baji or say nothing? Will Baji and Janna abandon her when she does not arrive at the appointed time? Her hands are shaking and she cannot think what to do. She can only hope to find help. Perhaps a policewoman? She begins to shout out, "Stop pulling me!" Yusuf pushes her hard against a wall, hurting her hip. He twists the skin on her forearm so that it burns.

"Where are you to meet her? The market? The Fort? The Mosque? Tell me now!" She is too scared to look at him. He shakes her shoulders, panting. She can feel the heat of his breath. Then Nafeesa sees a familiar shape not far away, just across the street. It is Baji! She has squeezed between two buildings and is watching them. She seems frozen in place. Nafeesa cannot move either. Yusuf, too, remains completely still. All three of them are paralyzed in the same moment when three men appear behind Yusuf and call him away from Nafeesa. "Wait here," he demands, then greets the men, putting his arm around one's shoulder. Nafeesa cannot hear what they are saying. When she looks to the area where Baji was watching, she is gone. Yusuf and the men begin to argue. It is heated and violent.

One of the men signals to Nafeesa. "Leave!" he orders, snapping his fingers and pointing at the street. For a moment she hesitates, afraid of them, too. Are they going to hurt Yusuf? "Now!" the man yells at her.

She grabs the plastic bag of groceries and moves in their direction, trying to squeeze between them and the street. Yusuf reaches out his long arm and grabs the dupatta around her neck, and for a second he chokes her and holds her gaze. His rage penetrates her. The men pull his other arm, releasing her and leading Yusuf down the hill in the direction of the mosque.

"Tell her she can never get away from me!" he shouts to Nafeesa over his shoulder. "Tell her I said to remember the cellar!"

***

The sky begins its late afternoon glow while Nafeesa weaves through the crowded market in Akram, running where she can, using her elbows where she must. When she rounds one corner, she runs smack into Baji. Her face is pale and her dim eyes scan the street. She lets Nafeesa take the lead up the hill. Near the checkpoint, under the Fort's sandstone tower, Janna sits in the driver's seat of her bullet-proofed silver Hyundai. She reaches to open the rear door for them, as Baji draws the dupatta across Nafeesa's face and whispers to her.

"Don't let Janna see your bruises and don't say anything about Yusuf stopping you on the street. The less she knows, the better. For her own protection." Baji steps back to let Nafeesa in first.She distracts Janna. "Let's stay away from Shahi Road," she says, "and watch for Mohan's truck."

Soon they are on the edge of Akram. The sun is low but still shines through clusters of clouds. The temperature is dropping. Nafeesa can feel Baji's hip up against her own. By her feet are two bags of supplies. She whispers below the traffic noise. "Didn't you disable his truck when you removed those wires? How could he follow us?"

"It just slowed him, wouldn't stop him. He is a mechanical genius and keeps lots of extra parts around. If he gets away from those men, whoever they are, he'll find a way to get that truck running again. Watch for it through the back window."

Nafeesa rearranges herself and kneels backward on the seat. Who were those men? What will happen when they let Yusuf go? Will he actually follow them into the mountains? The more she thinks about it, the more her bruised face throbs.

At the checkpoint on the western road, Baji takes their IDs and rolls down her window as Janna pulls the Hyundai alongside a young soldier. He peers through his large dark-framed glasses at the vehicle's interior, and Baji hands him two IDs and Nafeesa's passport and visa. He takes a second look at Nafeesa, who holds her dupatta modestly over her face. "The purpose of your visit?" he asks, and Baji begins babbling.

"I am her auntie and she is visiting. We're on our way to the foothills trail. You must know Mohan Ali, my husband—works for the Akram Mountain Shop? I teach at the Girls' Secondary School. You know it? Mohan's little hiking club ran out of food and water—someone was sneaking extras when the others were not watching—you know how some people can be— so we're taking provisions and showing my niece the beauty of Kashmir. In fact, I'm thinking she and I will just stay a bit so we can enjoy the evening sunset together. But our friend here can't decide whether to join us or go back now. Which would be better? We are so confused. What do you think we should do? Hmm?"

It is an old trick—throw a bunch of questions at them, local names and places, distract them with information and ideas, and cover it all over with the innocence of needy women. She flashes the young man her most motherly, teacherly smile.

The soldier raises his voice. "Madam, that is up to you. We just want to know who you are and the purpose of your traveling on this road." There is no female soldier to pat them down and the men do a poor, half-hearted job, neglecting to check the old woman's underpants where she has hidden a small pistol. Then the young man steps back from the car and clicks his heels with a swift salute. Janna pulls the car away from the checkpoint and back onto the dirt road.

"No need to rush, to draw attention," whispers Baji in a staccato beat. "To them we're just stupid women on a food mission."

Fifteen minutes later Baji's eyes cross a sweeping landscape. "Stop! This is the place. I recognize it." She exhales. And speaks softly. "People and politics may change in eighteen years, but mountains and valleys follow geologic time. Here is where we get out."

The area is vacant—north, south, east, west—no people in sight, no vehicles, nothing but Janna's car, the green and gold aspen on the mountain and the dirt road. Janna reaches for a box on the floor. "Now you are on your own," Janna says, handing the box to Baji. "Kashmiri delights. Sweets, so your heart does not forget me.

"My sweet friend, how could I ever forget you? You saved my life."

"We saved one another's."

"Come to Pakistan," Baji pleads, teary. "Meet my brother and my father. Our house is always yours." Baji kisses Janna's cheek through the open car window. She reaches in and wraps around Janna's shoulders a light woolen shawl embroidered with a pattern of black-necked cranes flying. "If you give a shawl to a woman, she is forever your sister," says Baji, quoting a Sindhi saying.

"Forever your sister," Janna vows through her tears and turns to hug Nafeesa.

When Janna drives away to return to Akram, Nafeesa's heart drops. That Toyota was her last safe place. She is afraid, and having difficulty breathing. Now there is only one way out and that is to follow Baji's path. They wave to Janna and unfold their walking sticks. Nafeesa clambers up the hillside toward the forest in the direction Baji points. She stops and turns to see Baji is struggling to climb, so she returns to her side, and they begin their hike toward Pakistan together. They follow the steep, pathless edge of the meadow close to the tree line. Baji leads with Nafeesa close behind carrying the heavier pack. The ground is dry and rocky with thick tufts of low growth. Nafeesa peeks over her shoulder repeatedly, watching for trouble.

"I'm glad to have your strong, young eyes to rely on," Baji says, smiling.

Midway up the hill, Nafeesa tugs on Baji's pack, hissing "Baji!" Rust-colored dust is flying at a distance on the road. A vehicle is coming in their direction from town. It is too far away to tell if it is military or civilian—or, possibly, Yusuf's truck. The two women fall to the ground next to bushy brambles and tall pines, flattening their bodies against the earth, remaining perfectly still. Nafeesa lets out a little yelp of surprise and fear. They watch

Janna's car move toward town. They are breathless, as the two vehicles pass each other in opposite directions. Neither slows and neither stops. Nafeesa can see it is a military SUV. She grabs Baji's hand.

No one notices two women up on the hillside, holding hands and scrambling together toward the cloak of forest, smiling at one another as they run, in a way that, under other circumstances, might have caused them to burst into laughter like young girls racing through a verdant landscape. At the entry into the quivering shadows of golden aspen, Baji takes the lead as Nafeesa keeps watch from behind. Nafeesa knows that now it is up to her whether the two of them survive that night on the mountain together. In the shade of early dusk, they are silent animals. At once Baji becomes younger than she is, and Nafeesa matures, carrying her own share and part of Baji's, too, taking responsibility for both of them, as a young woman should.

Chapter 6

Silent, Slow, Dark

Near the Line of Control between India and Pakistan, 2015

Nafeesa steps into the forest through a long line of cedars. There is a sudden trill of birdsong. It is another world, she thinks with pleasure. Her footing falters in the soft-packed pine needle floor, but she rights herself, inches her way, tree by tree, along the path she cuts with hand clippers as they go. Nafeesa has shed her doubts about Baji, who struggles to stand up straight with the daypack on her back. Although this hike may cause them both to suffer, Nafeesa recognizes she has the advantages of youth, and she is determined not to complain. At their first resting place she unloads some of her auntie's things and carries them in her own pack. Again, she feels the warmth of pleasure in her bloodstream, a softening now directed at her auntie, a form of love. Whether she is looking at crazy Baji or wise Baji, she is her Baji and that is what matters.

Baji promulgated her rules on the mountain: be silent, move slowly, hide in shadows, no signaling, only writing on small notepads they each carry. They remove their boots to lessen the sounds of footfall. Nafeesa cuts branches slowly, deliberately, her clippers lingering in the crotch of the limb until she can disguise the snap of it inside the whooshing wind or the trembling, clacking treetops. They rest as needed—no rushing ahead, no wearing themselves out, only one single step at a time. They will, if necessary, set up a tent, but only if it rains. They will adapt to the darkness and forgo the flashlight, although they pack one anyway. And to Baji's rules, Nafeesa adds a rule of her own. They will stay together no matter what.

In her flat palm, Nafeesa holds a compass, something she has never used before, but it is not difficult. She directs them away from the barbed wires and military towers, keeping the arrow pointing to her right. She continues to clip thin branches that block their way, and uses a hunting knife to cut the thick ones. She takes care to forge their path deep into the woods hidden by brush, staying aware of the forest's edge where soldiers may lurk. Later, when they turn southwest, toward Pakistan, Nafeesa will watch the compass's arrow float in its encased disc, pointing directly at her, as if to say that she is the one, she is true north.

Later, Baji tugs on the back of Nafeesa's coat and points to a small, moon-shadowed clearing. They stop to rest. The temperature drops and the heat of the day vanishes to wherever it goes, but the air is not yet cold. There is a comfortable coolness that will change soon enough. The two sit in a grove of aspen, unpacking their jackets and hats, shaking the canteen to mix the salted tea that they sip. They nibble dried apricots and crackers. Birds shriek and the almost-full moon rises in the east, pale and weak between two patches of clouds. A pop of distant gunfire reminds them exactly where they are. It is hard to believe the area is not a place of peace, that it is wired for war. But it is good, thinks Nafeesa, to be brought back from the reverie of the forest to the reality of the dangers around them. To be lost dreaming in a place like this can be fatal.

As the land rolls south, the hills become steep, and moving downhill takes a special effort. Nafeesa rocks herself backward as she descends and lets the weight of the backpack slow her down. Baji wobbles on the hillside, as if driven to fall forward. The constant braking is hurting her knees. She stops to rub her right knee, then her left. Finally, she sits on the side of the hill and scoots down between the aspens like an itchy dog. She grasps the smaller trunks and holds on as she goes.

Nafeesa waits. Now that the sun has passed them by, the pines silhouette themselves against the sky. How beautiful it all is! While Baji inches along, birds hunt for insects nearby. Five nuthatches–with pastel wings, light blue and gray, with pale coral breasts–dive and swoop, spreading out to tap-tap-tap on the trunks and fallen trees, seeking insects hidden in the dark interiors. Other birds shaped like tiny oil lamps climb upside down on tree trunks with their tails in the air. One suddenly squeaks as it emerges from a hole with a long cicada in its little beak. It flies to a high branch and begins devouring the bug while the others circle in to watch the feast, to nibble a fallen wing, to catch a stray fragment of cicada that might float their way.

Nafeesa checks her watch. They have been hiking for two hours. She estimates they have traveled a kilometer or two at the most. At this rate, it could be days before they cross the border. Suddenly she hears the crack of a branch, the clack of stone on stone as rocks loosen and Baji tumbles down the hill. At first Nafeesa is unable to find her—where is she? The sky is midnight blue and black without a thread of light. Nafeesa can hear her huffing and follows the panting to find her lying crosswise on the hill, her torso lodged against the trunk of a pine. Nafeesa kneels next to Baji, trying to examine her in the dark. She can see nothing. She wonders if she should use a flashlight. Baji must be reading her thoughts. Their hands grasp each other and Baji pulls Nafeesa's head to the ground next to her own. She points to the flashlight in Nafeesa's hand and shakes her head. "Silent, slow, dark," she reminds Nafeesa with a whisper in her ear. "I am hurt. Twisted ankle. Bruised ribs. Can't walk."

"Baji?" Nafeesa whispers, and she responds with a slow deliberate shake of her head—back and forth, back and forth, holding her finger to her bleeding lip, signaling "silent and slow."

"Get help," she says and exhales the words. "Find Beezah."

Nafeesa is shocked. Hiking in this strange way with Baji is one thing, but to leave her behind and go off on her own? That is unthinkable. She sees the searing pain cross Baji's face, and remembers her own fears–of wild animals, of getting lost in the woods, of being discovered by Yusuf, or jailed or killed by the military. And any of those things could happen to Baji whether I am with her or not. But how can I leave her? I do not know where Beezah is, or exactly what she is. Nafeesa begins to weep silently to herself.

Everywhere the forest darkens and the chill of evening settles on the woody floor. The birds are silent. The insects stop their constant chirping. Nafeesa shares her aspirin with Baji and helps her drink from her canteen. Nafeesa speaks not a word, but to the east a moonrise glow offers its dim assistance. She tiptoes around until she finds a flat, rock-free area large enough to pitch the small khaki tent Baji purchased in Akram. She has never pitched a tent before, but she does it. She returns again and again with supplies, spreads the unzipped sleeping bag on the ground inside, and invites Baji to climb in. Baji limps in silence, leaning, wincing, holding her hip.

Nafeesa sits half inside and half outside the tent, rearranging their belongings. What to take? What to leave behind? Water, compass, half the dried fruit and crackers, a little cheese. She lays the remaining food and water where Baji can reach it. She tries not to imagine what this scene might become if she never returns to it, but the images taunt her like a bully. Baji's flesh and the tent torn to pieces by hungry bears or growling wildcats, who sniff the air and claw their way to her. Or a corpse discovered inside the tent, starved–the food gone, the water bottle empty. Baji's ankle swollen to double its normal size, her ribs broken from useless efforts to escape. Or Baji's face with a bullet hole in her forehead, and a charred tent, with her remains inside, collapsed from the heat of a fire set by a raging husband. Nafeesa shakes her head to shake off the images in her mind.

Baji rests on her good side, then reaches toward the wall of the tent, arranging items in the dark. She hands the old donkey trail map to Nafeesa, and pulls a tiny book from her bag and places it on the tent's floor. She places the dripping top of her canteen onto the book and moves her lips praying soundlessly, invoking the Divine. Then Nafeesa recognizes that Baji is doing what she has seen Babba do so many times—prepare water for washing and water for drinking that one offers a guest. Baji is making a shrine. She is calling for help. Indeed, they need the intervention of Allah and any good spirit to watch over them. Nafeesa rests her mind on the altar her auntie has built and she offers her head to the elements. Do what you will with me, Nafeesa prays. But do not let harm come to my Baji.

Baji nudges Nafeesa with the flat of her hand, urging her out and onto the trail. She gestures that there is nothing to worry about, as if she is sending Nafeesa to the market or into the kitchen for a bowl of lentils. Nafeesa leans in and kisses Baji's cheeks and Baji kisses hers.

"I will go for help," whispers Nafeesa.

"*Allah hafiz*," whispers Baji.

***

Outside the tent, Nafeesa turns to zip up the tent slowly, silently in the dark. She pulls one small pack onto her back, checks the compass in her hand and the clippers in her pocket, and steps out on her own. They are not abandoning one another, she tells herself. I am simply going for help and Baji rests, and with time, her injuries will heal. Will I be able to find Beezah or someone else to help? There is no way to know unless I take the first step. The immaculate full moon has risen to a small penetrating hole in the sky. It casts a dim light by which Nafeesa checks the compass again and sees that its arrow points directly at her.

She steps south toward Pakistan.

With that step away from Baji, Nafeesa feels ripped apart–deep and physical, as if blood should be running down her legs, dampening the leaves and needles of the forest floor. The night is silent except for a distant noise—is it a roar? Is it the wind? She hears it to the east and then an identical sound to the west. Not close, but not far either. What is it? Nafeesa tries not to imagine anything except the next step forward. She relies on the stability of trees, reaching out, branch by branch, trunk by trunk. The farther south she goes, the more the forest clears; she has less cover and she no longer needs the clippers. Fresh air against her face is welcome and she keeps her lips together to keep thirst at bay. She has no idea how long it will be before she will find fresh water.

There are so many things Nafeesa tries not to think about—how long will it take to return for Baji and how will she find her again? Then she remembers she still has part of the old scrap of a shawl that her father recovered from the ashes of her grandmother's home. Nafeesa unravels it bit by bit and begins to count her steps. Each small piece of wool she breaks away from the cloth reveals a speck of the rich rosewood and spice shades that once the faded shawl had been. She is grateful the dyes have lost their vibrance and faded to natural, neutral colors. Every fifty steps she ties a small piece of dull thread to a low branch that she hopes will not draw the attention of Yusuf or a soldier or anyone else who might be in the area. The bits of the shawl will mark her path back to Baji. One inhale, and a few steps forward, exhale and another inhale and so on, as Nafeesa counts over and over from one to fifty, fingering the battered shawl, biting off the yarn bit by bit. She has to make it last. She makes a game of guessing which tree ahead will be closest to her count of fifty.

The moon reaches a height to penetrate the tall pines, casting shafts of light here and there. It is a relief to regain vision, but there are unidentifiable noises in the air so she stays in the shadows. There is a call and response pattern that grows louder as if, whatever they are, they are drawing closer. What is it? An animal growling. What? A bear or a lion? What will she do if attacked? Nafeesa has only her clippers in her pocket, a pitiful defense against wild jaws and fangs. Her heartbeat increases. She listens even more intently for the growls, if they are growls, and they come again and again—one from the north, one from the south, but farther away than before. She imagines two bears seeking each other in the dark and feels that she is trapped between them. She catches her breath to calm herself, to gather her senses. She opens her pack to take a drink.

Inside the bag, Nafeesa feels something unfamiliar—heavy, cold metal. She pulls out a pistol. Baji must have pressed it into her pack at the last minute, giving her the gun, leaving herself defenseless. Nafeesa feels sure her auntie must hear the same growls that she is hearing all around her, or other ones. She sits cross-legged, fingering the weapon, feeling its weight. It is loaded—six bullets—and a safety catch is securely closed. She has never fired a gun. Could she? She holds it with two hands the way police do on television, and raises it to her sightline, aiming first at nothing, then focusing her vision squarely on a fallen cedar at twenty paces. She imagines the cedar is a black bear. She keeps her finger steady but imagines squeezing the trigger. She begins to relax. Yes, I can do this if I have to, she thinks. She locks the safety, puts the loaded gun in the pocket of her jacket, pulls apart another bit of yarn and ties it to a spindly pine. She checks the compass and searches again for a way forward.

A loud panting and a clear, undeniable guttural growl stop her. Terrified, her breathing goes out of control as she moves away, closer to the Line of Control than she should, but farther away from the horrifying beast. But its low, throaty breath grows louder and louder. Should she stop moving? They say animals can see you in the dark only if you move. She stays still behind a tree, listening, waiting, her back muscles contracting, breath rising. Waiting. Nothing. Only the wind. The wind? Or is it a wild cat pausing, listening for her movements? To catch her shadow? Why has the growling stopped?

In a patch of moonlight that shines on a high rock to the west, Nafeesa sees something standing still. In her pocket she squeezes her palm around the pistol's handle. She will not take the weapon out, for fear she will use it and draw the military's attention. The Indian army camp is close. Surely there are patrols even closer. It is difficult to grasp what kind of an animal it is—a mountain lion, perhaps—its fur is light-colored and it is not large like a bear. She hides behind a bush for a safer, better look.

Then she sees it clearly—it looks like someone is riding on the back of a lion! When the lion turns its body, Nafeesa sees that its rider is a woman wearing a golden crown. She has seven arms and one of them holds a sword aloft. Unbelievable! But Nafeesa has seen this before! It is Durga! Kali! The one who causes fear to perish, the harbinger of happiness. Nafeesa is overwhelmed with the sight of this being she has pictured in her mind since childhood. But it is no vision; it is only a glimpse, for as quickly as Nafeesa recognizes Durga, she is gone—nowhere in sight. No growling. No throaty groaning. Is her mind playing tricks on her? At the same time, Nafeesa's heart and lungs quit their race, her fear subsides, and moonlight beckons her south.

She takes another step toward Pakistan.

***

As moonlight spreads across the thinning forest, Nafeesa moves at a quicker pace, climbing up and skidding down slope after slope, again counting to fifty, marking the trees as she goes. It becomes almost a dance, a playful, precise routine. As the land stretches into longer slopes, she becomes hopeful she'll come to the river soon, the river that will mark geography with the stamp of nationhood and she will be back in her native land.

Suddenly Nafeesa is starving, ravenous, hungrier than she can remember ever feeling. She thinks it must have been hunger that caused that hallucination of Durga. She has an enormous emptiness inside her, a pain crossing her belly, a sudden exhaustion of energy, something that brings her to an immediate stop, to her knees. With her legs folded under her, she bends forward to rest her torso against her thighs. Hiding behind an outcropping of rock, sitting in the dark shadow of it, she searches in her pack and discovers more crackers, dried fruit and nuts than what she divided between herself and Baji. Nafeesa realizes that Baji packed most of the food for Nafeesa, leaving little for herself. She bites into dried apple pieces, tearing them with her teeth, chewing, chewing, swallowing. I have to stay alert, she thinks, checking her watch. It is two a.m.

The steep path brings her close to the LoC. Silence and stillness are paramount. She waits, bites a tiny piece of sheep cheese that expands in her mouth as she chews–barely moving her jaw. Swallowing is difficult without drinking water, but she is determined to conserve what is left in her canteen at least until she finds more water to drink. The crackers are dry, too, crusty and hard against her teeth, but she takes time to soak each bite with her saliva, to let it soften in her mouth. And her tongue cooperates, miraculously adding moisture where it appeared that none existed, and her taste buds relish the pepper cracker and the tang of the cheese. Once she's had her fill, Nafeesa lies down on a pile of pine needles and sleeps.

When she wakes, it is still dark. It is like being blindfolded from the inside, she thinks, like someone pasted black eye patches over my brain. Nafeesa lifts the pack, which seems heavier than before. She considers leaving the gun behind. But what if she needs it to defend herself from a wild animal, or what if Yusuf has found Baji and is now looking for her? What if the threads she tied as markers lead him directly to her? No, she decides, I'm keeping the gun.

She thinks she hears talking nearby. Soldiers? Ground squirrels? Her imagination? She hikes in a slow uneven tempo to silence her footsteps down and up the next hill, using the compass to guide herself away from the militarized area and deeper into the woods. Hours later she is off-trail but the ground is even and without obstacles. A flash of light sweeps over her and she crouches, on alert like an animal. Military searchlights? Is it the beam of a flashlight in the hand of a soldier on patrol? The moon playing jokes? She begins to wonder which would be worse—to be captured by the Indian military or the Pakistani? At least with Pakistanis she can claim to be lost in her own country. But the gun! If they find it, they will suspect she is an Indian spy, or a threat of some sort, a troublemaker.

The light flashes again on a nearby clearing. Nafeesa freezes. There is a sudden pounding of hooves behind her, and Nafeesa jerks around, expecting to see military khakis. Instead, it is a solitary mule wearing a halter made entirely of snakes, and on its back is the most horrible woman —dark blue body, wild red hair, with a necklace of bloody skulls around her neck. A deep penetrating voice announces herself.

"I am the Queen of Armies. Protector of the Dalai Lama."

Nafeesa catches her breath. She recognizes the figure— Mahakali, the Tibetan daughter of the Himalayas— the one, they say, with power to recognize, by a simple roll of dice, who will live and who will die. Nafeesa wonders if she is dreaming or hallucinating. She is mystified. Again, she blinks and the image dissolves. Now Nafeesa is more awake than if she had slept all night, feeling humbled to have been chosen for the vision. She is ready to face anything, with or without the gun. Fearless, reckless even, and determined to keep going, she asks herself: which is worse, India or Pakistan? Both armies be damned! she decides. India and Pakistan together are no match for Mahakali's powers of protection.

***

The earth turns in the dark of night, and the bright spot of the full moon no longer walks with Nafeesa. There is a faint lavender glow to the east. The landscape expands. Below, a creek rushes away from the melting snowfall to the north, inevitably, she knows, it will intersect the Jhelum River to the west, and from there the Indus, Queen of all Rivers that runs two thousand miles to its final rest in the alluvial fields of Sindh and the Arabian Sea. These drops of water, she thinks, if they survive evaporation, will flow near Babba's house. She rests on the bank of the creek to contemplate the journey of this great water, hearing its rushing sound, feeling it spray against her face. Before she drinks, Nafeesa collects behind her lips what concentrated liquid essence of herself she can muster, and she breathes shallow breaths, holding it until her mouth is full. Then, like a wild goddess herself, she spits out hard into the water all of her intentions. *If the rest of her does not succeed in this mission, at least this much of me will return to Babba before he dies. Oh, tell him to wait,* she prays, *my river of life. I am bringing Baji back home to him. Tell him not to die.*

"Kulraj Singh is not dying yet." A voice booms the words from afar and on the other side of the stream. "He knows you are coming. He will wait, Nafeesa." Another strange creature—this one is a female human with no lion, no mule—just high-topped boots, and unforgettable eyes—one piercing blue, the other soft brown. A mane of gray dreadlocks hangs down her back, pulled away from her face, her face lined and wrinkled as if only lines created by laughter have been permitted to emboss themselves in her flesh, her flesh tight and close to her bones, her bones aligned as straight as the bones of a young woman and a long, ropy neck, a neck around which layers of prayer beads lie against her shirt, her shirt a dull dirty orange belted above her trousers, her trousers, men's trousers.

The vision rushes down the hill to the riverbank and holds her inviting arms open. Nafeesa skips from rock to rock effortlessly, and is drawn into the woman's warm embrace, cushioned by her body of protection. "Madam, are you a goddess?" Nafeesa asks. When the woman smiles, then Nafeesa knows the truth and she laughs out loud. "Or are you Madam Beezah?"

"Yes," she says to both possibilities. Her hard, warm body wraps around

Nafeesa, not letting her go.

"Please," begs Nafeesa, pushing back gently. "We must go back for Baji." Beezah surveys the landscape while Nafeesa describes the escape from Akram, Baji's accident, the decision to separate, her hiking alone all night. Nafeesa squats, filling her canteen.

"It is better to travel at night. Too many humans causing trouble in the daytime," Beezah comments, then asks directly— "This husband of hers, Yusuf. I remember him. You believe he has followed you?"

"Perhaps, perhaps not. The last time I saw Yusuf, some men were detaining him. If he did follow us, he was definitely delayed."

Beezah's strange eyes narrow. "We both need rest for what is ahead. My house is too far, so we will move deeper into the valley to the west and rest there until nightfall. Then we will find Baji and bring her back to Kotha to recover at my home. Follow me." With her walking stick in hand, she climbs, one slow step at a time.

Nafeesa cannot not shake the image Yusuf created in his story–of the naked Beezah circling the cedar, part crone, part old beast. She imagined a furry beast with sharp teeth, like something gory and green in a child's monster book, not like the real Beezah. She has so many questions, and feels shy about asking, but is desperate to know what is real and what is not. "I don't know how to ask you this, Madam, but do you sometimes take off your clothes to enter the forest?" When she hears her own words, she realizes how silly she sounds. Beezah faces her with a quizzical look. "I apologize," Nafeesa says, but Beezah is amused.

"No, continue," she commands.

"Yusuf wrote in a story that years ago when you helped them to cross over, you stripped naked and circled a tree several times in preparation to enter the forest. I am sorry. It's just that I'm curious about that. I shouldn't have asked."

"Naked?" Beezah laughs. "Me? Never. I am a modest woman. I don't do that for anybody, little girl." She laughs again. "Somebody has been making up stories to entertain you." Nafeesa blushes.

They continue their uphill climb. Hours later they rest in a clearing while the sun kisses the dew and everything glistens with life. "See how the sun dries the earth, offers its light, warms its cold places?" Beezah asks. Nafeesa nods. "The poet, Hafiz says that, unlike humans, the sun never says to the earth, 'You owe me.'" She cackles and the spaces in her mouth where teeth had once been become jetways of saliva. "Now does it?" she cries and her spittle lands on Nafeesa's face, but Beezah does not apologize. There is no apology about Beezah. No explanation. No defenses. She wipes her mouth on her sleeve.

Nafeesa finds herself with nothing to say. All she wants to do is eat and listen. Beezah leans back to pour fresh goat's milk from her canteen into her mouth. Nafeesa craves a taste. "And I brought along a second canteen," Beezah smiles, passing it to her. "Just in case." Nafeesa raises her brow. "I had a hunch I'd find someone who needed help today." Beezah also has hard eggs and Nafeesa eats two. Her bread is home baked and fresh. Beezah is excited by the few dried apricots Nafeesa shares with her.

"What happened to your face?" she asks.

Nafeesa has forgotten about the bruise from Baji's slap. "Ran into a tree," she lies.

Beezah sits cross-legged, meditating, her prayer beads clicking through her fingers. She is close enough that Nafeesa is comforted that she is there, but far enough that Nafeesa can cultivate her own thoughts. She wonders how Beezah found her, how she knew she and Baji were coming. And how did she know Nafeesa's name?

These questions buzz for a while, but soon other thoughts fly by. How far she has come from her disputes with her father to this mountain glade on the border of her country! She thinks that her life once seemed like a long train ride in a flat, uninteresting country, but now the terrain suddenly shifted, the train jumped the track, a bridge collapsed, and the car she'd been riding in now dangles above a river. Would it fall into the defeat below? Now everything is at stake—not just her future and her reconciliation with the past. Her soul is at stake.

When afternoon shadows start to spread and birds sing and swoop and insects silence to bewilder those hungry beaks, Beezah moves close to Nafeesa, her trousers touching Nafeesa's shalwar. Then Nafeesa hears the bear again.

"Hear that?" she whispers and Beezah growls back, imitating the sound perfectly. "Could it be a moon bear?" Nafeesa asks and Beezah roars.

"Cowbird," she snorts. "Sounds like a cow—unless you think it's a bear, that is." She slaps her leg. "In either case it's just an ordinary bird."

Nafeesa giggles at herself. She wants to tell Beezah about her vision of Durga. "I had a vision last night," she says. "It was when I was so afraid of those birds that I imagined were bears. Durga was riding sidesaddle on the back of a mountain lion."

"Really? A mountain lion!"

"Yes, she had a gold crown on and lots of jewels, and when I saw her, immediately, inside, I became unafraid. Oh, she was quite young and beautiful." Nafeesa stops, aware she's pairing the word young with beautiful, the way everyone does. In a glance she sees Beezah's blue eye wink. "It was you!" Nafeesa says. "You were Durga up on that rock!"

But Beezah just chuckles, holding Nafeesa's face, pulling it close to her own. The smell of rotting cheese on her breath is overwhelming, but Nafeesa braves the stench. "Now does this old face look like young and beautiful Durga? Huh?"

What can Nafeesa say? In truth, in some way that she cannot explain, Beezah's old face does look like young and beautiful Durga. Nafeesa says nothing.

"No," Beezah says "I have no powers like that. I'm just Beezah being Beezah all day long."

But Nafeesa is not so sure. Who was that Durga then, and that Mahakali on her mule, appearing for only a moment, and disappearing before her eyes?

"And when I was afraid of the soldiers finding me, another goddess appeared," she says. "She rode a white mule and had rings on her fingers—lots of arms, snakes, peacock feathers. From her mule hung a pair of dice."

"Sounds like you had a visit from Mahakali, the protector," says Beezah. "Very auspicious."

"Yes, just her presence renewed me. I felt ready to go on. It was like magic."

"Magic? I guess you could call it that." Beezah reaches behind her and pulls out a live, squirming green snake. "You mean she had dice hanging from something like this?"

Nafeesa's mouth gapes open and she pulls away.

"Harmless," says Beezah, "It's harmless. But you are the one who must roll the dice to know who lives and who dies. Mahakali's power is not mine. You are the one who saw her. Durga's power is not mine. No one owns that power. It is un-ownable."

Later, when the planet turns to disclose its diamond in the sky, the almost-full moon has waned a bit since the auspicious night of Durga and Mahakali. By its crooked, cockeyed light, they follow the trail looking for pieces of the old shawl. Nafeesa hunts low to the ground, wondering, was it here or was it there that the shawl surrendered its last thread, died as a shawl and became something else—a torn mass of fiber? Was it here or there that I ran out of thread from the shawl? I should find the marked path just beyond that point. She recalls it was on the other side of the stream feeding the Jhelum River, so she races ahead of Beezah after they cross over and begins scanning the bushes for a path.

"Is this what you're looking for?" asks Beezah, pointing to a bright piece of magenta string shining in a slant of moonlight. "Or this one?" and she reaches for a bush tied with a knot the color of a vibrant tangerine.

Nafeesa is confused. Yes, these are the pieces of the shawl she left to mark the trail back to Baji. But no, they cannot be the same ones, as they are alive with color, not at all like the dingy tatters she left along the trail. She shrugs and sighs. No longer is she questioning the mysteries that seem to arise from the dark when Beezah is around.

"Yes," she says, smiling. "Those are the ones I tore from the shawl of midnight."

The two women weave along the colorful path, silent and calm until, hours later, in a halo of moonlight they see the little tent. Nafeesa unzips it without a sound.

Inside sits a shadow of Baji before her little shrine, with its dried-up flower, its thimble of water, its three smooth rocks piled one on the other. A broad smile crosses her face when she recognizes Beezah. "I've been waiting for you," Baji whispers to them, putting her finger to her lips, reminding them to be silent and still.

Baji stretches her back and lets them pull her out of the tent. While Nafeesa stirs the dirt to leave no trace, Beezah massages Baji's muscles. Then they sip water and nibble chapati. Baji climbs on Nafeesa's back, and Beezah fashions a kind of sling out of the tent to carry it on her hip. Together the pack of three hike into the wild, slowly, little by little, step by step; then they rest, then hike some more, then eat, then hike, step by silent step. They stay silent, still, and dark. In the morning Beezah's hut is visible in the hills above Kotha. Soon they will celebrate Nafeesa's one rule: Stay together no matter what.

*** *

Beezah's hounds come running when they hear the three women tramping on the trail, and the goats and sheep begin their *maa-aa* and their *baa-aa*.

Beezah goes to them, scratching their floppy ears, calling each goat by name, dropping her pack to unlatch the pen so the sheep can race out to graze. The feeding troughs are empty. They have not eaten in two days.

Inside, Beezah sets sticks in the firepit while Baji eases herself down into a chair, groaning with relief. Nafeesa pumps water for Baji to take more aspirin tablets that Beezah hands her from her medicine bag. She wraps Baji's ankle with muslin and Beezah checks her work. Even though they are free to talk now, they do not break their wild, silent spell. Baji whispers please and thank you, but otherwise the only sounds are the cracking of sticks across Beezah's thigh, the thud of stuffed pillows tossed onto the rug, and the familiar hum of one another's breathing. Nafeesa's face has stopped hurting and she wonders if the swelling and bruising have subsided. She explores, but there is not a mirror to be found.

Baji is grinning her biggest grin. "Beezah, years ago you predicted that elephants and snow leopards would accompany the Queens of Heaven to open the gates to this reunion. But I didn't see any elephants or snow leopards. Did you?"

Beezah closes her eyes. "Answer her, Nafeesa," she says. "Did you see elephants or snow leopards? Or what did you see?"

"No elephants or snow leopards. Just a mountain lion and a mule, Madam," Nafeesa replies and they all burst out laughing. "And a snake," she adds, cranking up the hilarity.

"And the Queens of Heaven?" asks Baji, ready to giggle. "Did you see them, too?"

"I saw a blue-skinned, red-haired woman with a necklace of skulls ..."

"Ah," says Baji, lifting her eyebrows. "And what else?"

"A woman wearing a golden crown, holding a sword, riding a mountain lion sidesaddle." They are silent as Nafeesa finishes her description. "Durga," she says, "definitely Durga, but are those two the Queens of Heaven?"

Beezah steps up. "Well, through you, they opened the gate for Baji and me to be reunited," she says. "And for that, we thank you—and them."

Such strange talk is becoming natural for Nafeesa. Now her heart is open to the strange visions, maybe opened by those visions. But she worries still about their safety and she turns to Beezah. "I wonder if Yusuf might have followed us here. Are we safe from him now?"

"If he does, he will find something horrible, truly terrible, on the trail."

"What?" she asks, breathless, and Beezah smiles her practically toothless grin.

"His own mind!" she answers, slapping her thigh, laughing at her own wit.

But Nafeesa is not joking. "Baji, are you worried that Yusuf can find us?"

Baji reassures her. "Nafeesa, Yusuf has mastered the Himalayas by day, but the fact is, he is afraid of the dark—wild animal nightmares haunt him still. Cries like a baby, poor thing. If he did follow us, he surely has turned back by now."

She reaches out and takes Nafeesa's hand into her own, cupped and chapped and clinging. "You are wondrous, Nafeesa," she says. "Your courage and competence and devotion served all three of us. I see Meena in you. You are truly your mother's daughter. I love you so much." Nafeesa blushes from the bold expressions of love and warmth of Baji's words, and she is filled with satisfaction, power, and love. It is a feeling she cannot retain—the moment is almost too intimate for her. Something old squirms inside, then it too passes on.

"And Beezah loves everybody, so watch out, because it's a ferocious love." Beezah pushes herself up from the chair, returns to the wood pile. "We will rest here until Baji can walk comfortably again," says Beezah. "Yusuf won't find us. The military is not involved. The police are not looking for Baji. And we are not hungry, cold or lost."

Baji is relaxed and smiling. "In God's game, I've been found. Don't you feel it, Nafeesa? How we are each uniquely ourselves, but also part of it all. Do you feel it?"

But Nafeesa cannot respond. Something else is tapping at the door of her mind. "Babba," she says. "I feel the love of Babba glowing in me. He is the one who pointed me in this direction, and made it possible for me to come here. I came to bring you back to him." She kneels in front of Baji's chair and Beezah stops rummaging through the woodpile. "Baji, Babba is waiting for you. We should not stay here too long."

"He may already know we are on our way," says Baji. "He always seemed to know what was in my mind before I even said it. He used to say that he does not read my mind, but that sometimes he and I share the mind of God."

"Ah," says Beezah, leaning her hand on the stump of pine she uses for a table, savoring the words, "Sharing the mind of God. It is the way Lalla speaks to us: *The Lord has spread the subtle net of Himself across the world. See how He gets under your skin, inside your bones.*"

"I often feel Babba nearby," Baji continues. "I never doubt he is as close to me as the marrow inside my bones. Because he is, actually, isn't he physically in my DNA? And, Nafeesa, isn't he in yours?"

Nafeesa wants to respond how she now realizes she is a thread in the net of this family, and the family is a thread in the net of these people, and these people are a thread in the net of this place that they share on the spinning earth. Her realization is momentary, only a glimpse, the tip of a bird's wing, something subtle along the edge of her vision. She wants to respond to Baji's question, but what to say? It's a net? It's the smallest thing in the universe cut in half again?

Nafeesa's mind taps to a distant tune and her heartbeat quickens. She hears the hum of the breath in her body. Her spine extends, her hips rotate, and her shoulders move down her back to hold her heart in place. She rises from the floor, as Beezah rattles the edge of a tambourine against her leg and Baji snaps her fingers. Nafeesa sings a song. In her mind she is singing with Nanaa.

Now you must take a new kind of dance step,
A step into your own life as a woman.
And what kind of dance will that be, Nafeesa?
What kind of dance will it be?

Her wrists and forearms begin to spiral up into the air, and her hips shake in a wild movement that rumbles down to the soles of her feet, bones that pound the rug on the floor that lies over the remnants of death that are buried in the particles of clay underneath, where the wings of insects are becoming the dried molecules of birds, pine needles, the spray of the rivers and the hair of lions, all the elements of what they have walked through to reach that glorious hut, that container of her dance. The skin of a living drum resounds as her body twirls, faster and faster. Beezah's hut seems to expand as she spins, scarf in her hands, pants billowing as if a wind were rising from below. Nafeesa trusts it completely, this swirling, her arms embracing the air, her feet blessing the floor, her ears awake to the clapping of the hard hands of her auntie. She closes her eyes to spin and there is nothing else but That. Nafeesa dances as if entirely naked, sacred and alive. At the doorway is the familiar back of a woman, and when she turns around, Nafeesa sees that the face of the woman is her own. The mask of herself drops into her soul. She cries out, "I am Nafeesa!"

Then the tambourine slows, the clapping softens, sweat drips down her body and cools her skin. Nafeesa drops to the floor with her eyes closed. She curls up, her forehead on the floor, her knees folded under, her arms close into her sides, and her hands tucked into the pocket of her center.

Beezah speaks softly. "It is the dance of life," she says. "Now, like Lalla, naked you begin to roam. You begin to live in your soul. Then dancing, searching, roaming, is what you do. The mind reflects the world like a magic mirror."

"But where did my dance come from?" Nafeesa asks.

"Where does a sneeze come from?" asks Beezah. "Or a yawn?"

Nafeesa shakes her head. "I don't know."

"Exactly!" Baji responds. "I remember when Yusuf and I were here and we had an experience like this. Yusuf said that God was playing hide and seek with us. Remember, Beezah?" Beezah tilts her head and squints, playing, posing, waiting for Baji to say it. "And you said that God doesn't play hide and seek. That God *is* hide and seek! I never forgot that."

Nafeesa repeats it over and over under her breath like a mantra. *God is hide and seek. God is hide and seek.* "Those words are all that is left from the dance, all that is left for me to hold onto, but I can't hold onto them. They are words, spoken and then gone." She looks around the hut and focuses on Beezah. "Where do they go?"

"Do not search for God here or there. Search inside instead. Lalla says we are tied by a love-cord to this crazy world, and so we are, we truly are. If you search in this world, it is like pouring water into a cup of unbaked clay."

Baji looks at Nafeesa with strange eyes. "What is it, Baji?"

"You look different, Nafeesa," she says, hesitating. "Not exactly like you, or even like your mother. You look like . . . my mother. You look like your grandmother, the first Nafeesa!"

"Now I am Nafeesa," she says, glowing with a peace she has never known. "At last my grief has found a place to go. I will no longer seek the phantoms of my grandmothers, or my mother. I am no longer a baby without a mother, a girl without a grandmother or a niece without aunties," she says, realizing for the first time that the blood of her foremothers, the blood of her forefathers, runs through her veins as surely as the blood of her own womb bleeds with the moon. She has nothing to prove to anyone. She has only this life, and her ordinary and mysterious part in it.

Just then, outside the hut, the women hear a voice calling. "Nafeesa!

Nafeesa!" she calls out. It is Faisah! When Nafeesa opens the door, before her stand her two goddesses, Faisah and Lia, and an older woman. It seems to Nafeesa that Faisah and Lia have found a Beezah of their very own.

***

Rahima Mai pushes through the open door and into the hard embrace of her Auntie Beezah. Baji limps forward, leaning on Nafeesa's arm, to greet Rahima Mai, while Faisah and Lia wait their hugging turns. The six women try to fit inside, but the tiny house cannot contain the size of their reunion, so they carry their afternoon party outside.

Baji reclines on the string bed they drag from the hut, and the others sit, kneel, or squat on tree stumps when Faisah has rolled the heavy stumps close to the one wooden chair. "Here, have some rump cushions." Beezah tosses an armful of small pads and Nafeesa catches one to elevate Baji's foot, while Rahima Mai examines it. Lia places a pillow underneath herself, kneeling back on a blanket she has folded on the ground.

Rahima Mai examines Nafeesa's face. "Not too bad. A little bruised and swollen. Does it hurt?" Nafeesa shrugs. "Then nothing's broken." Rahima Mai turns to Beezah. "I don't suppose you have a bucket of ice in your freezer, have you, Auntie?" Beezah is stone-faced, and then the two burst out laughing at the idea of having the luxury of a bucket of ice in a freezer. Giggling is the primary way that Beezah and Rahima Mai communicate, and they alone have the backstory to their many inside jokes. But no one minds. Their joy is contagious—a reunion of relatives, a return to homeland, a pilgrimage to Kulraj Singh, a journey near completion, a coming of age. Rahima Mai sheds a few tears into the cup of goat's milk Beezah extracts from the nearby nanny. Faisah sits with Baji as they begin to fit eighteen years into a thimble of time. Together they relax with a shared understanding that each has come from her own unique distance and is now exactly where she belongs.

Beezah drapes a yellow print cloth over a pine stump for an outdoor table. Lia and Nafeesa pump water for rice, chop onions and carrots, boil water for tea, slice cheese, and Faisah picks apples for a baked dessert, mixing sugar, ghee, and barley flour in a cracked ceramic bowl. Then Beezah shows them how to prepare Himalayan apple pie.

"Old Tibetan recipe," she claims, "secret teaching found hidden in a wall." She laughs at her joke that nobody else understands. Beezah and Rahima Mai knead the flour and press out two circles of dough, filling one with the chopped apples and sugar mix, and laying the second one on top. They crimp the edges together and fry the entire dumpling in oil. They slide it onto a large platter, sprinkle it with chocolate powder, and while it steams and the chocolate is melting, they slice the pie into seven wedges and place the entire plate on the stump table. Beezah takes a piece to the outside of their circle and tosses it on the trail. "To feed the hungry ghosts," she says, and no one questions it. They eat with their hands, all from the same plate, leaning their faces over it, slurping bits of apple and crust, gobs dropping to the ground, dogs grabbing whatever falls their way, the women sucking their fingers, wiping their glazed lips with the backs of their hands, talking and eating and laughing together. Their pleasure is larger than that pie, than any pie.

"Hard to say which is sweeter—this pie or this moment," Baji says, inhaling the aroma, burying her nose in a slab of golden pie crust. She reaches over to pat Rahima Mai's sticky hand, then Beezah's, and they each in turn pat the others' while grains of sugar lodge in their teeth and under their fingernails.

Rahima Mai wiggles the pointing finger of one hand, holding a fistful of warm apple filling with the other. "You know, Nafeesa," she says in her most officious voice, "your Baji was not a good prisoner. Rather incorrigible, in fact. Day after day, when she was supposed to be working in my office, all she did was talk. Talk. Talk. Talk."

"And you loved it," Baji retorts. "'More stories,' you would say. 'More stories. More stories.'" She grabs Rahima Mai's wrists and forces the pie filling into her old friend's mouth. "Remember the curries you would bring from home?"

Rahima Mai nods, dripping apples from her mouth, panting from the hot, sugary dessert, gulping goat's milk from a clay cup. They wait for her to swallow and then Beezah uncorks a bottle marked *Apple Brandy*. "Don't drink much. It's a special recipe for special occasions." She pours a tall cup to the brim with thick, golden liquid and passes it around. Nafeesa wonders, since it's alcohol, and forbidden, if Baji and Auntie Faisah will drink it. They do. Everyone sips to her heart's content, and Beezah refills the clay cup.

When it is her turn, Faisah passes on the brandy refill. "I hate to bring it up, Baji, but can we talk a little business?" She looks around for permission.

"Yes, of course," Baji says, licking her fingers.

Lia throws a knowing glance in Nafeesa's direction and Nafeesa grins, holding back her index finger with her hand, mimicking Lia mimicking Faisah. They all give Faisah their complete attention.

"Yusuf's story says you died, Baji. We managed to get a government death certificate to prove it."

"I'd love to see that—proof that the old me has died." She wipes her fingers and takes the envelope Lia passes to her. Baji reviews it; Faisah continues.

"So tomorrow—if you are well enough for us to leave tomorrow," Faisah explains, "or whenever we agree to leave—I will send the certificate to lawyer Chaudry in Islamabad. He will file it, with a copy to the prosecutor, too. It is how these things are done. We can expect a dismissal of the case and quashing of the arrest warrant as a matter of course—perhaps in a matter of days. Then you'll be free to stay in Pakistan, but you can keep your Indian identity as Asma Mohan, I guess.

"Absolutely not!" Baji protests vehemently, definitely, passionately.

They all look stunned. "I am not running away any more. How can I continue my work if I am not myself? I am who I am and I will face the consequences. Disappearing, subterfuge, hiding, and camouflage—that was all Yusuf. It was not my way, and for me it became a trap, almost a fatal trap."

"You had to hide," Rahima Mai reminds her. "The court's verdict was about to be rendered when you escaped. We expected it would not go well. Have you forgotten?"

"No. But we'll never know what the verdict might have been—we did have a valid defense, you know. I might have been acquitted, or I might have been convicted and allowed to serve a prison term. By now I would be free."

"The sentence might have been worse than prison," Lia reminds her. Unconsciously she is squeezing her own neck as she speaks. Baji might have been hanged.

"True. And that fear of my execution is what drove me to Yusuf, to these mountains, to Beezah, to Kashmir and to my life there, and even back here now with all of you. Actions have their effects, do they not? One thing leads to another, moment by moment. It is my life that has brought me right to this day with a heart full of gratitude for each of you, especially Nafeesa who saved my life." She reaches Nafeesa's hand to pass to her the pleasure of knowing she is cherished. "Really," Baji laughs. "When has one woman needed so much saving?"

"One thing's certain," Lia says, dipping her fingers into cloudy water in a blue bowl where sticky sugar is dissolving, "if you appear publicly as yourself, proving Yusuf is falsely claiming your death, he will never work as a journalist again. He will lose any credibility he might have."

"I hadn't considered that," says Baji, remembering the love she and Yusuf once shared. She would do nothing to harm his reputation as a writer.

"So what are you saying, Baji?" Beezah asks. "Tell us what you want to do. We are ready for anything." She looks around for the light of confirmation. "Right?"

"Right!" Nafeesa and Lia sing out in unison.

But Auntie Faisah hesitates. She has been listening, trying to accept her sister's decision. "What is your plan, Baji?" she asks in a calm but distant voice.

"We continue the way that Nafeesa and I made it through the mountains, taking one step at a time, with our intention foremost, even when we are in the dark. Even when we know nothing, we are not afraid of the dark."

"Fine, but what is the plan?" Faisah repeats. "The plan?" She is irritated by the irrational tone the conversation is taking.

Baji speaks to her lovingly. "Faisah, you were by my side on every day of the trial and in my heart every day since. And still, you are fighting for me. What is the plan? We do what is most important. We go home and simply be with Abbu. Let him respond to the tenderness we will wrap him in. Listen and sing to him. Feed him and touch his body. Surround him with love, day and night."

"What about the arrest warrant?"

"I will leave that to you, Counselor. Call or write whomever you need to, but say that I am willing to face whatever consequences may come. If it means turning myself in, try to delay it as long as possible... at least until Abbu is taken."

They pass the brandy, sipping from the shared cup in silence now. Perhaps Nafeesa is a little drunk when she speaks. "Whatever we do, we are ready to move, and we are in this together." They all nod. She speaks for everyone.

In the morning, when Nafeesa, Baji, Faisah and Lia board the Muzzafarabad bus, they can feel the fabric of togetherness tearing apart. Still, their pain in leaving Beezah and Rahima Mai is lessened by the obvious delight the two take in each other and the reassurance that Rahima Mai will be safe hiding in Kotha.

***

From the bus window, drops of early rain shimmer on a distant patch of pines across a canyon. Above the tree line is one pine so tall and perfect its branches seem to spout like fountains. Closer to the road, a row of cedars with thick trunks stands firm. Above, the sky clears, becoming a perfect blue. Two hawks dance in the sky, free to cross any borders they like.

Baji sits next to Nafeesa in an aisle seat so she can prop up her ankle on a soft backpack. "Happy as I am to be going home, I have to admit that part of me wants to stay with Beezah and Rahima Mai. I feel impatient with all the noise on this bus—the chatting, babies crying, plastic bags rattling, the groan of gears shifting." Nafeesa squeezes her hand. She understands. There was something back there in the silence and stillness that she, too, wants to hold forever.

"Baji, how is your body feeling?" she asks.

"Truthfully, Nafeesa, my ribs are aching and stiff and the skin of my ankle cannot possibly stretch any more from the swelling. Still, I am grateful to be alive today to suffer these black and blue ribs, to feel in my spine each pothole on this mountain road." She pauses. "You know, when you were born, I was in prison and not able to hold you, or be with Meena when she passed away. Now *that* was suffering. This...puuh...this is only pain." Baji sighs. "On the other hand," she says, as she shifts position to take weight off her ribs, "it is a relief to be away from Yusuf. He has been living inside a fantasy. I worry how he will survive without me to support his dream of being the next Hemingway, the next Rushdie. Maybe he should thank me. Maybe now he will wake up to who and what he really is." Then Baji covers her head, leans against Nafeesa's shoulder, and closes her eyes.

Later it becomes difficult to take a deep breath inside the bus, in the stuffy stench of feet and armpits, spicy food and diesel fuel. Air conditioning adds a musty something to the air that tickles throats, and provides little ventilation. Across the aisle Lia slides a window slightly open and passes Nafeesa a napkin with a cold potato inside, then a plastic bottle of spiced tea that Beezah prepared for them. Nafeesa drinks the tea. She thinks about the sunny, half-drunken afternoon in the hills above Kotha, the stories they told—of escapes and goddesses, chance meetings and broken laws, hiding out and seeking truth. It was a birthday of sorts, she thinks, imagining the day her little life slipped out the end of Meena's.

In Muzzafarabad, Nafeesa helps Baji off the bus and Lia hurries ahead to find the toilets and benches for them in the depot waiting area. Later they will board another bus for Lahore to travel south, past Islamabad and past Gujrat, where Faisah will call Amir. The plan is for him to meet them at the Lahore depot and drive them to Nankana Sahib. With local stops, the entire trip will take ten hours.

Faisah searches for a spot to charge her mobile phone to call the lawyer Mumtaz Chaudry. There is an area of the depot with a bright green and white sign in Urdu where someone has printed, in English, "First Class Elite Important Business Section." Faisah hands some crumpled rupees to the matron and signals to the others. Nafeesa rushes to sit next to her.

"*Allahu akbar!*" Faisah shouts. "I'm getting a signal! The phone is work-ing! I'm calling Mumtaz Chaudry."

"Yes, I know, Auntie. Please let me listen in."

"Not appropriate," Faisah starts to say, but Nafeesa gives Faisah the double-whammy—both her sincere *namaste* hand gesture and her pleading puppy eyes. Faisah concedes. "Well, since there are no other first class elite important people in the section to overhear the conversation, maybe you can listen in."

"Faisah! Faisah!" Chaudry repeats through the squawking speaker,

"You're back in Pakistan!" Nafeesa can hear a kind of devotion in his voice. He missed her that much? "Just a moment," he says. "I must gather my papers."

Faisah explains the situation to Nafeesa. "Years ago, Tazi and I—he abhors being called Tazi, so, of course, I call him only that," she chuckles— "we collaborated on human rights cases. One lawsuit freed bonded laborers in the Malakwal area. It was difficult to convince witnesses to testify against landlords—the Ahmeds—they controlled everything—jobs, banks, politicians, personal safety—but we were good at it. Those were the good ole days." They hear his voice again.

"My condolences on the loss of Baji," Chaudry says formally through the speaker. "What a loss to your family, to Pakistan, to the entire world."

"Thanks, Tazi, but, guess what! Baji is not dead. That was only a rumor."

"What?" he squeaks. "*The Convoy* is a reliable publication. Everyone in our circle is talking about it. You were going to fax me a death certificate. Remember?"

"Well, I am with Baji now and she has a request. Since jurisdiction resides with the Shariah judges, she wants you to ask the prosecutor and the judge to dismiss the old criminal case against her. And to grant blanket immunity from any escape charges, of course. She's willing to turn herself in, if necessary."

"But Fai–*sah*," Chaudry objects, drawing out the sound of her name.

"Against my advice, too, but she's the client and is quite firm about it. Doesn't want to hide or be on the run any more, and she says she is willing to come forward and take the consequences."

"I'll see what I can do," Chaudry says, not sounding hopeful. "And please do not tell me where you are or anything else right now—so I can keep it clean with the court. This is tricky business."

"I understand. Just keep me informed what is happening at each and every turn along the way." She lowers her voice. "I cannot tell you where we will be, but please do everything to delay her appearance. We have something most important to do."

"I promise to call. And, Faisah, I am so glad Baji is alive. But let me go so I can work on this." He hesitates. "Oh, and come to the demonstration in Islamabad next week at the Faisal Mosque. We are organizing it now to protest the firebombing of an Ahmadi leader in Faisal Town some months ago. Two people died. You should come. The old gang will be there. In fact, you should speak. It would really rouse the crowd to see you again."

Nafeesa's eyes widen as she realizes that Chaudry is talking about the firebombing of her house in Lahore! There will be a protest of the murder of her Nanaa, and her great-grandfather! What would her father say about it? She knows then that she really does miss her father.

"It's hard for me to face the Faisal Mosque, Tazi. The last time I was there ...." Her voice trails off, as she recalls Meena's body collapsing onto her own, her blood spreading all over her and the speakers' platform.

"I understand, of course," Chaudry says. "So sorry. Maybe just as well. They expect a large counter-demonstration. It is possible the event will be banned."

"I'll think about it," she says.

"One more thing, Faisah,"

"Yes?"

"Call me Tazi again!" he begs.

They all laugh. Nafeesa loves listening to her auntie being so playful with her friend.

"*Shukriah*, Tazi Tazi Tazi. And Lia sends her love, too, Tazi Tazi Tazi."

They board the bus at four o'clock when the afternoon is reluctant to release the sky into its evening glow. Baji sleeps. Lia reads. Nafeesa's eyes wander from the backs of their heads to her Auntie Faisah, sitting next to her with her one eye glued to the landscape out the window. Nafeesa thinks about Yusuf's story. It is as if they are rolling backward through its pages, reversing the journey that he and Baji took— along the canyon road with the high, rough rimrock where the cliffs narrow and almost kiss across the canyon divide, past the brown rectangles of crops, fig trees and orchards, small birds nearby, large ones at a distance, the old British fort crumbling on the other side of the Jhelum, their friendly old river. The foothills are steep but the bus descends smoothly. On the Expressway, the bus picks up speed, the road darkens as night arrives. They whip past signs to Murree, the resort town where once an old Nissan was doused with kerosene and set alight. Near Pindi, Faisah's phone pings. It is Mumtaz Chaudry. It is a short call and when she hangs up, Faisah chortles soundlessly.

"What is it, Auntie? What did he say?" Obviously good news or something humorous. She teases and tickles her, but Faisah will not give it up no matter how much Nafeesa begs, no matter how many namastes and puppy eyes she throws her way.

"We'll be in Lahore soon," she whispers. "I'll save the Tazi story for everyone to hear on the drive to Nankana Sahib with Amir. I am dying to wrap my arms around my little brother, to feel the sweetness of him all around me. We will wait so he can hear the news with us."

And soon, there he is—Amir, so tall, standing at the practically empty depot with his one hand raised, as if they couldn't see him there. He runs to Baji, the mother he remembers best, but Faisah pushes ahead and wraps herself around him, while at the same time he pulls away from her, drawn to the sight of his Baji limping down the steps. Faisah will not let him go, so Amir more or less drags her with him toward the bus, and reaches his arms out in Baji's direction. Enormous, unashamed tears form in his eyes. Baji's face beams. She opens her arms, struggling to keep her balance as he comes close. At last, Faisah lets him go and he moves into Baji's embrace. She is crying. He weeps too, but stands there, letting her kiss his face over and over. Everyone is in tears at the sight of their obvious longing—like mother and son—the irreplaceable years of loss, and their enduring love.

"You are my hero," Amir whispers in Nafeesa's ear. "You brought them home to us." Then he scoops Baji up with his long arms and steps so lightly that the two of them seem to float. Nafeesa unlocks the doors to the SUV and everyone piles in, while Amir sets his Baji down in the front as carefully as if she were a gleaming porcelain tray of tea and biscuits.

He updates them on Babba's status. "Fair," is how he describes it. When the five of them are back on the road, Faisah tells them about the call from Chaudry. She begins casually and everyone strains against the background of noisy tires and traffic. They roll up the windows to listen.

"So, I received a call from the lawyer in Islamabad." She leans forward between the two front seats so that Baji will not have to turn around. "He was reporting on his efforts to convince the prosecutor and the judge to dismiss your case and quash the arrest warrant."

"And . . .?" Baji asks, but Faisah says nothing. When everyone quiets, she holds the silence just a moment longer, drawing out the drama of it.

"That's exactly what I asked Tazi—'And...?'" Faisah extends the sound of the word, not surrendering center stage for a second. "So Chaudry says: 'How could we have forgotten the efficiency of Pakistan's judicial bureau-cracy?'" She is mimicking his voice, a fast and rather high-pitched sound. "'Guess what!' he says: 'They can't locate any records of Baji's case. No court file. No warrant. In either court. In either Islamabad or Lahore. Nothing on the computers. Nothing in the file room. Any files older than ten years are destroyed. I had two different clerks check. Twice.'"

The car fills with clapping and laughter. Faisah interrupts them. "Wait! There's more. 'But what about the prosecutor's file?' I ask Tazi. And he says: 'I talked with a Mr. Zahur, who is the prosecutor in charge of that courthouse. He's a young man, very nice. You know what he says when I ask if he has an old file on the case, or if new prison escape charges would be filed?'"

"What?" they all call out, "What?" They can't believe their ears. "Wait. Wait," shouts Amir. He pulls the car to the shoulder of the road and turns off the engine.

"Tazi said that Zahur says, and I quote: 'Not only might there be a statute of limitations problem for us, and a witness location problem, but frankly, Mr. Chaudry, nobody here cares. Nobody has heard of this Ujala Ehtisham. We have rape in our streets and extremists planting bombs in our churches. Or haven't you heard? We have more important things to do than tend a dead file.' When Tazi offered to turn her in, Zahur hung up on him!"

"Did Chaudry say anything else?" Baji asks when the uproar subsides.

"Well, I thanked him for all of us and told him he was my hero. Then he became very solemn and formal. He said: 'You, and Baji, and Lia are the heroes. Mr. Zahur may not remember your family's sacrifices to protect women in Pakistan, but some of us will never forget.'"

Soon they enter Nankana Sahib, where the lit lamps of the Golden Temple glow in the darkness. As the vehicle crawls along the unpaved streets, Amir speaks. "I forgot to mention. Zeshan is here. He decided to stay overnight."

Nafeesa is happy she will soon see her father, and she is surprised she no longer feels the anger, the fear of him. Where did it go? she wonders. Ahead of them, the old house is dark, silent and still, the front gate lit only by the sliver of moon and a few stars. The hollyhocks are closed up for the night. All is perfect just as it is.

***

The car engine stops the heartbeat of their journey. Baji, Faisah, Lia, Amir, and Nafeesa emerge, relieved, wrinkled, aching, worried. Car doors close soundlessly, so as not to disturb the silence that belongs to the night.

Amir rushes ahead into the house. There is Zeshan at the gate, in his dark suit, with his fresh haircut and trimmed beard. He is a silhouette of formality and calm. He starts greeting them, swinging one bag over his shoulder, another bag over that shoulder, holding Nafeesa's elbow while she looks into his face. The others are busy gathering belongings, eager to see Kulraj Singh inside this private, ultimate refuge. They stand outside the door to the house while Amir takes a small flask of oil and prepares to drip a few drops across the threshold, as if he were the woman of the house, welcoming guests.

Faisah stops him. "We are not guests, brother." She pushes on the door, but Zeshan stops her. "Before we go inside," he says, "I must tell you that your father has taken a turn for the worse today." They gather like drops of water that are bound to fall, but still they cling. "He slept all day and ate little. I spooned a little vegetable broth into him shortly after Amir left. He choked on it, unable to swallow, unable to speak. His lips tried to shape a word, and he struggled with the effort, but he was unable to string any sounds together." Zeshan speaks clearly and softly. No one could have delivered such terrible news more kindly. The spines of Kulraj Singh's children tremble under the news that soon they will be orphans. "I have set up a bed in the shrine room," Zeshan says, opening the door. "Amir and I should move him there at once."

The next hour is not filled with the exuberance of reunion. Instead, they become a small procession in the candle-lit courtyard that surrounds the string bed on which their father lies. One by one they kiss him as he sleeps, his hands folded over the woolen blankets that cover his chest. His breathing is imperceptible. Faisah wonders if someone should check his pulse.

"Will he never hear my voice again, my farewell from this life?" Baji grieves.

"Will I never serve him tea again?" asks Amir, bereft.

"Or seek his advice?" says Faisah.

Lia is silent next to her, watching both Faisah and Kulraj Singh. Her beloved is losing her father. And Lia grieves for her and for herself, because she loves Kulraj Singh, too.

Nafeesa traces in her mind the circle of the path that Kulraj Singh's wisdom wove for her. She thinks there is something oddly right that each one of them is face to face with his death. She envisions Kali with the dark blue-breasted body and wild red hair–Kali, the goddess of time and death. "The time has come," Kali says. "He will return to his being beyond time."

Baji nests under the neem tree next to Kulraj Singh, whispering prayers, patting his arm, squeezing his hand, listening to his breathing that is practically soundless. Meanwhile, the others remove everything from the shrine room until it is as vacant as the day it was built. Amir and Zeshan drag the filthy rug outside, hang it over the cinderblock wall and beat it in the dark. Lia carries a bucket of soapy water and strokes the smoky walls by candlelight. Nafeesa sweeps with a stick broom while Lia creeps on hands and knees with wet rag fragments, wiping up the floor of ashes, incense, cookie crumbs, dead insects, and candle wax. Faisah and Nafeesa remove the old string bed, the dank pillows, the sacred photos on the wall. They re-make the bed with fresh sheets, pillow covers, a saffron-colored dhurrie. Then they lift up the small shrine whole and carry it to the kitchen table where they disassemble it, polish each metal bowl inside and out, scrub each flower vase. Nafeesa rubs with a soft cloth the framed image of a haloed Guru Nanak, the faded photograph of her namesake, her grandfather's Beloved. She and Faisah scrub everything clean and scent the room with cut stems of eucalyptus and sprinkle his bed with rosewater. They return the furnishings and the shrine to the shrine room, adding water to the offering bowls and bright marigolds to the vases. Amir lights fresh candles and tests a few notes on the polished harmonium, as its bellows inhale air and exhale music.

Kulraj Singh's face twitches when Amir lifts him up. With Faisah's help, he carries their father to the shrine room in procession. Nafeesa dusts a straight-backed dining chair for Baji, rubs grapeseed oil into the dried out old frame, and adds a pillow for the seat. Then she pulls apart the fresh white curtains that billow at the room's entry. Baji sits on the floor with her head in the crook of her elbow, which rests on the edge of the bed beside Kulraj Singh. Her face is close to his and she whispers to him. No, she is singing a lullaby!

> *Night is falling, stars are calling out:*
> *it's time to sleep,*
> *Close your eyes and see the One*
> *soon you'll be breathing deep*
> *Waheguru, stay with us tonight.*
> *Be our protection till the morning light*

Kulraj Singh smiles at his daughter. "*Waheguru*," he whispers. "*Waheguru.*"

For days the family takes turns timing the rise and fall of his chest, at first counting the respirations, then naturally, inevitably matching their own breathing with his. How shallow his lungs must be. How slowly they move. There is no window in the room, and although the curtains are light and wispy, they prevent the free flow of air. At first Nafeesa feels she will smother without more oxygen. By her third shift she is able to refrain from deep breathing, to resist that long drink of oxygen by keeping at bay the part of her that is driven to satisfy every desire. Even in his dying, he is teaching me, she thinks. Is it like this for the others? These moments are so private that the experience is something they might never talk about. And that seems right to her, too.

The outside world is invisible to them. Amir requests prayers at the Golden Temple. Young Sikh boys walk by day after day in their *jooras*, the blue cloth that covers their topknots of hair that has never been cut.

They know their "uncle" is dying inside. Adults, too, their hair wrapped carefully in dastaars, know that their "brother" is dying, and they keep to their ordinary tasks. Dying is part of living.

When the family is not sitting with Kulraj Singh, they each sleep for many hours. Faisah lays out a chore chart, more to give herself something to do than because they need it. Work has a natural flow, as they each anticipate the needs of the other.

"Aren't you hungry, Sugar?" Lia asks Faisah, and a bowl of dal appears for her. Faisah washes the dishes.

"Your shalwar is dirty, tsk tsk tsk," Amir teases, and Nafeesa finds her laundry in her uncle's arms and later she hangs his clothes to dry.

"You look tired," Baji says and Faisah naps. Then Baji rests.

"You look bored," Lia laughs and Nafeesa deals the cards. The game enervates them.

"I wish Reshma were here," Faisah confides to Baji, recalling their eldest sister. "Remember how she surprised us by helping with Baji's defense, and then by showing up when Meena died? How kind she was. Where is she now?"

"Yes, we should be together. If only we knew how to reach her in that cult she lives in. I know how Abbu has missed his firstborn."

Zeshan tries to blend with the family, but truly he is a misfit, even though they all love him. His offerings always begin and end with him. "I brought some groceries," he says, leaving bags in the kitchen for someone else to unpack, hinting, "I just love curried vegetables." Sometimes Zeshan brings chairs into the lavender field where he and Nafeesa sit by themselves to talk.

Sitting with her grandfather on his third day without food, Nafeesa offers him sips of water. She spoons a drop between his lips and the tip of his tongue curls out of his mouth and his eyes open, pleading for more. He drinks, drop by drop, for many minutes. It seems to be his only need. He casts his eyes in the direction of the photo of his beloved wife, Nafeesa.

Then he looks at his granddaughter.

"Are you in pain, Babba?" she asks. He blinks. She knows he hears her. He lies there without anxiety. She leans close. "Babba, I brought your daughters back to you," she smiles.

His wet lips move. *"Shukriah,"* he whispers, as if he is already calling to her from some other place. Then he falls asleep.

She places her head on the bed next to his and she dreams this dream:

There was a field filled with people looking up at the sky. They were hypnotized by the low calling of thousands of birds winging across pastel clouds. It was a collective flight of crows, rooks in a ballet of shifting shapes, twisting, morphing into hills and valleys, dark lines becoming round, and then merging in a collective reel, now up, now down, a family of families, that expanded and contracted in a swirling dance. Her grandmother, the first Nafeesa, watched from under an enormous orange jacaranda, with shrieking birds flying, calling out, demanding something.

When Nafeesa wakes, Baji's hand is on her shoulder. Babba is facing the photograph of his Beloved. His eyes look satisfied, as if they have finally had their fill. Then he gasps and exhales. The next inhalation never comes.

***

"We will wash his body as we washed our mother and our sister," Baji says and they bring bowls of water, shampoo, clean cloths and ropes, eucalyptus leaves, rose petals. Baji wipes her father's face, while Faisah washes his feet and legs, Lia his arms, Nafeesa his hands, and Zeshan his backside. Amir cleans his torso and private parts, his beard and hair. They each pat his body with folded cotton cloths, as if the patting might cause his nerves to remember them, his muscles might twitch a last response, his fingers might, in some autonomic reaction, press the sacred keys on his harmonium, or his eyes might pop open and his throat groan with pleasure at the warmth of the pure water they pour over him. But when his body does not respond to their touches, they know with certainty that his soul is migrating along with all those who came before in his particular line of creation, and extend back to what we have no other word for, so we call it the Beginning.

Then, along with all of the Sikhs of Nankana Sahib, who permit the Muslim family of Kulraj Singh the honor, they walk in procession to the cremation grounds—women leaving their homes, and men closing their shops and taking the hands of children, directing them through the back alleys and across vacant lots, behind houses and onto the open fields to recite a nighttime prayer as they set the husk of Kulraj Singh's body alight. Goats graze and chickens attend from their pens.

For ten days the family stays indoors and recites prayers, sings songs, remembers Kulraj Singh with gratitude and bittersweet calm. Then they pour his ashes into the Jhelum to mix at once with all the life and death that meet in that river. A shaft of light casts a pale rainbow on the water. A cloud passes overhead. Then it rains.

A breeze blows through the courtyard on the morning of their leaving Nankana Sahib, and sparrows peck at pieces of chapati that fall on the brickwork. By the time the family sips a last pot of tea together, doubts have become hopes, uncertainties have been transformed into plans, the powers of fate are renewed.

"Come with us to visit the U.S.," Lia begs. "All of you." She looks at each of them one by one.

Faisah rolls her eye. "We don't know yet just how long we will stay there, so please come and meet the Americans."

Baji shakes her head. "We still have work to do here in Pakistan. Abbu left a letter for us about land in Malakwal that our mother inherited decades ago as the sole survivor of the Ahmed feudals who owned and controlled that entire area. He wrote that she never claimed the land but that it is safe now to do so. Amir and I plan to turn it into a cooperative farm, and develop new programs for job training and to promote the rule of law and women's rights."

"Yes, I'm going to close up this house and move with Baji," Amir said. "It's time for me to make a change."

Then, for a moment, everyone was silent. Wait a minute, Nafeesa thinks. *What about me? I've found my way home and now everyone is leaving.* She thinks of her life in Lahore, Nanaa, Rufina, her father. She thinks of her life in Nankana Sahib with Babba and Amir. She takes a breath. She remembers the slap that woke her up, the donkey trail and Baji, Beezah and her dance. She takes another breath. She is free to go with any of them—to the U.S. or to Malakwal, if she wants to. They invited her. But, she knows, those paths are theirs, not hers. At least not right now.

"I will go back to Lahore," she declares and takes her father's hand. "There's one more thing I know I must do, Abbu. I want to speak at the protest rally at the Faisal Mosque next week. I have something to say and at last I have a voice to say it with." Zeshan looks alarmed as she continues. "And I want you to come with me." She sees her father relax.

"As you wish, Nafeesa," he says. "As you wish."

***

Above them, the birds of Pakistan circle out and back over the sunflower field. The hollyhocks bow at the side of the road, clouds part, and at last the wind calms. A familiar light and warmth spreads across the land, as the sun climbs, and all the young things, both those above ground and those below, wait, listening for their own music and the steps that will follow.

Author's Note

Almost twenty years ago I met a remarkable Pakistani, a woman who, for her protection, I will call Aisha. Aisha had worked as a grass-roots teacher for twenty-five years, and was involved secretly and personally in rescue efforts for a number of women condemned in so- called "honor crimes." As I listened to her stories, in my mind she became the "Harriet Tubman of Pakistan." As for myself, I had spent many years as part of the early battered women's movement in the U.S., so although the details of the abuse Aisha described to me were both extreme and strange, the details were also strangely familiar at the same time.

On the evening that I met my new friend, she showed us a video about honor crimes, a cultural, patriarchal practice (not based on religion) by which family members target and punish (sometimes through killing) another family member who is perceived to have trans- gressed norms, usually related to sexuality in order to restore the family's "honor." As we washed dishes after a small meal, Aisha and I recalled the courage of the abused women we had known, and, silently, with our hands in dishwater, we began to weep. Impulsively, quietly, I asked her if I could write her story. She agreed, and over the following months, we met every other week over cups of tea while I read and she commented on my first drafts. She loaned me numerous books, reports and studies about honor crimes in Pakistan which I studied as her devoted student. After many months of writing, I turned her story into fiction, both to protect her (she still is engaged in rescue work) and to give me the freedom to diverge from the facts of her life and to create the particular story that seemed to want to be told.

In January of 2004, I went to Pakistan for a month to gain the sensory experience and firsthand knowledge of the country. It was a kind of "Human Rights Tour," which Aisha and her family arranged. I visited schools, human rights offices, union organizers, medical clinics, law offices, anti-trafficking organizations, orphanages, courtrooms, child labor factories, a women's shelter, and bonded labor camps. I was invited into many homes and, as I was there during the wedding season, I attended several weddings—in a five-star hotel in Lahore, in a crowded home in Karachi, and in an open field in interior Sindh. Along the way, I interviewed a couple in hiding, and talked with one woman whom Aisha had helped to escape her family that had been determined to kill her. I came away with stories and an enormous respect for the people there who are willing to risk their lives to stand up for their rights and the rights of others. I also emerged with a more nuanced picture of the country and its people. I found them to be gentle and soft spoken. There's something very beautiful about a culture where people stop to pray five times a day. I wanted to do justice to that in my book.

Over the next six years I conducted extensive research, became involved in Pakistani human rights support, lobbied Congress, and completed my first novel, *My Sisters Made of Light*, published by Press 53 in 2010. Then I embarked on an extensive travel throughout the United States, and with the help of many old and new friends, was able to share in a network of concern for victims of abuse in Pakistan. From book sales and the generosity of my readers, we were able to raise $25,000 for the construction in 2016 of a safe shelter in Punjab, Pakistan for women and children escaping abuse.

Over the past seven years I wrote this sequel, a story which features some of the same characters and takes place eighteen years later. Although this is a stand-alone sequel, I took a few pages near the end of *My Sisters Made of Light* and used them as Prologue to *The Shawl of Midnight*, in order to create a bridge between the two stories. This novel is set in a world between worlds, both politically (Kashmir is contested land between Pakistan and India) and spiritually, as the mind responds to the silence and dark of midnight under the sky's uncertain protection. It is a world of birds who know no boundaries, of wide-ranging mountains that seem to have arisen forever from nothing at all, and of multiple sister-rivers that create all forms of life itself. The cultures humans created there mix together—both ancient and cosmopolitan—and its people are real. One is dying but is never alone; one is searching hopelessly for her dead mother; one gay couple struggles, as all couples do, to live together and still love one another; one older sister is just trying to survive; one brother is both nurturing and lonely; a husband transforms from hero to monster; and a father painfully learns to let loose the reins he has placed on his only daughter. The novel asks how people process their family traumas, their religious impulses, their countries' constraints, the ways they present themselves to others—and to themselves. *The Shawl of Midnight* explores the depths of family relationships, how people change over time and distance, and how we might discover through our own pressures and actions what we are shaped by—exactly what we are made of, and where home truly is.

Half of my proceeds from the sale of every copy of this book will be donated to nonprofit humanitarian service organizations in Kashmir and/or Pakistan.

Jacqueline St. Joan
Denver, Colorado, 2022

Acknowledgements

It has been almost twenty years since my travels in Pakistan and twelve since the publication of *My Sisters Made of Light*. I never really intended for there to be a sequel to that story, but the characters in Kulraj Singh's extended family stayed with me over the years, and my readers kept asking what happened to Baji and Yusuf after the prison escape. Somehow, and it is still a mystery to me, I knew, more or less, what happened to these characters over time, but the one I wondered about most was Meena's daughter, Nafeesa, who was born at the end of the first novel. I did not know her story and so I wanted to follow her into the future to find out what happened to her, to examine not only the ways that aging changes people (or doesn't) but also to expand on the questions raised in the prequel of how young women can survive, live, and thrive (or not) amidst whatever challenges their families and their cultures may throw in their faces. I wrote *The Shawl of Midnight* during the years my oldest granddaughters were coming-of-age and I watched them search for their own "hero's journey" within our family saga. I could recall my own coming-of-age story of those early adult years that are so critical, especially for females, in determining what life (or what dance!) will be. This book is part of that puzzle of life to be solved individually as pieces are moved around and drop in place or not. It is part of that human saga that crosses the borders of life's generations and re-generations.

Many people have helped me in so many ways throughout my life, including friends, family, and professionals who generously gave me their moral support, genuine encouragement, precious time and useful feedback during the years it has taken me to complete this book. First, I must acknowledge my Pakistani friend–whom I call Aisha, "the Harriet Tubman of Pakistan," for her years of rescuing women from honor crimes, whose courage and steadfastness inspired this project, and whose Kulraj Singh-like family guided and sheltered me during my research in Pakistan. I continue to hold in my heart the human rights workers and lawyers of Pakistan who remain unwavering in their commitment to the rule of law and the liberation of women and children. They are an inspiration to the world.

As I am writing about cultures that are not my own, I have tried to learn widely and listen deeply, to consult with those who have knowledge I lack, to only go where I am invited, to treat other cultures generously and to give back in return. But even with extreme care, mistakes can happen and corrections and criticism may be warranted. From the start I have felt entirely committed to presenting this extremely complex place, its history and its people convincingly (and lovingly). People tell me that my writing reads like nonfiction, perhaps because I have tried to present the area's historical background, political ups and downs, religious practices, and cultural dimensions accurately, as they were explained to me. I sought advice from writers, and relied on a fine little book, *Writing the Other: a Practical Approach*, by Nisi Shawl and Cynthia Ward. (http://writingtheother.com/the-book/).

I truly appreciate those who helped me personally to deepen my understanding of cultural issues, including Zahra Buttar of the College of Southern Nevada; Shahzadi Farah, Reena Gruijters-Gill; Tahira S. Khan, dear friend and author of *Beyond Honour: A Historical Materialist Explanation of Honour Related Violence*; Bano Makhdoom of "Chai Time"; Aakriti Pandita, medical doctor and writer extraordinaire; Basharat Shameem of the University of Kashmir, and Yousif Solangi of Radio Pakistan. One Pakistani reader wrote to ask me where I had grown up. He found it hard to accept that I'd not been raised in South Asia! A Kashmiri reader recently wrote that he was absolutely sure I had visited Kashmir. Sadly, I have not. In the end this body of work is fiction that draws on real people and circumstances and on stories given to me directly. It also relies on years of research, discussion, travel and constant questioning. The rest is the result of my intentions and my imagination. Any cultural errors are my own.

I am especially grateful for poetic translations of Lalla's *vakhs* quoted by my Beezah. The epigraph and a fragment used on p. 221 come from Ranjit Hoskote's *I Lalla: The Poems of Lal Ded* (Penguin, 2011). "At the end of a crazy-moon night," which Beezah recites on p. 167, comes from Coleman Barks' *Naked Song by Lalla* (Pilgrims Publishing, 2006). Five lines from "I traveled a long way seeking God" on p. 45 were taken from Swami Muktananda's *Lalleshwari: Spiritual Songs by a Great Siddha Yogini* (SYDA Foundation, 1981). And Jayalal Kaul's *Lal Ded* (Sahitya Akademi, 1973) was the source of Beezah's remembered "Impart not esoteric truth to fools."

I appreciate those who have guided me as a writer: my editors, Betsy and Neal Delmonico of Golden Antelope Press whose experience and precision helped to improve the manuscript, and Rusty Nelson, who tolerated my weeks of nitpicking his cover designs which came to a glorious fruition thanks to his patience and genius. I thank my FaceBook friends who weighed in on which cover image to select, that became the right one, of course. I acknowledge the kindness of Sandra Bond of Bond Literary Agency, Maureen Brady of Peripatetic Writers; authors and mentors Robin Black, Andre Dubus III, Alexandra Fuller, Linda Hogan, and Harry MacLean; Jordan Hart of Kahini Writers, Judith McDaniel of the University of Arizona; Robin Miura of

Blair Publisher; and Kevin Morgan Watson of Press 53. I appreciate the time and assistance I received from family and friends who became my intelligent beta-readers: Allison Bryson, Chris Bryson, Dana Bryson, Libby Comeaux, Linda Fowler, Phyllis Greene, Eileen White Hollowell, Patricia Madsen, Laurie Mathews, Molly Moyer, Heidi Reichhold-Caruso, Merilee Schultheiss, Rita Singer, Ronnie Storey, and Jennifer Woodhull. And for giving feedback on early drafts, I cannot forget my Denver writing group (Constance Boyle, Gregory Seth Harris—thank you for the Feesie correction!—Petra Perkins, Gail Waldstein, and Liz Westerfield); and my literary home in Colorado, Lighthouse Writers: Andrea Dupree, Mike Henry, and especially Rachel Weaver and her fiction workshoppers. Thank you especially to Josie Riederer, my social media maven, and to Genevieve Swift, media champ for their expert assistance, advice, and friendship.

As wide as my extended family has become, I owe the most to my children and their children, who nurture me in so many ways and let me love them in return. They are always the closest in my heart. Thank you for loving me.

If you loved this book, read its prequel!
Praise for *My Sisters Made of Light**

St. Joan writes with the passion of a life-long feminist and the insight of wide experience. She brings to her story what she brought to the law, a conviction that life is full of both struggle and purpose and that grace comes to us when we have no reason to expect it.

—**Dorothy Allison**, author of *Bastard Out of Carolina*

I started reading *My Sisters Made of Light* and could not put it down. It is a powerful story, well-presented, well-researched, and written with passion. The labor of duty became a labor of love. I read voraciously but have not come across a work which deals so effectively and skillfully with the cultural fault lines of Pakistani society.

—**S. Akhtar Ehtisham**, author of *A Medical Doctor Examines Life on Three Continents: A Pakistani View*

By weaving her far-reaching knowledge, experience, and imagination, Jacqueline St. Joan makes characters and settings bloom. The narrative movement is simultaneously dynamic and delicate.... *My Sisters Made of Light* is an exquisitely-told story.

—**Tom Popp**, managing editor of *F Magazine*

*Available through *www.westsidebooks.com* or *www.bookshop.org*

CPSIA information can be obtained
at www.ICGtesting.com
Printed in the USA
LVHW020810201122
733280LV00041B/2564